CW00434518

# APARTMENT SIX

## STUART JAMES

BLOODHOUND
— BOOKS —

Copyright © 2020 Stuart James

The right of to be identified as the Author of the Work has been asserted by him in accordance Copyright, Designs and Patents Act 1988.

First published in 2020 by Bloodhound Books

Apart from any use permitted under UK copyright law, this publication may only be

reproduced, stored, or transmitted, in any form, or by any means, with prior permission in

writing of the publisher or, in the case of reprographic production, in accordance with the

terms of licences issued by the Copyright Licensing Agency.

All characters in this publication are fictitious and any resemblance to real persons, living

or dead, is purely coincidental.

www.bloodhoundbooks.com

## PRAISE FOR STUART JAMES

'The author is gritty, raw and dark in his writing. He is also extremely talented. I would highly recommend this read if you love a dark thriller in the same vein as Stephen King. My book of the month.' – **L A Detwiler,** *USA Today* **bestselling author of** *The Widow Next Door*

'Great job. Well crafted, deliciously twisty and kept me glued to the pages.' – **Jennifer Jaynes,** *USA Today* **bestselling author of** *Disturbed and Malice*

'Tense and thrilling, with an ending you won't see coming.' – **Lisa Hall, author of** *The Party* **and** *Between You and Me*

'Fans of Mark Edwards will very much enjoy. Definitely a writer to look out for.' – **John Marrs, author of** *The Good Samaritan* **and** *The Wronged Son*

'A spooky read that will grab your attention from the very first page.' – **Natasha Harding from** *The Sun*

'A great read packed with twists and turns.' – **Caroline Mitchell,** *NY Times* **bestselling author of** *The Perfect Mother* **and** *Truth and Lies*

*This book is dedicated to my wife, Tara, who I love more than life. Thanks for being there for me every step of the way, in all aspects of my life. You're my hero.*

*Also my children, Oli and Ava, who I couldn't be more proud of. You are both incredible people who I adore so very much.*

*My mother and father, Jimmy and Kathleen. Love you guys.*

# TWENTY YEARS AGO

'999, what's your emergency? Hello, 999, what's your–?'

'Hello.'

'Hello. What's your emergency?'

'It's my mummy.'

'You sound very young, sweetheart, how old are you?'

'I'm five, but I'm nearly six.'

'Who's with you? Are you still on the line? Hello?'

'My daddy.'

'Okay. Can you put your daddy on the phone?'

'He won't come. He's in his bedroom. It's upstairs, and it's dark, and it's scary. He isn't here much, but when he is, he stays in his room on the phone talking.'

'Okay. I'm going to stay on the phone with you. Can you get him for me? Will you do that? You don't need to be frightened, okay?'

'I can't. I already told you he's in his room, and I can't get past Mummy.'

'What do you mean, you can't get past Mummy, my love?'

'She's lying at the bottom of the stairs, and she's not moving.'

'Listen to me; what's your name?'

'My name is Meagan. But Mummy calls me Meggy for short.'

'Okay. My name is Michelle; you can call me Shelly. Meagan, I need you to be brave, the bravest you've ever been. Can you do that for me, Meagan? Can you be really brave?'

'I think so. What shall I do?'

'I'm going to stay on the line; I'm not going anywhere. I'm going to get some people over who are going to help you. Is that okay?'

'My daddy did it, you know.'

'Your daddy did what, Meagan? What did your daddy do exactly?'

'They were shouting, Mummy and Daddy. Mummy was upset, she pushed my daddy and he was really, really angry, the most I've seen him shouting. I had to block my ears; then Daddy pushed something into Mummy. She's on the ground, and she's not moving, and I'm scared.'

'Meagan. Listen to me; help is on its way. You need to leave the house, do you understand? Leave the house now; I'm here. I'm on the line, okay? Move towards the front door quickly and get out of the house. Meagan. Are you there?'

'Yes. I told a lie. Daddy shouted louder one time when I scribbled on the table with my new crayon set. But this time was really loud too.'

'What are you doing, Meagan? Are you doing what I said?'

'I'm walking to the front door. Mummy's still not moving. When will she wake up? Do you think she'll still cook me pancakes for breakfast? She promised me, and Mummy never breaks promises.'

'Meagan, keep calm, don't look at Mummy and go out of the front door. Whose phone are you ringing from?'

'Mummy had her phone in her hand; I got it from her while she was sleeping. I know the password, three five five three. She doesn't like me playing on her phone, she says it eats the battery, but I only play games mostly. Oh, it's locked. I think Daddy locked the door.'

'Okay. Listen. Can you see a catch? Turn the lock and pull the handle as hard as you can.'

'I am, but it won't pull. I'll go to Daddy. He's strong.'

'No. Do not go up the stairs, do you hear me? I need you to stay down. Can you do that for me, Meagan?'

'Mummy's still sleeping. Oh, I think Daddy is out of his room now.'

'Meagan, you need to listen. What's your favourite hiding place? Somewhere you are never found? Think hard.'

'Well, let me see. Once I hid for a long time in a cupboard where the noisy monster is. Mummy says it eats clothes.'

'Okay. Move to the cupboard as quickly as you can. I need you to go fast, Meagan. I'm on the phone; nothing's going to happen to you. You believe me, right?'

'I'm going now; Daddy's coming. I can hear him at the top of the stairs.'

'Move fast, Meagan; you need to hide. Go quickly. If he calls you, don't answer, do you understand? It will be our little game.'

'Okay. I'm here now. The monster is quiet. Sometimes when it's eating the clothes, it hurts my ears.'

'Okay. We don't like monsters, but it won't hurt you. Are you inside the cupboard?'

'I'm inside. I've shut the door. It's dark in here. I don't like it. I want to come out. Daddy's calling me. He sounds angry.'

'Meagan, nothing's going to happen. You understand that? As long as you keep as quiet as you can and don't answer Daddy.'

'He's running around. I can hear him breathing.'

'Okay. I'm here, and you're safe, but do not answer Daddy, you got that?'

'He's saying bad words. He calls Mummy that word all the time. Bitch. Mummy says that word isn't nice. What's a bitch?'

'Your mummy is not that word. Your mummy is brave, Meagan, and so are you.'

'I think he's in the room; he's standing with the monster that eats the clothes. Now he's pounding it with his fist. I don't think he likes the monster.'

'Meagan, don't speak for a minute. Please, you have to keep quiet.'

'He's moving; I think he'll find me. What should I do?'

'Stay very still, keep crouched on the floor and keep as quiet as you can. Remember the game, my love.'

'He's standing at the cupboard door. Now he's looking around.'

'Stay still Meagan; you can do this.'

'He's gone now. I think someone's at the front door. I can hear people's voices. Someone rang our bell. Daddy's running; I can hear his footsteps. It sounds like they're trying to break our front door.'

'Oh, thank God. You did amazing Meagan; you're the bravest little soldier I've ever met. I'm so proud of you, okay.'

'Okay. Can I come out now?'

'In a minute. Wait until the officers come and get you. I'll let them know you're in the best hiding place ever.'

'But what if they can't find me?'

'They will; they're going to help you, Meagan.'

## PRESENT DAY

The alarm clock sounded. Meagan jumped, slapping her hand on the snooze bar. 8.30am. She held her breath in anticipation, waiting to see if her husband stirred. She froze, taking the room in. Everything was correctly placed. She lay still, fighting the knot in her stomach. The anxiety had already started. She waited, staring over at her husband. Once she was sure he was asleep, Meagan eased the blanket back slowly, twisted her body and stepped onto the wooden floor.

She knew where the floorboards creaked: over by the wardrobe, the second slat out from the bedroom wall. The upstairs hallway just outside the bathroom: that was a large area and a definite no-go. The third step from the top of the stairs.

She had left her fresh clothes on the stool in front of her dresser. It was unthinkable to open the wardrobe door at this time of the morning. The bedroom door was open; just as well she'd remembered to leave it that way last night.

Meagan grabbed her clothes, held them to her chest and left the room.

She wouldn't dare use the power shower in the upstairs bathroom, the one with all that space and the newly fitted jacuzzi bath with the extra jets.

She crept along the upstairs hallway, easing her way through the top of the apartment. Then she placed her foot on the stairs and went down, avoiding the third step from the top as if it were spread with hot coals.

On the ground floor, she reached the bathroom at the back of the kitchen. Meagan took a deep breath, inhaled and let out a sigh. She could be herself again, if only for a short while.

She ran the shower, removed her nightgown and stood under the hot water.

Once finished and dried, she wrapped her hair in a clean towel and got dressed.

Meagan hosed the shower clean, first getting rid of the suds from the tiled wall, making sure every hair disappeared down the plughole. Then she stood the shampoo bottle in line with the shower gel, hung the flannel back on the hook, and placed the used towel in the laundry basket.

Meagan looked down; a wet footprint marked the bathroom mat.

Panicking, she went to the kitchen, removing several sheets of the thick tissue from the roll above the sink. Some sheets of kitchen paper were hanging down. She wrapped them back onto the roll, making sure it looked neat.

In the bathroom, she got onto her knees and patted the water stain on the bathroom mat, absorbing every drop of moisture. Most of it disappeared into the kitchen roll. Meagan thought about setting up a hair dryer. But it was too risky. She kept dabbing until the stain on the bathroom mat had completely gone.

She stood back, making sure it couldn't be seen, her eyes sweeping over the spot where the water had been.

Meagan pulled herself together and stared at her reflection. She was beautiful, with high cheekbones, full lips, dark brown eyes and silky shoulder-length black hair. But she may as well have looked double her age for how she felt about herself. Her husband had taken every drop of confidence away and flushed it down the loo, draining her of self-belief with his constant cruel jibes, sarcasm, his sneers and continuous insults whenever she said something until she couldn't feel any worse about herself.

She looked deep at the woman she'd become, feeling deflated, pitiful, inadequate. Then she reached for her make-up bag. She applied a small amount of foundation and blusher and finished with deep red lipstick.

She quickly threw on a white blouse and knee-length tartan skirt, deciding to carry her black boots to the front door so as not to make any noise.

Meagan was creeping along the hall when she heard a voice from the kitchen.

'Where are you going?'

She froze, her heart racing, an anxiety knot rising in the pit of her stomach. 'I'm meeting a friend for coffee.' Her face flushed as she struggled to meet her husband's eyes. She watched him wiping the counter with a dishcloth. He looked up.

'Would you care to explain the mark on the worktop?'

Meagan dropped the boots she was holding, moving towards where her husband stood. 'I'm sorry, I'll take care of it.'

'But you didn't, did you? That's my point. I had a late night last night; a few boys turned up I hadn't seen for ages. I'm hungover, Meagan, and now I have to deal with this.' He raised his voice. 'It's not really on, Meagan, is it? Do you see where I'm coming from here?'

She reached for the cloth, and her husband whipped it from her hands.

'I'm sorry, it won't happen again.'

'Sorry, sorry, that's it? Are you, Meagan? Are you really? You know how hard it is for me, surely?'

'Yes, I know Rob, I get it. Honestly, I'm sorry.'

Rob stepped forward, running his hand along her face. Her body was shaking with fear. She could see how he adored the feeling of being in control; the way he made her wince, the authority he demanded and the respect she gave back.

Meagan blinked, she flinched, pulling her head back as Rob looked into her eyes. He waited for a minute, enjoying the faces she pulled and how she grimaced, then dropped the cloth on the floor by her feet.

'I'm going back upstairs. By the way, I'm hungry. You're not going out.' He left Meagan standing alone in the kitchen.

Once her husband was out of sight, Meagan picked up her phone from the kitchen worktop, tapped in the name Sarah, and sent a text.

I can't come. Rob is sick. Sorry. Another time.

She stared at the text, thinking how shitty a mate she was, letting Sarah down: one of her oldest friends. A reply came back a few seconds later.

Oh Meagan, I'm already halfway there. Can't you meet for an hour? I'm sure Rob can sleep off whatever is wrong with him. I've been looking forward to the catch-up.

Meagan looked at the phone, bouncing it in her left hand, contemplating the result of meeting Sarah and going against her husband's orders.

She tapped a message back.

Okay, I'll be there for ten as arranged. See you then.

Sarah responded with a thumbs-up emoji.

～

Meagan made some coffee, toasted two slices of bread and loaded up a tray. Once upstairs, she was pleased to find the bedroom door open. Rob was out for the count, sleeping off his hangover. She watched him breathe in and out.

*How I'd love to pour this coffee over your fucking head, smother you with the cushion and watch as you struggle to take your last breath. Your final vision of this world would be me, ripping the life from your body until your face drained and your eyes rolled back – you evil bastard.*

She placed the tray on the cabinet beside the bed, then moved slowly out of the room.

Downstairs, Meagan quickly glanced in the mirror hanging in the hall. She edged her way to the front door, pulled her boots on her feet then eased the door open. She tiptoed along the communal hall, quickly descending the two flights of stairs.

Outside, the bright sunshine caused her to squint. She realised she needed her shades. *Too late now: I can't risk going back and waking my husband.*

The King's Road was already bustling with families, couples and tourists peering at maps, pointing, phones held in the air, recording the great London life. She suddenly felt sadness, watching these people, smiles on their faces, light hearts, happiness, conversation. How she wished this was her. She pictured Rob standing beside her, linking arms, walking along the street, him on the outside, unable to draw his eyes away, letting Meagan know she meant something, she mattered.

Meagan imagined her husband taking an interest in her conversation, asking about her day, how she felt, what she'd like to do at the weekend.

She fought to clear her head; this was her time: she needed to relax and enjoy herself. She pushed open the door to the coffee shop. The bell sounding above the door caused her to jump. Sarah had already arrived and was standing in the queue.

Meagan fought past the crowd of people, steering her body away from a smartly-dressed guy gripping more cups than his fingers allowed. A young woman wiped a table down to her left side, looking up and offering a welcoming smile.

The smell of coffee was overpowering. The shelves at the back of the counter packed with bean jars. Steam emanated from machines, coughing and spurting with more noise than Meagan could bear. People at tables were tapping on laptops and talking on phones. The staff were shouting out people's names and lining up cardboard cups on the counter.

Meagan felt dizzy. Panic washed over her body and she held onto the side rail, dropping to her knees.

Sarah came running over. 'Meagan, what's up, lovely? This wasn't how I pictured us greeting.' She laughed, helping her friend to stand. 'Are you okay? Did you fall, hun?'

Meagan took a deep breath, held her head up and composed herself. 'I'm okay. Wow, not sure what happened. I'm fine, I'll be fine. Can we go outside?'

'Sure. Look, I'll walk you out and bring the coffees over. Still a large latte, three sweeteners?'

'You got it, yes.'

Meagan was pleased to find the garden quiet; the chill in the air kept the crowd inside. She sat, waiting for Sarah, worried that Rob would wake, come and find her, grab her hair and pull her across the table in front of everyone.

'There we go. So, how have you been, lovely?' Sarah glowed. She looked genuinely content, fit, healthy. It was as if she hadn't a care in the world.

Meagan suddenly felt envious and then guilty for thinking this way. 'Oh, I've been good, keeping busy, you know. You look simply lush, my love,' Meagan stated.

They laughed, and Meagan was happy for a brief second.

Sarah took a sip of her coffee, glanced at her friend, watching her tremble, her lip quivering. Meagan struggled to hold the cup still.

'Are you sure you're okay, Megs? Something's troubling you, I can see it. Talk to me; I'm your oldest friend, after all. You know whatever is said is between you and me, lovely.'

Meagan broke down, sobbing at the table, unable to control herself.

Sarah jumped up, moving round the table and crouching by her friend. 'Hey, what is it, Meagan babe, what's up?' She removed a small box of tissues from her handbag, passing them to Meagan and watched as she dabbed her eyes.

After a minute, Meagan regained her composure. 'Everything is up; I can't cope, I swore I'd never be the fucking victim and look at me, a shell of the woman I once was.'

'Is it about your father? Look, Meagan, I understand you feeling like this, I do, call it a fixation, uncertainty, doubt if you like, but he's gone. The horrible things he did all those years ago, you watching him killing your mother, terrified he'd get you and do the same to you, I get it, lovely. But he's dead; he can't hurt you anymore.'

Sarah was right. Her father had died in prison a couple of years ago. Meagan couldn't even attend the funeral. She hadn't spoken to him since the night of the incident.

Sarah placed a hand on Meagan's arm, consoling her friend.

Meagan wanted so badly to talk; it wasn't just her father, Rob was going to kill her, she knew it.

Sarah took a sip of her coffee. 'How're things with you and Rob?'

Meagan stumbled across her words, struggling to find the correct way to describe her husband. 'He's still the same. Arrogant, selfish and the second biggest arsehole I've ever met. My father being the first.'

Meagan saw the pity in Sarah's eyes, how her face dropped. 'Meagan, I'm so sorry. You need to get out before something happens. I've told you, come and stay with me. I can help. All you have to do is ask. You know that, right?'

Meagan was distracted, staring across the empty tables. 'I've met someone.'

'You've what?' Sarah placed her coffee in front of her, tapping the rim of the cup with her finger.

'His name is Oliver. We met a few times on the way to work.'

Sarah held her shocked expression for a moment. 'Oh, Meagan. Are you sure that's a good idea in light of your situation?'

'I like him, Sarah. He's a gent. He talks to me, takes interest and he's bloody fit too.'

'Okay. You need to be careful though. I don't need to explain what will happen if Rob finds out.'

Meagan wanted so badly to tell Sarah everything, but she had to leave as quickly as she'd arrived, otherwise, her husband would let loose. Meagan had to do something. She knew only too well her life had to change.

On the short walk back to Albuquerque House, Meagan thought about Sarah; they'd been friends since childhood, living across the road from one another, inseparable.

She reached the shabby apartment block, fished the keys from her purse and opened the front door. The post had arrived. It was lying on a small table to the left of the dreary communal hall. Meagan walked past. The lift had been out of service for weeks with no sign of getting repaired. The walls had started to peel and were looking worn. Graffiti tags were scribbled on the white ceilings.

Meagan went up to the second floor, passing a family struggling with a pushchair.

The apartment she shared with Rob was at the top of the stairs, the first on the left. She stood in front of the door looking down at the word *welcome* written on the doormat as she placed the key in the lock and gently turned it.

In the downstairs hall of her apartment, she removed her jacket and hung it on the coat stand, then took off her boots and placed them on the shelf under the stairs, lining them up and making sure to close the cupboard door.

She listened. The apartment was quiet. To any visitor arriving, it would seem peaceful, a tranquil home, calm and serene. Meagan stared down the hall; nothing out of place, she was sure.

She reached the bottom step, creeping up the stairs, avoiding the third step from the top. How she'd love to get into her bed, rest, maybe buy a book for herself and read; or blast the radio, open the windows and dance.

She reached the bedroom, pausing. Her heart pounded. A feeling of complete dread rose from the pit of her stomach. Her husband was out of bed.

Meagan stepped backwards, struggling to function. Her head was clouded, spinning like a Ferris wheel. The bedroom door slammed shut, causing Meagan to jump.

Rob had been standing behind it and was now next to her. 'Where were you?'

'I-I needed to go out. I didn't feel well.'

Rob crossed the bedroom floor, running his hand through his long black hair, his fists clenched.

Meagan went to the bed, pulling the duvet straight. 'Did you eat your toast?'

'I thought I made myself very clear.'

Meagan looked to the side, out the window, anywhere to avoid her husband's gaze. 'You did, Rob. How are you feeling?

Did you sleep enough?' She desperately tried to change the conversation and distract her husband.

'Where did you go, Meagan?'

'I went out to get air, that's it. I felt dizzy and needed to clear my head, so I sat outside on the step for ages. I'm not sure what it was, but I'm okay now.'

Meagan searched her husband's face for a reaction, gauging his mood and waiting to see what he did next.

A loud beep came from her handbag.

'Pass me the phone,' Rob demanded.

'Rob, come on.'

'I said, pass me the phone.'

Meagan fought back the tears. She wanted to collapse with the anxiety she was feeling, longing to run down the stairs and never come back. She reached into her bag and handed the phone over, struggling to compose herself, her heart throbbing with fear.

Rob read the message from Sarah aloud, a wry smirk on his face. 'It was great catching up this morning. Stop worrying so much, speak soon, luv ya chick.' He looked across at his wife.

Meagan tried to talk; but her tongue had jammed and was stuck to the roof of her mouth.

'So talk to me, Meagan, because I'm really not getting this. I'm trying to understand what you told me when I specifically said that you were not going out. Do you still struggle to follow simple instructions?' He came closer, watching the fear in her eyes, her reaction. 'Do you want to explain it to me, Meagan, huh?'

'I–?'

Rob threw the phone to the floor, stamping on it and cracking the screen. 'Shut the fuck up a second; I'm talking. Tell me where you went!'

His wife was silent; she'd given up, it was pointless trying to explain.

14

Rob grabbed Meagan behind her neck and rammed her head into the bedroom wall.

~

Oliver Simmonds shared an apartment in Chelsea with his long-term girlfriend who'd recently decided she wanted more.

*'It's not you, Oliver; it's me. You're the kindest, most generous person I've ever met, and you deserve better.'* She wanted to remain friends, stay in touch, call over, share the occasional glass of wine. Why the hell would he want that? Claire had packed her belongings, kissed Oliver's forehead and left, just like that.

For the rest of the day, he never left his bed. He was numb, completely distraught and unable to function.

It was Saturday morning. Oliver had just taken a shower and, with a towel wrapped around his waist, he stood looking through the window over Chelsea Harbour. The Thames was so tranquil as the sun reflected on the calm water. Chelsea Bridge was packed with people walking back and forth. In the distance, he saw the Shard, towering over the London skyline.

The apartment was quiet, only the dull sound of the radio in the background and the occasional footsteps from the apartment next door. Oliver felt safe here. He worked in Mayfair as a PA for a high-class law firm. He had no aspirations to be a lawyer himself; he was a simple guy who preferred a stress-free, easy lifestyle.

The apartment was rented. He only moved in because his ex – Oliver hated that word, but that's what she was – had decided she wanted the best apartment, the largest bed, the best view. Now he'd have to move. Somewhere cheaper, the ground floor, out of town.

He popped two pieces of bread into the toaster and filled the kettle with water.

His mobile phone sounded from the side unit, alerting him to a text. Oliver picked up the phone and opened the message.

I'll do it.

He held the phone closer to his face; his body trembled with excitement as he read the message for a second and third time. He thought about what to write back, not wanting to sound too enthusiastic. He tapped the buttons and started to write, hovering his forefinger over the menu, deleting, tapping again.

Are you sure?

A moment later, another message.

Yes.

He smiled, digesting what had just happened, unable to believe the message he'd received. It was a pinch-yourself moment, and suddenly you're awake, lying in bed, realising it was a dream which has changed your mood.

But this was real. It was happening, and Oliver couldn't wait.

## THREE MONTHS EARLIER

Oliver was a man of routine; bed at 10.30pm with the radio playing in the background. He'd read for thirty minutes, no more. His alarm clock sounded every weekday morning at 6.53am. It was plugged into the socket to the right side of his bed; he slept on the left, a light sheet covering his large frame. The window was cracked open as the fresh air helped clear his mind, so he could sleep better. The London traffic wasn't a problem on the fourth floor.

He jabbed the snooze button once, then jumped up and got ready for work.

A queue had already formed going into the station and swept along Gloucester Road ending at the junction of Cromwell Road.

On the platform Oliver stood momentarily, taking in the crowd. He saw morose faces pushing, shoving, charging forward, seemingly unaffected, like cattle being placed in a pen. He watched the doors being forced shut, packing everyone together.

It was something he'd never get used to; these were the same people who probably holidayed in the Mediterranean, walking along the beach, their loved ones in tow, feeling the warmth of the sand as their feet sunk a little further into the hot grains, strolling, enjoying the heat, the early morning solitude, wallowing in the space and relaxation.

Oliver wondered how they adapted. How could people honestly live like this? Every morning of their working lives, struggling to get to the place that helped pay their bills, mortgage, rent, food.

He sighed deeply, joining the back of the queue, watching as people tapped their phones, smirking to themselves, texting messages to people they'd probably just left.

A woman in front of him slowly shuffled forward liking Instagram posts on her screen, pressing the heart emoji to let them know she approved of their picture. Oliver could smell her perfume as his body was forced against her by a couple nudging from behind. She'd opened a WhatsApp video and was giggling to herself.

Oliver glared at the monitor. The next train would be here in two minutes. He looked left, seeing the lights of the last train disappear through the tunnel. A crowd formed behind him, pushing, barging, oblivious to personal space. He turned, edging to the side, his face pressed into the back of a guy's jacket. 'Sorry, didn't mean to knock against you.'

The guy looked towards Oliver; he didn't answer. Instead, he gazed along the row of people, waving to a work colleague.

Oliver waited impatiently, thinking about Claire. It was just over a week ago that she'd left, walked out of his life, planting a kiss on his forehead and heading out the door. So casual, so cold.

He tried to forget about her, move on with his life, but everything made him think about Claire. They'd travelled to work together, meeting afterwards for a drink before going back to the apartment and curling up on the sofa to watch the latest boxset.

Through the tunnel at the far end of the platform, Oliver could see the lights coming towards him. He pushed forward, catching his leg on a bag and barging hard into the woman in front. She hardly flinched, turning to offer a smile.

'I'm so sorry, are you okay?' Oliver asked.

As she looked at him, Oliver noticed her split lip as if she'd been punched hard in the mouth. He wanted to ask her about it, feeling he needed to know what had happened, to make sure she was okay. He knew he couldn't: that would seem nosey, and besides, she'd probably tell him to piss off.

'I'm fine, really, don't worry,' she answered.

Oliver immediately noticed her expression; pitiful, desperate, her face unfocused and blank as if she'd been suddenly dropped into the moment and was unsure how to react in public.

He found himself raising his voice with the noise of the train. 'Well, if it's any consolation, I've been pushed from pillar to post. I don't know how I'm still in one piece; the crowds get worse, people are so rude. I'm Oliver by the way.' He offered his hand.

The doors opened, and the lady disappeared into the mass of people.

'Sorry, excuse me. Thanks.'

The doors shut, Oliver squeezed into a gap, grasping the rail above. As the train pulled off, he watched the frustrated faces; a young guy in a smart grey suit, puffing air from his cheeks, flicking a look at his wristwatch and placing his briefcase beside his feet.

Music blared from the earphones of a woman next to him who was bouncing her head in time to the loud beat. To his left, an elderly guy was flicking pages from an oversized newspaper, struggling to fold it backwards, obstructing Oliver's view. He glanced at a story over his shoulder and got a nasty look in return as the guy turned the pages away from him.

Again, he thought about Claire. They'd do this journey every morning, commuting to work; he'd never noticed how hectic it was while she was by his side.

The train came to a halt; people started pushing through the doors. More commuters got into the carriage, causing Oliver to grip the bar above tighter, determined not to move. He suddenly spotted the lady with the split lip, around ten feet from where he stood. She looked towards him. Oliver was certain she smiled, though he couldn't be sure. *Play it cool, Oliver, don't act like a love-struck teenager and make a fool of yourself, mate. Smile back, be subtle, friendly.* Oliver lifted his arm and waved, knocking the pages from moody-paper-man next to him.

'Watch out, you bloody clown,' he snarled, stooping towards the floor, gathering the pages.

'Sorry, I didn't mean to do that,' Oliver confirmed.

The guy looked at Oliver. 'Imbecile.'

Oliver blushed, looking towards the lady with the split lip. She was pretending to look past the two men, laughing to herself.

The train slowed again, edging into another station. Oliver picked up his rucksack and placed it over his shoulder, pleased to see the woman preparing to exit the train.

He shuffled towards the door, stepping out onto the platform, spotting the woman making her way towards him. 'Well, we survived another morning,' Oliver proclaimed.

She looked at him, amusement in her face. Oliver extended an arm, again introducing himself. 'I'm Oliver; my journey isn't always that adventurous.'

She brought her hand forward, hesitated slightly, then limply placed her hand in his. 'Meagan, good to meet you, but I'm running late.'

'Oh, here, let me get your bag, I'll walk with you, that is if you don't mind? Where do you work? I'm a personal assistant for a poxy law firm.'

'Do you ever stop talking?' A wry smile appeared across her face, and her eyes lit up, only for a second.

Oliver couldn't take his eyes off her. 'Yeah, I do babble when I'm nervous, not that I– Here, let me get your bag.'

'There's no need, really.'

They walked along the platform, side by side. The crowds had dissolved, and Meagan seemed to appreciate the company, someone to talk to. Oliver was pleased she seemed responsive and not the type who'd look down her nose at his friendly approach.

As they made their way out onto the bustling street, Meagan offered her hand. 'It was good to meet you.'

As she walked away, Oliver stood, oblivious to the crowds, watching her disappear along the street.

It was two days before Oliver saw her again on the way home from work. His boss had asked him to stay late and sort out paperwork that had been overlooked. Oliver was the last to leave the office, punching the alarm code in and switching the lights off.

Walking along Oxford Street towards the station, he saw her. She had her head down.

'Meagan, hey, you okay?' he asked, excitedly.

As she looked up, he saw the purple bruise across the top of her eye. Her body language was closed, uninterested as she attempted to move out of his path.

Oliver ignored the swelling on her face, not wanting to seem like a pest. 'Are you getting the train?' he asked, aware he sounded a little too enthusiastic.

'Look, leave me alone. You don't know me, you know nothing about me. Don't talk to me again. I'm not your friend. Understand?'

She raced into the station as he stood, shocked, unsure what he'd said to piss her off so much.

But that night he struggled to get Meagan out of his head. He couldn't stop questioning why she'd been so cold. He was sure he hadn't been rude. He ran the conversation over in his mind, dissecting every moment. Something was wrong; that much was obvious. He thought about the first time he'd seen her, the badly cut lip. *Okay, that happens, no alarm bells there. But the bruise was ugly, like she'd been punched intentionally.*

He slumped on the sofa, thinking about her, wanting to know what was going on in her life. It was ridiculous, adolescent; Oliver had only just met this woman. It was none of his business, but he had to find out about Meagan. If she needed help, Oliver would offer it.

She was like a child he'd found sobbing, and he was unable to turn away.

The following evening Oliver left work at just gone 5pm. The afternoon had dragged slightly; he'd had a couple of invoices to print and new clients to add to the company's database. Most of his spare time was spent thinking about Meagan. He was becoming obsessed, struggling to push her image from his mind.

He stood on the street outside his office, glancing at the brass plate above the doorway. People were rushing past and traffic was at a standstill on the road heading towards Marble Arch.

Oliver checked the time. He'd seen Meagan the night before around quarter to six. He had time to kill. Stepping inside a coffee shop, he ordered a latte with a cheese and ham sandwich and sat at a side table.

At 5.30pm, he went out to the street. It had got dark; the sky was a blanket of thick dark clouds. He hoped it wasn't obvious to Meagan that he was looking out for her.

Oliver walked towards the station, then stood in an alley to the left of Bond Street Station to shelter from the rain.

Crowds of people headed towards him. He waited for twenty minutes; there was no sign of her.

*Come on, where are you? Maybe I've missed her. She could have come out early and rushed home.*

Oliver waited until 6pm, then called it a night.

He sat on the train, feeling a little disheartened and foolish. As the doors began to shut, Oliver saw her running frantically, pushing her hands out to stop them.

She got in the carriage. Oliver watched her looking for a seat and she made her way towards him. He contemplated turning away, hiding, struggling to stem the excitement, anticipation rushing through his body.

'Hey, Oliver, right? Can I sit?'

Oliver moved his rucksack, making way for her to settle beside him.

She looked at him as she wiped her soaked jacket. 'I'm glad I bumped into you. I wanted to apologise.'

'There's no need, really.' He noticed the bruise, more apparent now, a deep purple which had worked further down her face, the swelling almost closing her right eye.

Meagan turned towards Oliver. 'I was rude to you; you were only being friendly.' She looked away. 'I'm not used to it, to be honest.'

Oliver struggled to understand her sudden interest. 'You want to talk about it?'

Meagan paused, contemplating. 'Not really.'

As he sat beside her, taking in the sweet aroma of her perfume, he watched her hand shaking as she wiped a small trace of blood from the cut. Her lip was slowly healing. He wanted so badly to help make everything right. She seemed so vulnerable. Like a child lost in a busy playground, unsure where to turn, calling for their parents.

She bent forward, pushing her head into her hands. 'Oh God.'

Oliver felt the nervous energy; her legs trembled, she tapped her shoes on the floor, her tension surreal. She wore a wedding ring, and gold hooped earrings. A silver bracelet dangled from her left wrist, catching the light. Oliver loved the fact she had expensive taste.

They walked out of the station together, side by side. Meagan thanked Oliver for looking out for her and being so concerned. She leant forward, and kissed his cheek. He flushed as he watched her turn and walk off along Kensington High Street.

She'd been gone a couple of minutes when Oliver suddenly decided he had to follow her; this was his chance, he needed to find out her story.

He walked in the opposite direction, then stopped, quickly glancing behind. Meagan was out of sight. His heart pounded, and with an overwhelming rush he realised what he was about to do. Oliver couldn't help himself.

He turned, walking back to where Meagan had been a minute earlier. He was jogging now, the rucksack bouncing on his shoulder. Reaching a street corner, he gazed along the row of houses and small tower blocks. The streets were empty. Ahead of him were a couple of houses to the left side, he guessed she could have gone into one of them, but they were further down. She'd had to have moved fast, and her apparent state of mind would most certainly prevent this.

He peered along the side street to his left, a hundred yards further along, seeing a turning to the right. Oliver moved quickly, past the expensive semi-detached pads with their fancy front gardens and lavish cars parked out the front. He could smell an open fire, smoke billowing from the rooftop across the street. It had turned cold. He saw his breath forming in the air like a cloud of smoke as he panted, wanting to be at home now, stretched out on the sofa, warm and secure in his temporary apartment.

There was no sign of Meagan. He stopped, quickly glancing behind, crossing over the side road. A middle-aged lady dressed in a nightgown came out from a house, dumping a rubbish bag in a bin out the front. She watched Oliver as he gazed behind him, stopping and then walking along the pavement. He crossed back over the road, and she quickly went inside, shutting the front door. He realised how suspicious his behaviour must seem.

Oliver reached a side road to the right, about to give up, cold and in need of a warm shower. He spotted Meagan, around fifty yards along the secluded street, walking alone, bag in hand, unaware she was being followed.

Oliver kept well back; he couldn't risk being seen. Meagan would most certainly view it as weird behaviour, jeopardising his chances of getting to know her better.

She continued walking for another five or six minutes, with Oliver behind, keeping as hidden as possible.

He watched as Meagan stopped outside an apartment block. A guy dressed in a smart suit approached her. She looked startled. Oliver assumed it was her partner; it looked like he'd been waiting, watching her move along the street. The guy in the suit raised his voice. Oliver moved closer, hiding behind a parked car, ten or so yards from where Meagan and the guy were standing.

He asked her why she was late, shouting, getting in her face, calling her names.

She stepped back, pleading with the guy to calm down, not to make a scene on the street, then he lashed out, punching her on the temple with his right fist. Oliver watched her lying on the floor as the guy stepped back, peering along the street, watching to see if anyone was looking, then he kicked her in the stomach and calmly walked back across the street.

Oliver froze, unable to digest what had unfolded in front of him. He wanted to go over, help her, tell her everything would be okay. But would it? What could he do? This guy was a brute, nothing less; the scars she bore were due to this evil bastard. He was the reason she was so unhappy, a nervous wreck, deflated, demoralised, and her spirit destroyed.

He was about to walk across the street towards her when Meagan got to her feet and went inside the apartment block.

Meagan reached the stairs. She held onto the railing, clawing her way towards apartment six.

Her husband was pissed off. He had accused her of getting home late, assaulted her and humiliated her in public, not caring who watched. She wanted to call the police and let them know what was happening. They'd give him a warning, maybe a telling off. What then? What would happen when he returned? She dreaded to think about it, what he'd do when he came back.

She reached her apartment and opened the door. The lights were off inside, the place silent.

Meagan held her ribs, wincing with the pain. She was pretty sure they were broken.

In the kitchen she took a packet of painkillers from the drawer, popped a couple into her mouth and swallowed them with a glass of water. She kept the light off, moving slowly in the darkness. Meagan wanted to leave, fill a small bag with clothes, then get out of here and never return.

But Rob told her on numerous occasions while standing over her that if she ever left, he'd hunt her down. He'd told her that if she involved people he'd deny everything. He'd find her and bring her back.

Meagan had to be patient. She knew if she stayed long enough with Rob, she'd achieve her aim of a divorce settlement.

She climbed the stairs, supporting her weight with her right hand, gripping the rail to steady herself. Meagan winced, the pain unbearable.

Once she reached her bedroom, she lay on the bed unable to muster the strength to remove her clothes.

Oliver stood outside on the path for a few moments. He'd watched Meagan's partner crossing the street to a black Jaguar, pulling out a set of keys. A car alarm beeped, the lights flashed once, then he opened the driver's door and got inside.

Oliver kept low, ducking behind another vehicle further down the road. He watched the guy take out a phone, laugh to himself, then pull off down the street.

Oliver contemplated going over, getting into the building, finding out where Meagan lived and getting her some help. He crossed over the road, trying to gain control of himself, feeling like his mind had been taken over, possessed. Oliver knew the consequences; he knew what would happen if the bastard returned. He'd probably get the hiding of his life, but he couldn't stop himself.

He eyed a list of apartment numbers on a frame to the left-hand side, then pressed the bottom one for a couple of seconds.

He waited, debating whether to go again and try the same one. *This is such a stupid thing to do. What do I say when they answer? Oh, hi, it's me. Yeah, me, you know. Open the door; I'm getting soaked out here.*

Oliver pressed the second and third buzzers, stabbing the buttons for a few seconds, waiting and repeating the process. He was about to move his finger further up the line when he heard a voice.

'Can I help you?'

Oliver crouched apprehensively, moving his mouth to the box, suddenly realising the voice was coming from behind where he stood. He spun round, facing a menacing-looking guy who was gripping a bunch of keys. He was tall, at least six-two, dressed in jeans and a white shirt with a smart dark jacket. He had short grey hair styled forward like a crew cut. Oliver could smell his expensive aftershave. The guy bounced his keys, throwing them up and whipping them from the air, impatiently waiting for an answer. He paused menacingly, waiting for a reply.

Oliver was dumbstruck, struggling to communicate, to think of something, anything to come back with. *I have a parcel; visiting a friend in the block; I'm a plumber, and there's been a report of a leak on the top floor.*

'I asked you a fucking question. What are you doing outside the building?' The man moved closer to Oliver, staring through him. Oliver watched the guy's breath in the cold night, like steam coming from an old train. He wore black gloves on his clenched fists. He was looking around, stepping closer.

Oliver's heart raced, pumping adrenaline through his body. The two men were suddenly distracted by the sound of heels tapping along the ground, moving towards them. Oliver glanced past the guy with the gloves, watching a woman dressed in a long brown coat, balancing a mobile phone between her shoulder and neck, searching for her keys in a small beige handbag.

'Hey. Bloody cold isn't it?' Her declaration was aimed at both men.

As gloved-guy turned to answer, Oliver raced past them both, heading for the street and disappeared down the road.

After a few minutes, Oliver stopped to catch his breath. He bent forward, panting heavily, his cheeks burning, his hair damp. He gazed back up the street to make sure gloved-man hadn't followed.

Oliver disliked confrontation, and felt aggravated with what had happened. *What the hell was his problem? The dickhead looked like he was ready to attack me. For what? Standing outside an apartment block? What was he so concerned about?*

Oliver weighed up the consequences of going back, getting inside the building and finding Meagan. He deliberated for a few seconds, then decided to go home, take a shower and eat. He couldn't think about anything else. He felt completely brainwashed, obsessed with the woman he'd met on the train. Meagan lying on the ground at the front of the apartment block, and the pain she'd suffer in the morning, haunted his thoughts.

∽

Nine days later Oliver saw Meagan again on the way home from work.

He'd kept busy. Work was demanding. His boss was pressuring him because they had new clients so the team had to work late, get in early and make an impression.

Oliver's first thought of the morning and the last at night was of Meagan. He wanted to see her, to make sure she was okay, still alive. He feared the worst. He searched for local news articles about her. When he couldn't find anything, he went to the apartment block and waited outside, keeping hidden as he watched people going in and out of the front door. He never saw her. The bastard who'd beaten her showed up on the odd occasion, parking his black Jaguar outside Albuquerque House, waiting in his car, talking on the phone, casually walking over to the building without a care in the world.

It was early evening. Oliver left the office at around 5.20pm. He ambled slowly towards Bond Street Station. The rain was heavy. Pedestrians knocked into him and his path was obstructed with umbrellas of various shapes so he found himself repeatedly stepping aside to avoid being hit.

He made his way into the station and stood on the platform as crowds gathered behind, edging forward.

He got a seat towards the front of the carriage, and there she was, standing at the door. Oliver anxiously fixed his tie, moving it one way then the other. His cheeks reddened as Meagan made her way towards him. He wanted to jump off the seat, race towards her, run hand-in-hand with her through the carriage and out onto the street. He needed to keep calm, relax, not look desperate. She was alive; he was thankful for that.

'Can I sit?' she asked.

Oliver moved across to the empty seat as Meagan joined him.

'Wow. It's good to see you. How have you been? Maybe that's a stupid question.' Oliver immediately realised he'd sounded over-enthusiastic. She looked fresher this evening. The bruise around the top of her eye had almost disappeared, and her lip had healed. As the train pulled out of the station, Meagan winced, the pain in her ribs still evident. Oliver started to ask how she was after the bastard had kicked her, but managed to bite his tongue at the last second.

'I'm surviving, I think.' She chuckled. Oliver was pleased to see her face light up. She moved her body towards him, staring at him. 'I don't know anything about you,' Meagan stated.

'Well, why don't we change that? Have a drink with me.'

Her expression suddenly dropped as if she'd seen a spirit walk through the carriage. The glow from her face evaporated. It was as if her body had closed into a ball.

Oliver looked at her. 'I'm sorry if I offended you. I didn't mean anything by it.'

She took a moment to compose herself, gathering her thoughts. 'It's not as if I don't want to; I simply couldn't.'

Oliver gazed out the window at the black tunnels, light from the small lanterns catching his eye. 'Are you married? You must be, that was a daft question. A woman like you.'

'I have a partner, yes, but we don't get along. I'm going to leave him.'

They noticed an elderly gentleman sitting opposite, looking over the magazine he was reading, watching the two of them, listening intently.

The train was slowing. People were getting off their seats, pushing towards the doors.

'So why don't you just leave, if it's not working out, I mean?'

Meagan dropped her head; she fiddled with her hair, then pressed her fingers together. 'It's not that easy. Let's say that I need to time it correctly.'

The train waited at the platform for a few moments as more commuters got on, struggling to find standing room. People were gripping the bars overhead, determined to hold onto their space as if their lives depended on the one spot they had, like a baby holding a small cuddly toy.

Oliver watched Meagan. The way she moved, the negative energy which seeped from every pore of her body, how she struggled to hold her head up for more than a few seconds. He reached out and pushed her hair out of her face. He watched her flinch like she was preparing for a slap.

'I'd never lay a finger on you. I want you to know that.' Oliver spoke as if reading her mind.

She sighed, pushing out a hard breath, struggling to contain her emotions. Then she sat up, pushing her shoulders back as if to rid herself of the pain. 'I don't think you would; I'm not suggesting you're like that.'

They sat in silence while the train passed two more stations. Oliver didn't want to seem desperate, and Meagan appeared frightened about where their friendship would lead.

As the train pulled into their stop, Meagan jumped up, insisting she needed to walk out alone. Oliver thrust his card into her hand as she made her way to the platform and out onto the street above.

Meagan fished the keys from her handbag, opened the main door of her apartment block and went upstairs to the second floor.

She was nervous; her legs were shaking, eyes wild. She opened her front door, listening for any movement. Rob's car had gone from the street. It didn't mean anything, he rarely parked in the same place. He had once told Meagan it was safer that way, whatever that meant. Her husband was rarely at home. Recently he had been spending his time at bars, casinos, his club. He gambled most evenings. 'It's the only way to deal with the frustration,' he had told her. It was either that or take it out on his partner.

Meagan removed Oliver's card. She looked at his phone number, wanting so badly to call him, to leave the apartment and never return. The hallway was dark, still and void of life. Meagan flicked on the kitchen light switch, taking in the long, wide room. She was slightly more relaxed now. She wished it could be like this every night – without Rob.

Meagan went to the fridge, leaving her heels on, making as much noise as she liked. She opened the fridge door, the light temporarily straining her eyes, then banged the door shut and turned on the radio which was placed by the side unit. She turned the volume to full blast, then sang at the top of her voice. She jumped around the kitchen, banging pans on top of the electric hob, opening and shutting the doors of the units underneath the sink.

After a minute, exhausted, she turned off the radio and sat down on a stool by the breakfast bar.

She sat in silence, thinking she should eat, but the hunger was leaving her body. Meagan wanted to sleep; again, she contemplated calling Oliver. But it wasn't a good idea.

Suddenly she heard something outside; it sounded like an argument.

There was shouting, a man raising his voice, swearing. Meagan switched off the light in the kitchen and went down the hallway. As she reached the front door, something pounded against it, like a fist or a heavy object. She stopped and backed up.

It was time to call Oliver. Rob had gone out and probably wouldn't return until the early hours.

She cautiously walked up the stairs to her bedroom, reaching into the back of her underwear drawer for her spare mobile. She dialled the number on Oliver's card.

He answered on the second ring, confirming his name. 'Oliver Simmonds.' His voice was cheerful.

Meagan whispered, trying to force the urgency of her call. 'It's me, Meagan.'

'Hey, Meagan. Wow, you called. I didn't expect you–'

'Something is happening in the communal hall outside my apartment. I'm not sure what's going on, Oliver. A woman is screaming; it sounds like she's being attacked. I'm frightened. The front door thumped a second ago, and Rob's out.'

'Okay. Take it easy. Breathe. Is the front door locked?' Oliver listened to Meagan as she went slowly to the door.

'Yes, it's locked. I'm scared, Oliver.'

He paused, talking calmly into the phone, keeping her relaxed. 'Meagan, once the front door is locked, you're safe. You understand that, right? Are you still there?'

'I'm still here.'

'Okay. What are you doing, Meagan?' Oliver could hear her shuffling about, the phone reception cutting in and out.

Again, Meagan whispered, keeping her voice as low as possible. 'I'm looking out of the spyhole. It seems quiet.'

'Okay, maybe they're gone. I'll stay on the phone if you like.'

'I'd like that.'

Oliver listened, the fear evident in Meagan's voice, obvious panic. 'Are they gone? Meagan, talk to me.'

At the front door Meagan listened for a second, then whispered, 'I think so. It's quiet now; they must have gone. Sorry to call you like this. It's not how I imagined our first phone call, if I'm honest.'

'Hey, it's fine, I'm just glad you called.'

'Rob is out most evenings; I hate being–'

There was another loud thump on the front door. Meagan cried out, 'What the hell? They're going to get in, Oliver, whoever's out there is trying to get into the apartment.'

'Meagan, is the front door shut? Is anyone in your apartment?'

'No one is inside. The door's locked but someone is either trying to get in or falling against it, maybe being attacked. What should I do?'

'Wait, keep as quiet as possible; move away from the door. Don't let them know you're inside. Do you hear me?'

'Yes. Yes, I hear you.'

Meagan waited for a couple of minutes. Only her light breaths informed Oliver that she was still on the line.

'I think they're gone, Oliver. I haven't heard anything for a few minutes now. It's quiet.'

He heard a clink, and then the squeal of a hinge. 'What are you doing? Meagan?'

'I've got to see what's happening.'

Silence. Then, 'Oliver, are you there? Oliver.'

'Yes, I'm here. What's going on, Meagan?' He needed to know what she was doing.

'I've opened the front door; I need to make sure whoever was out here isn't trying to get into one of the apartments. Call it neighbourhood watch, if you like.'

'Meagan, please, don't be stupid. Go back inside. You'll get hurt. Are you listening to me, Meagan?'

'I'm walking along the communal hall. The apartment doors are all shut, it doesn't look like there's any damage. Maybe it was kids. They often get in here, smoking their shit.'

'Fine. Okay, well, now you know it's safe. Please listen, Meagan, and go back inside. Lock the door where it's safe.'

'I'm just looking. I need to know.'

'What's happening, Meagan? Are you back inside?'

'No. I'm going down to the first floor. Just stay on the phone. I feel safe hearing your voice.'

'I don't believe this. Please, go home. Leave it, Meagan.' Suddenly, Oliver heard her voice, the phone seemed to drop and there were ruffling sounds in the earpiece. 'Meagan. Talk to me, please.'

'Shit, shit, shit.'

'What? What can you see?'

'I'm on the first floor… And there's a woman lying–'

Oliver could hear a raised voice.

Meagan paused. 'She's trying to speak. A guy is standing over her; he's wearing black gloves, he's leaning over the woman, his hands are around her fucking throat, Oliver.'

Oliver recalled the guy who had challenged him recently while he stood outside the building. He also wore black gloves. 'Is she alive?'

Meagan froze, struggling to produce the words, sounding confused. 'I think so, but her body's twitching. He's lifting her, putting her over his shoulder. She's not moving, Oliver.'

'Go back up the stairs, Meagan, get inside and lock the door. Now.'

Meagan followed Oliver's instructions, stepping back onto the stairs and racing up to the second floor.

Oliver heard the door banging shut and the lock being engaged.

'I'm by the front door. I can hear him; he's outside, Oliver. I'm watching through the spyhole. I can see a shadow. I think he's passing my door, moving along the hall.'

Meagan held her breath for a moment, then continued. 'He's opening a door on the second floor, my floor. He's a fucking neighbour.'

Rob sat at the bar, swigging a double Jack Daniels, straight. He watched as the bartender wiped a glass with a tea towel and placed it on a shelf above his head.

Rob turned, facing the stage. A woman in a tight bikini was gyrating in front of him, slowly removing her clothes. The music was loud, a slow dance track from the nineties. He got off the stool and took a seat by the edge of the stage. He watched how she moved, her smooth body glistening with oil, her perfect figure, then he dipped into his pocket and drew out a fifty-pound note, placing it into the side of her underwear.

She smiled, giving Rob a provocative wink. When she'd finished dancing, she strutted towards him. 'Hey, you wanna take this further, boss?'

Rob smirked, taking her hand as she led him into a back room where she continued the private show. There was a large bowl of cocaine on a table, and the door was shut and locked.

Meagan stood in the hallway of apartment six; her body pressed against the wall, arms by her sides, her right hand loosely gripping her mobile. Oliver was still on the phone, trying to calm her down, struggling to digest what had just happened.

'What if he comes for me, Oliver? A neighbour's just strangled a woman and dragged her into his apartment.'

Oliver listened as Meagan struggled to gain control.

The lights were out, the apartment in darkness. Feeling her way towards the living room to the right, Meagan crept over towards the window. The thick, heavy curtains were closed, keeping whatever light there was out of the room. She went to the window, her hands shaking and her body numb from adrenaline. She pulled the curtain slightly to the right and peered into the communal hall. Meagan listened intently. 'It's too quiet, Oliver.'

She recalled the day-to-day sounds she'd become accustomed to hearing. The lift as it passed through the levels, a robotic voice announcing the second floor; a neighbour playing jazz, the music blaring from his living room. She recalled the old lady who lived upstairs pulling her shopping trolley behind her, moaning about the lift but also frightened of small spaces, cursing about the stairs getting harder to manage and the smell of piss in the landing. And there was the oversexed couple at the end of the hall, who often stopped at the top of the second floor to seduce each other on the way to their apartment.

'Should we call the police?' Oliver asked.

Meagan went back to the hall, crouching down by the front door. 'Rob would lose the plot; he never interferes with neighbours, ever. He'd never say hello when he meets them in the communal hall, ask how they are or wish them a pleasant day; they aren't important to him.'

'Charming,' Oliver said.

'Secondly, the guy down the hall would know I called. He'd find out, and what then? He'll come for me, Oliver. I have to do something. I have to help her.'

'Meagan, no, don't interfere; there's nothing you can do. Just leave it the fuck alone.'

Meagan jumped up suddenly, moving towards the front door. 'I have to find out.'

'Meagan, don't be stupid. Leave it alone. I'm begging you. Stay where you are, do you hear me?'

Removing her shoes, she slowly opened the front door, looking along the communal hall, seeing it was empty. She spoke into the phone. 'Stay with me, Oliver.'

She listened to his raised voice as her hand dropped by her side, still gripping the mobile phone.

Meagan went down the stairs, glancing behind her, listening intently. Rubbish had piled up outside an apartment on the first floor, white bags filled with something rotten. She passed through a haze of flies and the stench was unbearable. The next apartment along had a plaque nailed to the door with an Irish greeting: *céad míle fáilte*, in black letters. She held the rail at the top of the first-floor landing leading to the ground floor, steadying herself she made her way to the ground floor. There was a cupboard to the left by the communal front doors which was always unlocked, containing the mains stopcocks for each apartment.

She pulled the front door, holding it open. Standing out on the street, Meagan looked at the panel to the right and jabbed a couple of buttons. She held the phone to her ear.

'Where are you? Are you outside? Is that traffic?' Oliver quizzed her.

'I'm by the front door. There's a couple of apartments on my floor, people I don't know. I'll try them first.' Her heart was pounding, feeling a trickle of perspiration rolling down her face. 'There's no answer.'

She could hear Oliver shouting, telling her to go home and forget what she'd seen.

Meagan jabbed the buzzer again. 'Come on; I know you're in there, answer the bloody phone. I'll try another one. Gloved-man has to be in one of them.'

Meagan looked into the hall from outside, searching for a shadow coming down the stairs. She lifted her hand, debating whether to press again, pushing the button and waiting. 'Answer, you prick.'

'Hello.'

Meagan froze, unsure what to say.

'Who's there? Hello.'

Oliver was mute, listening to the calamity unfold before his ears.

Meagan heard the phone being placed back on the hook. She pressed the buzzer again, longer this time.

'Hello. Who the fuck is there? I'm coming down.' The phone was again placed back on the hook.

Oliver's voice came down her phone, raised to get her attention. 'Meagan, for Christ's sake, leave it while you can.'

Meagan quickly went back into the communal hall. She could hear footsteps charging down towards her from upstairs. She took a deep breath, opened the cupboard and stepped inside.

A small halogen light hung above her head, so she could see where she was standing. Water dripped onto her leg from one of the pipes. She held her breath; gloved-man was outside the cupboard door.

'Shit, Oliver. What have I done? Shit. Shit. Shit.' Meagan heard the front door open; gloved-man stood outside the building. Suddenly the front door shut. She edged forward, cracking the cupboard door open slightly, looking out through the gap. Gloved-man was walking down the steps and moving along the street.

Meagan charged out of the cupboard, the door smashing against the back wall. 'Oliver, I'm going to lock him out. It won't keep him for long, but it should slow him down.'

She spun around, quickly going back up the two flights of stairs. 'Oliver, he's left his apartment door open.' Then she added to reassure Oliver that she was still safe, 'The front door downstairs hasn't opened, so he hasn't come back in.' She stood outside gloved-man's apartment, bending forward to ease the stitch that had just developed. Her face was flushed, and her legs had momentarily weakened. She glanced along the corridor. The light was still flickering towards the back of the building.

She brought the phone to her ear, making sure that Oliver was still with her. 'If something happens, call the police. You'll hear if it goes wrong, Oliver.'

He hesitated. 'I'm calling the police anyway. You're in severe danger, Meagan.'

'Listen Oliver, if you call the police, Rob will kill me, it's as simple as that. He's warned me time and again never to interfere with the neighbours. I'm on my own here. I'm going to get to the woman; she could still be alive. Trust me, I know what I'm doing.'

Meagan reached her hands forward, pushing the front door wider, and stepped into the hallway of gloved-man's apartment.

She whispered as softly as possible. 'Hello. Are you okay? Hello. I'm here to help.' Meagan waited for a response. 'I'm going to help you. I live on this floor. Are you all right?'

She slowly went down the hall. The apartment was pitch

black, lit only by a small glow coming from the landing upstairs in front of her.

'Hello. Can you hear me?' Meagan pulled a cupboard door open to her right, and a small light came on. On the floor were a mop and bucket, a couple of shelves filled with DIY objects, light bulbs, tools and an array of plugs.

She gently shut the cupboard, moving towards a room to her left. She opened the door, finding a bathroom. Meagan pulled a light cord above her head. She leant back, covering her mouth with her hand, letting out a scream. 'She's dead, Oliver. The woman from the communal hall is lying in the bath, sunk into the water.'

There were footsteps outside; someone in the communal landing was coming towards the door where Meagan was standing.

'Shit.'

'Meagan, get out of there. He's going to come back; you'll be next. I'm coming over.'

She didn't answer.

Meagan closed the bathroom door, going along gloved-man's hallway. She opened the closet door in the hall, stepped inside and closed the door gently. She held her breath, frightened to move, listening to Oliver's voice over the phone and hearing footsteps where she stood.

She saw a shadow lurking outside. Through the slight gap between the door and the frame, she saw the shadow move. Gloved-man was coming along the hall. Meagan crouched, her body aching, listening intently.

'What am I doing here? He's going to kill me! I'm such an idiot. I can't escape. Help me, Oliver.'

Meagan listened. The apartment had gone silent. Her heart raced, she was suddenly dizzy, feeling claustrophobic, needing to get out of the closet. Her anxiety level increased tenfold, and gasping for breath she pushed the door open slightly, enough to see the hallway.

The apartment door was open to her left. Along the hall she saw the bathroom door had closed.

Meagan slowly stepped out of the closet, holding her breath, edging towards the front door. She heard a splash of water. Gloved-man groaned, talking to himself.

'I think he's in the bathroom, Oliver. I can hear water, he's taking the dead body out of the fucking water, probably lifting her over his shoulders. I can hear water dripping.'

'Please, Meagan, just get out,' Oliver demanded.

Meagan went to the front door, edging slowly, glancing behind every couple of seconds, treading as carefully as possible on the wooden floor. She reached the front door and shut it gently behind her.

Quickly, she went to her apartment. A voice from behind startled her. 'Where are you going?'

Meagan stiffened, her body numb. She turned, fighting the feeling of terror. 'Rob, I didn't hear you come up.'

'Where did you go?'

Meagan quickly turned the phone off. It was the spare that Rob didn't know about that she kept hidden at the back of her underwear drawer. She cut off the call to Oliver and shoved the phone in the back pocket of her jeans.

'I wanted to see if the lift was working. The old lady upstairs is struggling, and it's not fair. Let's go inside, I'll make you something to eat.' She peered at gloved-man's apartment, hoping he wouldn't come out. *Is Rob going to check my pockets?*

'Sounds good.'

Meagan opened the front door, leading Rob by the arm. He was high, sniffing like crazy, his eyes wild. Once inside apartment six, he pushed Meagan against the wall, rubbing his hands over her body, lifting his knee and placing it between her legs. Grabbing her hair, he pulled her head back, planting sloppy kisses on her neck.

'No, Rob, I'm not in the mood. I'm tired and just need to rest.'

He slapped her face, leaving a red mark across her cheek, then pushed her harder against the wall.

'Rob, I can't. I don't feel great, please.'

Again Rob lashed out, this time punching his wife in the stomach, watching her double over. He helped her up, grabbing her by the neck. 'I make the fucking rules.'

He undid his belt as Meagan cried out, holding her throat with his left hand.

The door knocked. Meagan sighed with relief, exhaling a hard breath from her lips.

Rob quickly let go of his wife's throat. 'Who the hell is that?' As Rob opened the door, Meagan stepped back.

The old lady from upstairs was standing at the door, looking concerned. 'I'm so sorry to bother you both, I have a power cut and was wondering if you're affected?'

Meagan brushed herself down, inviting the lady inside, thankful for the little saviours in life.

As the old lady came into their apartment, Meagan peeked out to the hall. The door to

gloved-man's apartment was still shut.

It was late by the time the old lady left their apartment. Rob went up to take a look at the electrics and found the main fuse board had tripped.

The old lady thanked them for looking after her and said to call her if ever they needed anything, proclaiming to Meagan that Rob was a total sweetheart and to hang on to him.

As Meagan walked her to the door, a knot developed low in her stomach and fear rose through her body. But once she'd closed the door she was relieved to find that Rob had already gone up the stairs to bed.

She messaged Oliver once she knew it was safe.

I'm fine. Thanks for tonight. Rob's home, he's just gone to bed. I know it was stupid. I just wanted to help.

She watched the screen as Oliver typed:

Don't do that to me again. I was worried sick. Fuck's sake, Meagan. What were you thinking? You could have got yourself killed. You're too vulnerable to go doing stupid things like that. Promise me you won't put yourself in a position like that again. I've been pacing the floor.

She wrote back.

I promise. Look, I've got to go. Rob can't know I have this spare phone. I'll see you soon. xxx

Over the next couple of months, Meagan and Oliver met most mornings on the station platform and often on the way home from work. The trains were packed, and they talked whenever it was safe, not wanting to draw unnecessary attention to themselves.

Meagan often sat opposite Oliver, occasionally touching his leg with hers, giving him a flirtatious smile, or holding eye contact with him. Oliver struggled to stem his lust, and Meagan needed her husband out of her life.

She often imagined how life would be with the stranger she met on the train; he was winning her trust the more they met.

Oliver fought with the rage, the sheer hatred he had for her husband. The more he saw Meagan, the more marks he noticed appearing on her face, her arms, and how she fought to hold onto her confidence. He witnessed her downfall day by day. He knew time was running out.

He was desperate to help; he had to do something before the bastard killed her.

Finally, when Oliver was at breaking point, his chance came.

The train was unusually quiet on the way home and Meagan came into the carriage a few seconds before the doors closed. He watched her as she approached him. Meagan struggled to contain her enthusiasm. Her spirits had lifted and her body language was alive as if she had a surge of electricity racing through her veins.

She sat beside him. 'How was your day?'

'Oh, busy as usual. You look like you're going to burst.'

'I need to talk to you. Rob's going away for a couple of days next week. He has business of some sort in Spain, so I'll be on my own. He's leaving next Tuesday, and he's not back until Friday lunchtime.'

Oliver was unsure of what to say, but he knew it would give them time to gather their thoughts and try to sort things out.

'Wow. That's great. It is, isn't it?' Oliver was unsure if Meagan's plans involved him.

'Oliver. It's bloody amazing. I've never looked forward to anything so much. I'm going to spend as much time with you as possible.'

Oliver placed his hand in hers. 'That sounds like a plan.'

Meagan saw Oliver a couple of days before Rob was leaving for Spain.

As she boarded the train on her way home from work, she saw Oliver sitting alone, dressed in a smart suit, well-groomed and cleanly shaven. His black hair was swept back, and he was looking over documents.

As Meagan approached, he looked up, his face gleaming. 'Meagan, hi.'

'Mind if I sit?' she asked.

He placed the papers into his rucksack, making room for her to join him.

'I'm glad to see you, Oliver. How have you been?'

He smiled, clasping his fingers together and pushing them out in front of him. 'Oh, you know, keeping busy, tired of commuting, in need of a holiday.'

They both laughed. 'And you?' He scanned her face, trying to read her expression. He saw faint scratches along her cheek.

'I'm okay, I think. Look, is the drink still on offer?'

Oliver's face flushed as a rush of excitement raced through his veins. 'Hell, yeah. You mean you and me?'

'Yes, just you and me.'

'Of course. Absolutely it's on offer, Meagan.'

She looked flustered. 'Good. I'll message you as soon as Rob's gone.'

Oliver and Meagan held eye contact as the train slowed to their stop.


*Present day.*

Now, Oliver stood in the living room, holding his phone, still excited by the message he'd received earlier, thinking about the last three months.

He looked at the screen again, a smug grin across his face, struggling to contain his emotions. Meagan was going to meet him for a drink. The woman he met on a train, the person he couldn't stop thinking about.

He wanted to send a text, tell her how he felt, thank her for agreeing to meet. *Calm down; it's just a drink. You know she's married, and it's wrong. Nothing can change, but maybe it can. Meagan is obviously unhappy; her partner is abusive and beats the shit out of her regularly. I've seen the marks; she can't make a life with him. He's a brute, a persecutor of the highest order. Finally, it's my chance to make a difference. Get closer. Gain her trust. Win her over.*

Oliver went to text her, then closed the phone, deciding it was better to wait. She'd agreed to meet him. What more could he ask at this moment?

Meagan messaged Oliver on Sunday; a short, to the point instruction.

My husband is leaving Tuesday afternoon for Spain. Let's meet at a pub close to Kensington for around seven. Don't reply to this message. Meagan.

A second text came through with the address of a pub. He knew it well; Oliver had been there a couple of times with his ex. He recalled the great food and a large beer garden.

He opened his phone, marking the date and time, simply writing: *drink date.*

Oliver had struggled to contain his excitement; he'd kept busy, throwing himself into work, keeping his head down. However hard he tried, he thought of her, the woman from the train. Meagan. Her image splashed across his mind like a newspaper scattered over the floor.

He arrived at around quarter to seven. The pub was busy even though it was early evening.

As he scanned the bar, he saw a handful of couples sat at round wooden tables. The place was lit by candles on white shelves along the wall and the sound of pool balls were clacking in the distance. A guy was leaning over the counter chatting to a woman while she served the drinks and a group of lads were at the bar, plonked on high stools, guzzling shots of whisky. Oliver imagined they wouldn't last the night.

He went to the bar, contemplating where to sit. He was nervous, unsure of himself, thinking he shouldn't get involved. *It's too late for that now.*

The tall young woman behind the bar informed him she'd be with him in a minute.

Oliver removed his phone, checking for messages, silently hoping Meagan had cancelled.

'What can I get you?'

As Oliver went to order, the door opened and Meagan walked in confidently. She was wearing a bright red dress under a long brown coat. She had her hair up, held in a bun and tightly pulled back. Her face was beaming and she looked breathtaking.

'Hello, glad you could make it.' Oliver leant forward, kissing her cheek. He helped her out of her coat, inhaling the strong perfume.

'I'm glad I came.' They laughed nervously. Oliver realised the barmaid was getting flustered waiting for his drinks order.

'What can I get you?' Oliver asked, taking the drinks menu from the bar.

Without taking a look, Meagan suggested a large gin and tonic. He ordered a pint of lager, and they made their way to a table in the far corner.

'So.' Oliver took a swig of his drink. 'Sorry, I'm nervous, I'll admit. Shit, why am I feeling like this?'

Meagan sipped her gin and tonic. 'So am I. I don't do this as a habit, meeting strange guys behind my husband's back, but I wanted to talk to you. In private.'

Oliver was concerned. 'I'm all ears.'

As they sat in the warmth, ensconced by the open fire, listening to the crackle of the burning wood, Meagan poured her heart out. She didn't hold back. She told Oliver everything; her sham of a marriage, how Rob treated her, his nights out, the club he owned, his drug usage, the mood swings, the menacing behaviour and extreme abuse. How she couldn't leave her apartment. Rob only allowed her to work as a nanny to bring her own money to the table. He permitted it when he found the woman she worked for was divorced and lived on her own with a small child.

She explained his jealousy, constant suspicion and overbearing possessiveness.

Oliver sat listening, never taking his eyes off Meagan, watching how she moved, the way she grew in confidence as the night progressed. Her eyes occasionally scanned the room and she would bite her bottom lip as if realising where she was; out of the apartment, her safe place. Like a prisoner released to the outside world, struggling to find her comfort zone, pining for the world they once knew.

She spoke for nearly an hour, barely taking a breath, flushed with the heat and a little dizzy with the alcohol.

As Oliver returned from the bar with more drinks, Meagan looked at him, her expression firm, serious. 'I want to ask you something.'

Oliver placed the drinks on the table in front of them, spilling some and mopping it with a paper mat. 'Go ahead.'

'What I'm about to say may strike you as a joke. You may take it as a laugh and think I'm having you on, messing around even, but I've never been more serious in my life.'

Oliver stared straight through her, suddenly giddy, a surge of adrenaline racing through his body. 'What is it, Meagan? You can ask me anything.'

'I want you to kill my husband.'

## 4

## TWENTY YEARS AGO - BEFORE THE PHONE CALL

'Meagan, I'm not going to keep asking you. Put your shoes on. We're going to be late for church.'

'Which ones?'

Her mother looked down, beginning to lose patience. 'You know, Meggy; you're just being awkward. Honestly, you get more difficult by the day, young lady.'

'But I don't know which ones you mean.'

'You do, now quickly go and find them.'

'I don't. That's why I'm asking. Is it my school shoes? The black ones? Daddy said they were dirty.'

'The white ones, Meggy. Did you look under the stairs?'

Meagan traipsed across the hall, holding her favourite toy, a small grey rabbit she named Arthur. She opened the cupboard, finding her shoes on the back shelf beside the pots of spices her mother had stored.

'Got them.' She held the shoes up for her mother to see.

'Great. Thank you, right, let's go. We can't be late.'

Her father was sitting in the car, pressing the horn furiously. Meagan and her mother opened the door and sat in the back of the vehicle. 'What was the holdup, Tricia? You're lucky I didn't go.'

Meagan looked across at her mum, making a sneaky face behind her father's back. Tricia decided to keep quiet; the only way to avoid an argument. It was Sunday morning, the family were going to church, and the last thing Tricia wanted was confrontation. They'd done nothing but shout at each other the last few months.

Meagan struggled at school. She had nightmares, cried frequently and fought to cope. She hated her parents fighting; it made her feel sick.

They pulled out of the drive and headed along the quiet road. Her husband looked behind, eyeing Meagan and his wife. 'I asked you a question.'

'Oh, for heaven's sake, Sean, leave it.'

He slammed the brakes, undid his seatbelt and got out. He wrenched Tricia's door open. 'I didn't get that. Do you want to repeat yourself?'

Meagan held onto her mother's arm, trying to make it better.

'I'm sorry, I'm just a little stressed.' Tricia attempted to ease the tension.

'Get out of the car,' her husband demanded.

Tricia looked at her husband, unable to believe he'd do this. 'Please, Sean.'

'I said, get the fuck out.'

Tricia kissed her daughter on the head, slid out of the car and stood by the ditch on the quiet lane. Sean shut the door and forced his wife behind the vehicle as Meagan tried to listen to what her father was saying; he was shouting, spit coming from his mouth. Meagan knelt up, pushing her head towards the glass at the back, watching her father shout, her mother nodding. Suddenly, her dad pulled his hand back, striking her mum across the face. Meagan gasped, placing her hand over her mouth.

A few seconds later, her father came back, got in the car and drove off.

'Daddy, why did you do that to Mummy, making her walk?'

Her father's eyes never left the road ahead. 'Because Meagan, my sweet child, she doesn't follow the rules, she chooses to disobey me, and that's what happens.'

Meagan thought for a second. 'Daddy, I didn't think adults have rules.'

'We still need to follow instructions, Meagan, do the right thing. It's just that Mummy didn't. She broke my rules, and these are the consequences.'

'What's consen– conqe–?'

'It means you get punished, Meagan, plain and simple. Stop talking now.'

Meagan watched as the rain poured from above, pelting against the window, the condensation thick on the glass, worrying that her mother would get a cold and be sick for ages.

Sean parked the car on a side road. The rain had eased slightly, the clouds were a thick dark grey, drifting slowly above.

Sean lifted his daughter out from the back seat, and they made their way to the church.

Meagan sat with her father, looking around at all the odd-looking people. Old ladies with head scarves, men wiping the rainwater from their brows, tucking the handkerchiefs back in their jacket pockets, altar boys and girls going to the front, carrying lots of objects. She wondered if she'd be allowed to do this soon.

'Daddy, I want to bring gifts to the front. Can I do that?'

Her father glanced to the side. 'You can't talk, I've told you many times, Meagan. How on earth could you do a job like that when you never stop talking?'

There were a few minutes left of the service when Meagan heard a racket towards the back of the church. The door opened, her mother stood in the passageway, rosy-cheeked and breathing deeply. Her hair was soaked, water dribbled down her face. Meagan smiled, and her mother's face glowed as she spotted her daughter.

Meagan beckoned her over, but her dad hadn't saved a seat.

Meagan listened as the priest gave a final blessing, then she raced to her mother.

Sean went outside to the car.

'Are you okay, Mummy?'

'I'm fine; come on, let's go.'

As they stood by the outside of the church building, Tricia watched as her husband drove out of the car park and headed back towards the house. The rain had started again, and this time it wasn't going to stop anytime soon.

Meagan was pleased to get a lift home with her best friend's parents. She and Sarah sat in the back, laughing at everything the adults said. Meagan listened to her mother, making excuses as to why her dad had driven off and left them in the rain. She watched Sarah's mum give a subtle tut, glancing towards her husband, shaking her head.

'Why are you tutting, Mrs Tunney?' Meagan asked.

Sarah's mother turned round from the front. 'Never you mind, Meagan. Being nosey will only get you in trouble.'

Meagan looked at Sarah, and they both giggled.

Tricia leant towards the two girls. 'Stop acting silly now, come on. We're lucky to get a lift home.'

Meagan watched the wiper blades racing left and right, the condensation forming heavily on the front window. Mr Tunney wiped the glass with the back of his hand. He cracked the window open slightly, causing a spray of water to hit the three of them in the back seat.

The girls screamed, and Mr Tunney told them to keep it down.

'Mummy. Can Sarah have a sleepover in our house? Please, please Mummy?'

'Meggy, it's a school night, you know the rules: no sleepovers when you have to get up early.'

'Why are there rules? Daddy says you don't follow his rules. Does that mean I don't have to follow yours?'

Tricia looked at her daughter, gearing herself up for the next bombardment of questions. They were never-ending, and the more she answered, the more Meagan came back with, like a continuously looping conveyor belt.

Mr Tunney pulled up to his drive. Tricia got out of the back seat, thanking them for the lift, and Meagan followed.

As Tricia looked across towards the house, her heart sank as she saw her husband's car in the drive.

The rain had eased, the clouds breaking slightly, allowing light through, lifting Tricia's spirit ever so slightly. Meagan pointed to a captivating rainbow in the distance. Her eyes were wild as she pulled her mum's hand, pleading her to bring her closer to the spectacle.

Tricia jumped as she placed her key in the front door lock. Sean flung it open from the inside, causing her to cry out.

'You made it then?' Sean asked.

Meagan stepped forward. 'Daddy, why did you leave us?'

He turned, walking back towards the kitchen. 'Dinner is nearly ready.'

Tricia removed her jacket and placed it over the stair rail. 'I'm not hungry. You and Meagan eat. I'm going for a lie-down.' She kicked off her boots and went up the stairs.

Sean paused, standing in the downstairs hallway in disbelief, shocked his wife would do this to him. 'You really aren't going to eat after the time it's taken?'

'I told you, Sean, I don't feel well.'

She listened to him move towards the kitchen, slamming the oven door and hammering the food on the table.

She undressed and lay on the bed, frightened of what he'd do and frightened of upsetting their daughter.

As Tricia drifted off to sleep, she heard footsteps coming towards her. She jolted, briefly wondering where she was. Meagan was at the door, shouting, 'No, Daddy, don't.'

As Tricia sat up, Sean lifted the jug of steaming gravy and proceeded to pour it over Tricia's head.

She winced in pain, the liquid burning her skin. He then scrunched the potatoes in his hands and crammed them into her mouth, until she vomited.

Meagan was distraught. She screamed out. 'Stop it, Daddy. Stop it, you're hurting Mummy'.

She heard her mother scream as she rushed to get water and help cool her face. Meagan was crying, struggling to understand why her father would treat her mother so cruelly, why he'd hurt her every day, making her cry, smiling when she got upset, laughing when her mother begged him to stop and leave her alone.

Sean left the room as Meagan stood at her mother's bedside, dipping a flannel into the water and dabbing it on the deep burn marks.

## 5

## PRESENT DAY

Oliver sat in front of Meagan, unsure if he'd heard correctly. His legs were trembling and his arms were numb so he was unable to reach forward and sip his drink. *Maybe I misheard her. A sudden lapse of concentration on my part, like when you're talking in a crowd, and you're sure you hear someone behind you say something shocking. You zone out temporarily, debating whether to go to the person you've never met and tackle them, question their last remark.*

*'What was that, pal? What did I hear you just say? My wife's a minger? I'm a dickhead? I don't belong in a pub like this with normal, decent people, is that it?'*

*Even though you're sure someone made a remark, you carry on, ignore it, put it to the back of your mind.*

The problem was, Oliver *had* heard what Meagan had just said. He had heard every terrifying word. *So what now? Do I brush over it, tell her how attractive she is? Ask her how her day went? What has she planned for the coming week? Tell her what I'd love to do to her? What I've been fantasising about?*

Meagan searched Oliver's face. 'Did you hear me?'

*Shit, it's real.* Oliver sat forward, finally pushing the sense of paralysis from his body. He took a deep breath, sipped his beer, then placed the glass in front of him on the soggy beer mat. 'I'm getting my head around what you've asked me. You want me to kill your husband? That's what you said, right?'

Meagan leaned back, crossing her legs, her shoe dangling from her foot, her leg bouncing. 'You heard correctly.'

Oliver paused, debating his answer. 'And how do you think I'm going to do that? Follow him home, jump out from a cupboard and place a carrier bag over his head until he's limp? You're not thinking straight, Meagan. I can't just go around murdering people. It's against the law for a start. Have you thought about that?'

'I've thought of nothing else. I've been with my husband for almost three years; I can't explain what it's like to live with such a vindictive bastard, worried every day I'm with him will be my last. You've seen the cuts and bruises, you know what I'm going through. I can't leave the apartment; he watches my every move. Do you think I'd be here tonight if he wasn't in Spain? I tiptoe through life, terrified of what he'll do. His temper is getting worse, Oliver.' She looked up, tears in her eyes, so pitiful. 'He's going to kill me unless we do something. You're my only hope. I have no one else to turn to. He's told me on more than one occasion if I ever leave, he'll hunt me down. He said there's no escape. He won't let me leave. Not ever. You have to help me, Oliver. I'm begging you.'

Oliver stared, his head fuzzy, his mind racing, confused, contemplating his dilemma. He'd fallen for Meagan big time, was unable to think of anything else. She sat in front of him, asking for help, pleading with him. Scenarios played out in his mind, a mass of outcomes. Meagan was desperate; she wanted out of her marriage and this seemed to be the only way.

Oliver took a deep breath, steadying himself before speaking. 'I want to help, honest, but there must be another way? What if I break into your apartment, kill this evil bastard, then what?'

Meagan answered like she already had it all worked out. 'I'll leave for the evening. The communal hall will be easy enough to get into; I'll give you a key, then you can make your way up the two flights of stairs to apartment six.'

'Then what?' Oliver watched Meagan's face as she thought of an answer.

'It's up to you what you do, how you do it.'

'Up to me? Funnily enough, Meagan, I don't make a habit of this. Okay, I've watched films about murders and read novels about murders, but it doesn't make it easier for me. I haven't a clue where to start. I can't just google "how to murder the husband of a woman from the train I've fallen for".'

Meagan laughed. Oliver thought how rare that was: he'd known her a few weeks and could recall just a handful of times that he'd seen her face light up.

'You'll work it out. It's my only hope, then we can be together.'

The next evening Meagan arrived at Oliver's apartment at 7pm sharp, wearing a red blouse, knee-length skirt and black boots.

Oliver opened the door, quickly poked his head out to the hall to make sure they weren't seen and then greeted her with a loose hug and showed her inside.

Meagan welcomed the smell of garlic and tomatoes in the air as she walked along the hallway. 'Wow. Something smells good.'

'Thank you; let me get you a drink.' Oliver could feel the anxiety rise, his body shaking. *Breathe Oliver, just breathe.* He clenched his right fist into a tight ball to rid the temporary paralysis.

'Red wine, please,' said Meagan.

Standing by the drinks cabinet in the living room, he poured a large red wine.

She walked over towards the window, taking in the view of

London at night. 'Wow. That's incredible. I don't think I've ever seen anything more magnificent.'

Oliver handed Meagan the tall glass. 'It is pretty incredible, isn't it? Sadly, the rent is unaffordable.'

'Oh, Oliver, I love it. I've never seen anything more beautiful.'

He walked up behind her, wrapping his arm around her waist. She turned, smiling, the tension evident on her face. Oliver placed his drink on the coffee table, holding Meagan close, moving his head forward to kiss her.

She pulled back slowly, placing her finger on Oliver's lips. 'Not yet. Not until it's done. It will give us something to look forward to, make it worthwhile.'

That rejection made Oliver want her all the more.

As they ate, Meagan scanned the living room, the high ceiling, thick white walls, a few Banksy pictures hanging low and a Formula One calendar. She took in the heavy shelves with images of Oliver and another woman and photos of Oliver's family placed neatly to the front. The plain décor was warm and inviting, with oak beams on either side of the room. A large, curved plasma screen on a dark wooden stand was set in the middle of the wall with speakers on both sides.

She spooned the pasta into her mouth, jazz music playing in the background. 'I could get used to this.'

Oliver looked up from his plate. He'd been spinning the food with his fork; his mind was confused. 'How serious are you?'

Meagan paused for effect. 'Deadly.'

'Okay, what's the plan? You want me to kill your husband? Why have you never done it?'

Meagan looked over her shoulder, towards the shelf filled with photos. 'Who is that?'

'She was my partner for two years. She just left one morning without an explanation.'

'People can be cruel. Believe me, I should know. In answer to your question, I've never had the guts. I witnessed firsthand my mother... the abuse – no, not just abuse, the torture, the fucking living hell she went through each day. I swore I'd never let it happen to me, convinced myself I'd see it coming. Rob was kind in the beginning. When we first met, he drove a taxi. He picked me up from a wine bar and slipped me his number. He was good-looking, a real charmer. I agreed to go for a drink as friends as I was, like you, on the rebound. We had a great couple of months, the best restaurants, weekends away; he couldn't do enough for me. We married quickly, but within a year, it all changed. It's like he turned overnight. Now I'm just another pathetic victim like my mother.'

Oliver never let his eyes wander. He was listening to every word, sympathising with Meagan's story, thinking, *God, I want to be with her.* 'Okay, I'll do it. I don't want to make an issue of it, so when it's done, we never talk about it again, understood?'

Her face lit up. 'Understood.'

Meagan explained that her husband was due back from Spain tomorrow evening. She wanted it done fast, as soon as he returned.

Meagan would leave an autoinjector in the storeroom of the basement hall. The autoinjector would contain botulinum, an extremely fast-acting poison. She gave Oliver clear instructions where to find the autoinjector and described how to work it. The toxin would cause Rob immediate muscle paralysis, closing down his respiratory system leading to his death. She also told Oliver where to find apartment six. His instructions were clear. Break into apartment six, stab the autoinjector into her husband and leave.

She said, 'I'll be out; I can't watch, I'm afraid, I'm not brave enough, Oliver. Besides, you'll be able to concentrate on the job in hand. If, for whatever reason, you need me, you have my number. You know what you have to do.'

They finished their meal, then Oliver walked Meagan back to her apartment. As she waved goodbye, Oliver stood outside, struggling to curb the complete dread in the pit of his stomach.

## 6

TWENTY YEARS AGO - BEFORE THE
PHONE CALL

I t was three days ago that Meagan had witnessed her father
cruelly burn her mother with the gravy.

Meagan struggled to sleep. She would wake in the night,
crying out, with visions of her father doing the same to her.

Tricia didn't leave her bed. She'd developed the flu, with cold
sweats and high temperature. Meagan frequently checked on her
mother, making sure she had everything she needed.

It was Wednesday evening. Sarah had come over, Meagan's
best friend from across the road.

Sean was out working and wouldn't usually come home until
late. He worked at the local council and his days were taken up
with meetings, speeches, and helping local businesses – a regular
pillar of the community in the eyes of the neighbourhood.

The girls were sat on the living room floor, combing their
dolls' hair and talking about school.

Meagan heard the key in the front door, and the menacing
figure of her father appeared in the hall. She felt sick, worried her
father would lash out in front of her friend.

She listened as he went up the stairs, opened the bedroom
door then slammed it hard.

'What's wrong with your daddy?' asked Sarah. 'Is he in a mood again?'

Meagan pushed herself up from the floor, and went to the living room door. 'I don't know, but he's gone to Mummy and Mummy isn't well.'

'Shall we go see?' Sarah asked.

'No. He'll be angry if he catches me listening. It makes him shout. You stay here, okay? I'll be back soon. Comb this one's hair now and make her look pretty.' Meagan tossed another doll towards Sarah, who placed her hands out, dropping it on the floor. 'Be careful. She's not well, just like Mummy.'

'My daddy says your mummy is lazy.'

'She is not.'

'Is too.'

Meagan shut the door so she couldn't hear Sarah anymore. At the foot of the stairs, she listened. There was total silence. As she reached the top of the stairs, she paused, hearing her father's voice.

'Is that it? You're just going to lie there and do nothing? This is all because of Sunday. I told you I was sorry. What more do you want?'

'Please, Sean, I'm sick; let me rest, please.'

'You've been resting for three fucking days; nothing is getting done in the house. Do you expect me to do everything?'

As Meagan stepped forward, she saw the door open, and she hid. After a couple of seconds, it closed again.

'I'm telling you something; I won't stand for it for much longer. Get out of bed.'

'Sean, please, I can't move; my body is crippled with pain.'

Meagan quietly opened the bedroom door and found her father at the bedside, slapping her mother around the face.

'No, Daddy, don't hit my Mummy.' Meagan leapt on her father's arm, swinging like a pendulum.

He wrestled her off, cursing as he left the room. Tricia burst into tears, apologising to her daughter for what she'd just witnessed.

Meagan leant in, placing her arms around her mother. 'I hate my daddy.'

'Meagan, don't say things you don't mean.'

'I do, Mummy. He's just like Jimmy Mertock at school, picking on the girls. Jimmy tried to kiss me once. He's all spotty.'

Tricia laughed, wincing with pain, and laid her head back on the pillow.

'Mummy, why do all the ugly boys try to kiss me?'

Tricia ran her hand through her daughter's hair. 'Baby, you have to kiss many frogs before you find your prince.'

'So why not just go straight for the prince, Mummy?'

'You know something, I've never thought of that.'

Meagan joined Sarah downstairs in the living room, listening to her father slam doors and stomp around the house like a petulant child.

Sarah looked up while combing the doll's hair. 'Is your mummy okay?'

'She's fine. Daddy burnt her on Sunday, and now she's not well.'

Sarah's eyes widened. 'How?'

'I'd rather not talk about it.' She looked at the doll in Sarah's hands. 'You've done a very nice job. She'll really find a prince looking like that.'

The living room door burst open and Sean walked in, instructing Meagan it was time for Sarah to leave.

'Daddy, she's only just come. Can't we have a little more time? Please, Daddy.'

'I said Sarah needs to leave.'

Sarah stood, wiping the creases from her skirt. 'Thanks for having me. I enjoyed being here.'

Meagan sniggered at how polite her friend sounded.

'Off you go now, we'll see you soon,' Sean instructed.

Meagan lifted herself off the ground. 'Daddy, you need to walk her across the road.'

'She's big enough to do it herself, Meagan. Off you go, Sarah.'

Meagan watched her father, shocked at how dismissive he was. As Sarah left the room, Sean walked up the stairs and into the spare room at the back of the house.

'I'm sorry, Sarah. I can come with you, if you want? I hate my daddy.'

'It's fine. I'll be okay. I'll see you soon, if you like.'

Meagan walked to the front door with Sarah and stood there until her friend had made it home.

A few seconds later, Sarah's father came barging out of their house, charging across the road.

Meagan quickly shut the front door, feeling guilty about the incident with her friend.

The doorbell rang, causing Meagan to jump. 'Daddy, someone's at the door. Daddy.'

'I heard you the first time.' Sean went downstairs.

He opened the door and found Mr Tunney standing with his fists clenched. 'Don't ever do that again.'

'Do what?'

'You bloody well know. Letting my daughter walk home on her own. You of all people, being a father yourself.'

'I don't know what you're talking about. I've been upstairs the whole time. I didn't even know Sarah was here.'

Mr Tunney looked towards Meagan. 'Is this true?'

Sean moved forward. 'Don't bring her into it. I suggest you communicate better with your child and arrange collection in future. As I said, I've been upstairs the whole time.'

Meagan and her father watched Mr Tunney turn on his heels and walk out of their front garden.

Meagan went to the front window in the living room, thinking how sad she felt for Sarah and Mr Tunney. She was also shocked and angry that her father could stand at the door and tell such lies.

## 7

PRESENT DAY

Oliver had barely slept. He was lying in bed, his head was cloudy, and his eyes struggled to focus as he glanced around his bedroom. He stared at the alarm clock: 6.53am.

He lay, scanning the ceiling, his body cold and clammy. He'd been awake for hours, pondering the responsibility on his shoulders.

Rob was returning from Spain early this afternoon. Oliver planned to break into apartment six this evening. He had to be patient, let Rob settle. Meagan had told him her husband suffered whenever he came home from abroad. The drugs, alcohol and God knows whatever else he put in his body would knock him out. It would make Oliver's job much more manageable. He'd sleep for hours; his tiredness always got the better of him.

Oliver was worried sick, unable to comprehend the task ahead. He had to go through with it, make it happen. *Then I can be with Meagan. That's all I want.*

In the kitchen he made a coffee and sat at the table. In the distance, he glimpsed the Shard and the River Thames.

He sat in complete silence.

There were so many things that could go wrong. He feared

being seen walking up the communal stairs, a neighbour confronting him, firing questions. He was worried about the guy that Meagan had seen, the man in gloves who'd questioned Oliver outside the building. Meagan had acted ridiculously, trying to help, witnessing this person's brutality and putting herself in such a precarious situation.

It seemed she was surrounded by wicked men.

Whatever had gone on in that building, the body in the bath wasn't Oliver's responsibility.

He also worried that Rob would get the better of him, struggle free, then what?

He wanted to message Meagan, but they'd decided not to communicate until it was over. They couldn't risk leaving a trail.

Oliver sat in the kitchen, sipping his coffee, wishing it was this time tomorrow and it was all over.

After Oliver finished his coffee, he showered, dressed and left his apartment. He planned on going to work to take his mind off the task, to keep busy, try and act as normal as possible, avoid suspicion. He wanted to see Meagan, hold her, tell her everything would be okay, that it was all in hand, plain sailing and straight-forward. But would it be that simple? So many things could go wrong.

They'd agreed that meeting up at the station may jeopardise their plan; they couldn't risk being seen together, now that Oliver knew what Meagan wanted him to do.

He passed the crowds of people on the way to the station; men and women in suits, blurred figures, mobiles balancing on their shoulders pressed to their ears, loud voices, briefcases swinging – just another day.

Oliver struggled to concentrate. His head was rushing with thoughts, his body aching with anticipation.

As he got to the station, he waited on the platform, too fright-ened to look around in case Meagan was there.

Once he reached the office, he got his head down and threw himself into his work.

~

It was late morning when Meagan's phone alerted her of a message; a short, one sentence text.

Getting on the plane, see you in a couple of hours. Rob.

Meagan felt weak, uncertain she could go through with it, but the plan was in action, and she had little choice. This was the first step to her new life. It had to be done.

She switched off her phone, because she feared Rob would use some app to locate her, quickly dressed and left apartment six.

She walked along the King's Road fighting the paranoia, certain that people were staring, watching her, judging. She crossed the road, entering the same coffee shop where she'd met Sarah a few weeks ago.

It was busy. There was a queue of people standing impatiently waiting to order, tourists planning their day, office staff getting a quick caffeine hit at the end of the busy morning.

A waitress greeted her, furiously wiping a stubborn stain from the edge of a table, her finger pushed into a J-cloth. 'Hi. You want to take a seat?'

Meagan shook her head, her mind going into overdrive. *Maybe she knows. Why did she ask me the question and not anyone else? Singling me out and not the others?* As Meagan watched the waitress move behind her, she fought a helpless feeling as she reached into her handbag. She was considering calling Oliver, telling him to forget they'd ever met.

The waitress greeted an elderly couple coming in through the front door arm in arm. The spotlight was on them, the waitress fussing, asking them to take a seat. *See, it's not just me. Get a grip. Breathe woman, breathe, you can do this.*

Meagan ordered a latte and sat in the corner of the room. She had time to kill. Her mind drifted once again to Oliver. She wondered if he wished it was only time he was killing.

Oliver left the office at 5pm sharp, heading back to his apartment. He needed to go through everything in his head and plan this evening, get it right.

Meagan had given him the code to the front door of the building and explained where her apartment was. She only had one key to the apartment so Oliver would have to find a way to break in. 'Damage the door a little,' she'd said. *Not a problem. My grandad was a locksmith and taught me the tricks of the trade.*

He'd find an autoinjector containing botulinum in the storeroom of the basement hall. Meagan described where he would find it. His orders were clear. Break into apartment six, stab the autoinjector into her husband and leave.

He contemplated how it would play out, how he'd feel: taking the life of another person, watching him take his last breath, ending Rob's existence. He pictured Meagan to make it all seem worthwhile. Oliver suddenly felt ill; he couldn't eat, his body was shaking uncontrollably. He wanted to call Meagan, see if there was another way. He already knew the answer.

He left home at just past 8pm and made his way to Albuquerque House.

As he stood outside, he looked up at the four-storey building, the path leading to the front door and the lights at the front of the block.

The side road was practically empty, a couple of buses and the occasional car passed as he looked to the High Street.

Apartment six was on the second floor; he'd enter the building, keep as silent as possible, go to the basement, get what he needed, then slowly creep up to the second floor.

He punched in the code to open the main door. The numbers were so small. Now he understood why the residents used a key. It took him several goes, tapping, re-tapping, pressing cancel and trying again. Hearing a loud clunk, he pulled the door towards him.

Once inside, Oliver made sure the place was safe for him to move. There were no security cameras. Meagan had told him the building was often vandalised, and they'd been ripped off the walls.

Oliver stood for a moment, struggling to stem the nervous energy which had built in him. He breathed deeply, in and out, steadying himself by placing his hand on the wall.

*Okay, just relax, Oliver. You break in and poison the bastard. Remember what he's doing to Meagan. How cruel and evil the fucker is. If anyone deserves this fate, this ending, it's this fucker. You can do this, just go to the apartment, break in and bang. Take him out.*

Oliver slowly made his way down to the basement.

## 8

## TWENTY YEARS AGO - BEFORE THE PHONE CALL

Tricia had finally recovered from the flu. She was feeling better.

Meagan had made toast and brought it up to her mother's bedroom, placing it on the side table. 'I made you food, Mummy. It will help you to get well.'

Tricia sat up, watching her daughter, wishing it could just be the two of them. 'Thank you, Meggy, you are a sweetheart.'

When Tricia came down a short while after eating, she found her daughter colouring a picture with crayons.

'Mummy, are you better now?'

'I am, my lovely; I'm much better. Where's your father?'

'In his room; I heard him talking on the phone. Mummy, why is Daddy always angry?'

Tricia crouched beside her daughter. 'Honey, it's okay. He has lots to deal with. You need to understand that, okay? Sometimes adults behave in a peculiar way. It doesn't make them bad people.'

'I think Daddy's bad.'

'Oh Meagan, don't ever think that. Your daddy loves you more than anything.'

Tricia went to the stairs. 'Sean, are you hungry?'

When he didn't answer, she asked Meagan, 'No Sarah today?'

Meagan looked up. 'Her daddy is angry. I don't think she's allowed over.'

'Why?'

Meagan explained what happened the other night; Sarah's father coming over, shouting at their front door.

'Okay. Look, get something warm on you, we'll go and see them.'

They spent a couple of hours at Sarah's. The girls played in the garden on the climbing frame, bouncing on the trampoline and overeating. Mr Tunney made coffee for the adults and produced a homemade cake from the oven.

'Wow. That looks incredible,' Tricia said. 'I have to ask, does it contain nuts? I have a severe allergy.'

Mr Tunney assured her it was safe to eat.

Meagan listened to her mother apologise to Mr Tunney about Sarah, assuring him it would never happen again, explaining how ill she'd been and unaware of what had happened.

It was getting late. Meagan looked exhausted. Her cheeks were a bright red colour, her face full of cake and she struggled to keep her eyes open. Tricia made an excuse, keen to get home. Sean would be expecting them.

She couldn't face another confrontation.

As Tricia opened the front door, Sean was standing in the hall. 'You're up then?'

She paused, feeling anxious, fighting the start of a panic attack. 'Yes. I'm feeling better. Did you eat?'

'Where were you both?'

Tricia's face reddened, a rash developing on her chest. 'We

popped across the road; I wanted Meagan and Sarah to spend some time together. Do you want something to eat? I can cook something. How about eggs?' Tricia made her way past her husband, who was blocking her path.

'You heard what happened during the week, yet you went behind my back.'

Tricia looked at her daughter. 'Meagan, why don't you go play in your room?'

'I want to stay with you, Mummy.'

'Am I getting this right? Please tell me if I've missed anything?' Sean was trembling, looking like he'd explode.

'Please, Sean. Not now. I didn't do it to piss you off, I promise.'

Meagan looked at her father. 'I asked Mummy to bring me. It's not Mummy's fault.'

'Meagan, don't talk when I'm talking. Do you understand? How many times have you been told not to interfere when adults are talking?'

Tricia tried again to protect her daughter from what she feared would unfold. 'Meagan, baby, please go to your room.'

Her daughter whispered, 'I'm not leaving you, Mummy. I'll protect you, don't worry.'

'I'll ask again. Why did you disobey me, Tricia, when you're well aware of what happened during the week?'

Tricia flipped. It was fight or flight, she had to make a stand. 'Sean. For Christ's sake, you let a five-year-old child go home on her own. What if someone grabbed her? Or she was knocked over crossing the road? Why would you do such a thing?'

'You're such a bitch, you know that?'

'Daddy. That's a bad word. You can't say that to my Mummy.'

Tricia crouched, moving her hand through Meagan's hair. 'It's okay, baby. Daddy is just tired. He didn't mean it.'

Suddenly, Sean lifted his foot back, booting Tricia in the side of the face so that his wife fell hard on the ground.

As she winced, he kicked her in the ribs, a loud crack echoing through the hallway.

Tricia cried out, 'Sean, stop. Please, not in front of Meagan.'

As Tricia moved her hand to protect herself, Sean stamped on her fingers, twisting his foot, crushing her hand until it turned purple.

---

## 9

PRESENT DAY

Oliver found the storeroom in the darkness. He wanted to use his phone as a torch, but it was too conspicuous. He needed to keep in the shadows, move unnoticed. He slowly stepped along the cold concrete floor, feeling his way along the dingy corridor with his hands waving in front. The basement of the building gave off the odour of a crypt. The murky air was filled with dust particles and he struggled to breathe in the congested atmosphere.

Oliver dragged his left arm along the sharp wall, rough stones cutting the tips of his fingers. Finally, he touched a door handle towards the end of the corridor. He pulled it downwards, opening the heavy door. He removed his phone from his pocket and switched on the torch. Then he closed the door behind him.

He welcomed the light, adjusting his eyes, sweeping it across the room.

The storeroom was barren. Thick pipes clipped to the bottom of the wall gave off an uncomfortable heat.

Straight in front of him was a wooden shelf, with a bulging envelope in the middle.

Oliver picked it up, took a deep breath and made his way back out of the dark basement.

On the second floor the communal area was dimly lit and empty. He could hear water dripping in the distance. A light bulb flickered towards the end of the hall. Behind him, the lift bell rang continuously, the doors opening, bouncing awkwardly and closing unevenly, like they'd become disjointed.

He moved along the communal hall, edging the fire door open, scanning the apartments from the roof space outside. He watched the windows, seeing a couple towards the end of the block. Oliver moved closer, making sure Rob was asleep; it didn't bear thinking about if he was up, walking about. Then he went back inside.

Oliver had to be quick. He listened intently, scanning the area, knowing he had to move fast, in and out. He couldn't be seen – that would jeopardise everything.

He felt for the envelope in his pocket, making sure not to open it until he was inside apartment six.

Again, Oliver drew the phone from his pocket, moving the light towards the front doors. He was pleased to see they looked flimsy and he thought he wouldn't have a problem getting inside. *Apartment six. It's got to be one of these.* He recalled what Meagan had said, the clear instructions. Suddenly, his head was cloudy. He stumbled backwards, struggling to see, the building spinning like a carousel out of control. Oliver knelt, pressing his forehead to the ground. *Come on, you can do this. Be strong.* He urged himself to finish the task, pushing himself upwards. He was dazed, confused, struggling to understand his surroundings, a temporary mind-block.

He pictured Meagan's face, her disconcerted appearance, the fear in her eyes, her blank, empty expression. The telling signs of how she suffered at the hands of her husband. He needed to do this, for her, for them.

He'd become doubtful. He struggled to hold the light, his hands trembling. He was overwhelmed with nausea. His lips were dry, a cold chill rising through his body.

He moved back towards the stairs, shining the light at the door in front of him. A brass shape was hanging on a screw. He squinted his eyes, his vision again became blurry, but he was positive it said number six. He was certain.

'Yes, you beauty. Let's do this.'

He made sure the stairs were empty, waiting to see if he could hear anyone. Silence. No one coming down from above, no one coming up from below.

He peered towards the back of the building, watching the flickering light dance, seeing it suddenly go out, causing the hall to go into darkness.

Oliver held the torch in front of the door, aware of his heavy breathing. There was a dull noise ringing in his ears probably due to his stress, fear and anxiety. He took a step back, removing a bank card from his wallet, inhaled and jimmied the card in the lock. *Too much noise! Get a grip, Oliver, you can do this.* It sounded like scratching, nails being drawn down a chalkboard, then a heavy clunk like a hammer against steel. The lock loosened, the door flung open and suddenly Oliver was inside apartment six.

He found himself in a narrow hall. A soft light came from the kitchen towards the back, allowing him to see a little.

He held his breath for a moment, waiting.

Firstly, Oliver needed to find Rob. Meagan had said he'd be upstairs.

He shut the front door gently, moved along the hall and reached the stairs.

*Great, I'm inside,* he thought. *Find Rob, keep calm and as silent as possible.*

Oliver crept into the kitchen. He stood in the silence, listening for a sound, anything, a telltale sign that Rob was awake; a shift, footsteps, heavy breathing. It was quiet, so very quiet.

He backed out slowly, opening the door to his right; a closet filled with boxes and household cleaning materials, a pack of yellow J-cloths, a mop and bucket and a heavy-looking yard brush.

He closed the cupboard door gently, satisfied that no one was down here, then slowly went upstairs.

As he reached the top, Oliver found the bedroom to the left.

He listened outside, pushing his head closer to the bedroom door, again waiting, trying to be patient, understanding the need to rush, but he had to be careful, prioritise, make sure it was safe.

He placed his elbow on the large door handle, pushing it downwards, and the door budged slightly.

Oliver peered through the gap, gazing inside. A figure was lying on the bed, dressed in jeans and a shirt. The guy looked out of it, possibly drunk, or unconscious, maybe both.

Oliver stood by the bed, listening for any movement. He watched the chest moving slowly; light breaths in and out.

As Oliver stood motionless, fighting with the dread and panic that had suddenly taken over, he pulled the envelope from his jacket, removed the autoinjector and jabbed it into the guy's arm.

Oliver watched as the large figure suddenly jolted, his body beginning to spasm, kicking out, and a few seconds later he went completely limp. Oliver stood over him for another few minutes until mucous spilt from the guy's mouth, foam covering his lips. Then Oliver turned and left apartment six.

## TWENTY YEARS AGO - BEFORE THE PHONE CALL

M eagan stood outside her mum's bedroom, her ear placed against the door.

She was listening to her father, shouting, calling her mother a lazy bitch.

Of all the words she'd heard, that was the one her father used the most. She knew it was a cruel word. She saw it on her mother's face so many times; the embarrassed look whenever her husband had said it to her while Meagan was present.

Meagan hated that word, it rhymed with other horrible words; that's how Meagan worked out if a word was good or not. *Bitch* rhymed with *itch*. Something Meagan hated. Her friend Molly had a cat that was riddled with fleas, and Meagan had heard Molly's mother mention it, hence that was why Meagan had stopped visiting the house. She couldn't stand the bites.

*Bitch* also rhymed with *titch*. Jimmy Mertock, the school creep who persistently tried to kiss Meagan, had called her that word many times. It also rhymed with *snitch*, another word Jimmy called the girls when they told the teacher on him.

Meagan listened, her mouth open with shock. Her father was moving around the bed. 'You're a lazy bitch, good for nothing. I do everything for you, do you hear me? Without me, you'd be worthless. You understand what I'm saying?'

'Sean, please,' her mother begged.

Meagan heard a loud slap. She knew it was her father's hand across her mother's face.

Tricia was crying, then another slap. Meagan was shaking as she pulled the handle of the door and entered the room.

'I can't do this anymore, I can't. I don't want to live.' Her mother was sobbing, hugging a soft pillow, shaking desperately.

The words rang out. Meagan stood in shock as her father again lifted his hand and slapped his wife. He spun round, a look of shock on his face, then hurried past his daughter and across the landing to his room.

Meagan moved towards her mother, eyeing the bandage that was tightly wrapped around her hand. 'Are you okay, Mummy?'

Her mother attempted to sit up, wincing in pain. 'I'm all right, sweetheart. What have you been doing?'

Meagan dismissed the question. She looked towards her mother's dresser. 'Shall I comb your hair?'

Tricia smiled. 'That would be nice.'

As Meagan reached for the brush, she quizzed her mother. 'Why do you want to die, Mummy?'

'Oh, baby, I don't want to die. Don't ever think that. How could I leave you?'

'Does Daddy make you want to die?'

Tricia waited, attempting to speak, unsure how to answer, then changed the subject. 'Come up onto the bed and sort my hair out. Have you seen Sarah today?'

'I've been watching telly. I think I'll go see her later. She has a guinea pig, you know.'

'A guinea pig, huh. Well, you'll have to go and see.'

As Meagan combed her mother's hair, Tricia fought back the tears, struggling to stem the lump in her throat. She thought how difficult it must be for her daughter, having to witness the cruelty inflicted on her. She knew how a child's life is mapped out from early memories and how so often her daughter observed Sean's behaviour.

As Meagan gently ran the brush through her mother's hair, she told her about school, who her close friends were, the kids she disliked, the teachers that always seemed cross and how Jimmy Mertock always tried to kiss her.

Tricia laughed as Meagan scrunched her face when she said his name. 'I think that maybe you like Jimmy Mertock?'

'Yuk. I do not. He's creepy, that's what Sarah says.'

'Well, Sarah is wrong to say that about Jimmy. He's just struggling to contain his emotions. Now, what do you say we go downstairs and eat?'

'But I haven't finished making you look beautiful, Mummy.'

'Meagan, it will take a lot more than combing my hair to make me look beautiful. Come on.'

Tricia edged her way to the kitchen, and proceeded to make poached eggs on toast. Suddenly she heard Sean stomp down the stairs, shouting from the hallway. 'I'll be home this evening.'

He shut the front door, and Tricia listened to the car pulling off the drive, breathing a sigh of relief, finally able to relax.

After they had eaten Tricia asked Meagan to clear her plate and wash up. 'You can visit Sarah and see her guinea pig.'

Meagan sighed. 'Can't Daddy do the washing-up?'

'No arguments, Meagan, come on. I'll have a quick freshen up, and I want it done by the time I come down.'

'Fine.' Meagan moved her plate to the sink. 'I hate Daddy.'

'Meagan, please. We've been through this.'

Twenty minutes later, Meagan was holding Arthur the rabbit in her hands, while she and Sarah chased the guinea pig around the garden.

The adults were inside, drinking coffee.

'I want a pet. My daddy always says no. My daddy hit mummy this morning.'

Sarah looked up. 'Why does your mummy allow him to hit her?'

'I don't know. I think he hates her. He called her a horrible word too.'

'My daddy loves us,' replied Sarah.

Meagan thought about what Sarah had just said. 'Well, Daddy loves me. Just not Mummy.'

'He can't love you if he hits your mummy.'

'He does love me. Don't say things like that, Sarah.'

'He hates your mummy, and he hates you too.'

'He does not hate me.'

'Yes, he does. My dad says he's a pig, just like Arthur.'

'Arthur's a guinea pig; they're tinier. And you copied me. My toy rabbit is called Arthur. I thought of the name first.' Meagan moved away from her friend and went inside. She didn't like how Sarah teased her. Usually, they got along well, but Sarah seemed to enjoy goading Meagan about her dad, which always upset her.

Tricia and Meagan spent another couple of hours with the Tunneys.

Suddenly Tricia's face turned scarlet. Mr Tunney spoke, but Tricia couldn't register the words. As she looked through the living room window across the road to her house, she watched Sean's car pull up on the drive.

## 11

PRESENT DAY

Oliver walked out onto the street, the cold air slapping him hard. He was breathless, struggling to compose himself. All of a sudden, it dawned on him what he'd done and he was already wrestling with his conscience. Oliver questioned how Meagan had such a hold over him.

*I've just killed somebody. I poisoned him, watched him draw his last breath. I did that. Maybe he deserved it for the things he'd done, but killing him, that makes me just as bad.*

Oliver struggled to push the thoughts from his head. He needed to get out of there and home before someone spotted him.

He fought with his paranoia, images flashing in his mind of someone seeing what he did and calling the police; vans turning up with dogs sniffing his scent, racing after him down the quiet street; the police finding him in his bed and cuffing him, leading him out of his apartment, past his concerned neighbours. He heard the whispers. *Yeah, Oliver is his name, a right bloody nutter that one. He was always a weird sort of guy. Never mixed with people. A total oddball if you ask me.*

Oliver assembled his thoughts, going through the last few

minutes, recalling the incident. He'd got inside apartment six, gone upstairs and poisoned the guy. Had he been seen entering the building or on the second floor? Could anyone have heard?

He stood still, composing himself. He needed to call a taxi, but there'd be records, a file kept by the controller, who would be happy to help. *Oh yes, he did call. It was late. I thought something was up, you know, he sounded odd. He was breathless and struggling to get his words out. I knew straight away he was a bad one. I told the driver, I warned him, 'don't pick this weirdo up'.*

He started walking along the street, conscious not to look out of place, taking it slow. He couldn't look conspicuous and draw attention to himself. He slowed, easing to a stroll, looking over his shoulder.

*God, what have I done?* He thought about Meagan, trying to ease his conscience, tackling the guilt. Everything was for her, for the shit she goes through each day. He pictured her face, her beautiful features, the cuts, bruises, the beating her partner gave her outside the apartment block. It ran through his mind like a recording.

Oliver imagined being sat in the cinema watching the show, rows of people drinking Coke and stuffing their faces with over-sized tubs of popcorn. Rob putting the boot in, Meagan wincing, the watching crowd booing, throwing rolled up paper napkins at the screen.

Suddenly, Oliver rides in on a huge white horse, somersaults onto the street. He races up the stairs to apartment six and rescues Meagan.

Everyone is cheering, queuing to shake his hand after the short production. Rows of people lined up in the cinema aisles are clapping, whistling, patting him on the back.

He thought about calling Meagan. *It's too risky.* Maybe just a text to tell her it's done? *No, it's time to lie low, under the radar. If anyone finds out what's happened, the first thing the police check is phone records.*

Oliver tried to remember who had been at the pub the night he met Meagan. Panic set in. The barmaid? No, she was more interested in the guy at the end of the counter buying her drinks and flirting.

The group of youths knocking back whisky chasers? They wouldn't have noticed if a bulldozer had rammed through the front door. Besides, they left a little after Oliver arrived, probably landing in a nearby ditch. He recalled a couple who were playing pool, sharing peanuts and a bottle of red wine. Oliver was sure they hadn't looked over.

He needed to pull himself together, gain control, get home.

Oliver pictured the guy lying in bed. He pictured injecting him with the autoinjector, the way his body had spasmed, the noises he made.

He leant over into a bush and vomited.

Oliver closed the front door to his apartment, fastening the double lock, sliding the security chain in place. He leaned against the wall, using it to support his weight. Regret washed over him. He struggled to come to terms with the act he'd just carried out, running it over and over in his mind. He'd just killed a man, ended his life, terminated his existence. Oliver was freaking out. He needed to hear Meagan's voice, speak with her so she could make it all okay, bearable. He knew it was impossible. They'd planned to keep their distance, no contact.

Suddenly he thought of Claire, the girl he had shared so many great times with. He could call her, leave the apartment, go to her. She said they could remain friends. Maybe that's what he needed; to get off this rollercoaster and hide.

From the living room window the lights over West London were blinding. Oliver reached out, pulling the cord of the heavy blinds, watching them fall, listening to the crunching noise as they bounced, darkening the apartment suddenly. *Where was Meagan? Did she say I could call, or was she calling me? How long can I wait? I need to speak with her, find out the plan. We can go through this together, organise what to do next.*

He was distracted by a siren in the distance, an ambulance, police maybe. London had sirens day and night, it was a city that never stopped. It was getting nearer, louder, coming towards him.

Oliver quickly went to his bedroom window, which over-looked the street. He was struggling to contain a panic attack that had threatened since he'd left apartment six. He wiped the sweat from his forehead. The heating was off, the apartment chilly, but Oliver now felt on fire.

The siren was almost on top of him, blaring through his head. He looked to the ground below the window: flashing blue lights, a large vehicle with a ladder on top. A fire engine, not a police car. He watched as it passed the building, turning right into a side street. The noise disappeared in the distance, a faint whirring sound fading into the background.

Oliver paced back and forth across the kitchen floor, rubbing his fingers together, reaching for the fridge, closing the door, moving toward the window, lifting the blind slightly. The nervous energy was all too much; he needed to rest, take a bath, read. *I can't concentrate! How can I do any of these things?*

He lay on the sofa, picked up the remote control and flicked through channels to find the news. A reporter was standing outside the prime minister's house, talking about NHS staffing. He turned the volume up slightly, and after a few minutes, two people appeared sitting in a studio, briefly going through local news bulletins from earlier today. Nothing about apartment six.

He was safe, for now.

~

For most of the day, Meagan had sat in the coffee shop. She was buzzing from the effect of caffeine, numb from sitting in the same spot at a table near the front.

She needed to be seen, that was important in case anyone asked questions later.

She began to have doubts about whether Oliver had gone through with it. Had he broken into the apartment and done what he had promised? She imagined him at the last minute, turning back, going home, never contacting her again. It would kill her, him backing out, changing his mind, deciding it's not what he wanted, leaving Meagan to live the rest of her life with her bastard of a husband.

She wasn't brave enough to do it herself. Meagan couldn't comprehend killing someone, especially Rob; he'd overpower her, looking into her eyes, that smirk, the snarl starting from deep within, his face, the evil expression and the spell he'd cast. She'd bottle it, collapse in a heap and have to face the aftermath.

A shiver raced down her spine and goose pimples rose on her arms.

'Another coffee?'

She jumped. The waitress was standing in front of her.

Meagan glanced at her watch. It was getting late. Rob would be home, unpacking his clothes; he'd take a shower and then get into bed.

'Go on then, thanks.' Meagan smiled as the waitress passed a menu across the table, dropping it in front of her.

'No, just the coffee, thank you.'

'Very well.'

The waitress had been working all the time Meagan had been sitting there, approaching her every half hour or so. Meagan made sure she spoke with her, asking her how she was, making it obvious when she'd finished her drink and wanted another.

She debated whether to call Oliver. Her phone was still switched off for fear of Rob and his tracking apps. She couldn't risk it. She needed to stay off the radar and away from Albuquerque House.

The waitress returned, Meagan gratefully accepted the drink, commenting on the rain, how cold it had got.

She sipped her coffee, looking at the walls, up at the ceiling, distracting herself.

People came inside, brushing water from their coats, smiling at her as they went to look at the menu behind the counter.

She watched couples hand in hand, families settling down after shopping, storing large expensive labelled carrier bags under the table beside them, talking about the theatre, films, news, sport, laughing together.

Meagan found herself becoming envious. She and Rob would never have this type of relationship. Her life was a mess. Meagan thought back to when she first met him, how they laughed, held each other, talked for hours and made crazy, passionate love every moment they could. The continuous text messages whenever they were apart. They ate together at the best restaurants, went to the best bars and walked home arm in arm. Nothing else existed and no one else mattered.

How could it happen? How could Rob change so quickly? Sarah had warned her. 'He's not for you, hun. You could do so much better. Give it more time.'

Thinking back, maybe he bullied her into the relationship, and she was too green to see past it and realise what was happening.

Meagan rechecked her watch. It was getting late. *Oliver must have visited the apartment by now.*

She finished her coffee, paid the bill, then stood. She had a sudden head rush as she reached down to take her handbag and the room spun. She breathed, in and out, steadying herself. Then she waved to the waitress and went out onto the street.

The cold air was too much. Meagan's cheeks felt flushed after being in the warmth all afternoon. A bus passed, soaking her with rainwater. She moved slowly, not wanting to draw attention, her head down, her frame slouching. Her mind buzzed. Meagan regretted drinking so much coffee, with the caffeine pumping through her veins. *This is it, girl. Time to see if Oliver has come good. Be brave now, be very, very brave.*

She crossed over the road, looking up at the four-storey building.

## TWENTY YEARS AGO - BEFORE THE PHONE CALL

Meagan awoke and raced into her mother's room, jumping on her bed.

The covers were pulled up, the bed neatly made.

'Mummy, where are you?' She waited for a response, pulling herself across the bed to the other side, leaning towards the ground and hanging forwards, her hands on the floor. Meagan peered under the bed.

'Mummy?' She glanced towards the dresser, seeing her mother's comb, the small mirror, the make-up bag with the zip half open, a lipstick balancing on the closed jewellery box. Everything was as Meagan had remembered yesterday.

'She must be hiding.' Meagan shouted out, 'I'll find you, Mummy. Don't worry.' Meagan climbed off the bed, raced excitedly out to the hall and went down the stairs.

She went into the garden, looking in the usual places; the garden shed towards the back, behind the rack of tools, the tall cabinet, under the wooden workbench. 'I know you're here somewhere; I've just got to find you.'

Meagan left the shed, looking towards the miniature pond that contained a small collection of goldfish and a ceramic fish spilling water from its mouth. Behind was a small patch of wood-land that had large oak trees. Meagan recalled hiding there with Sarah a couple of times.

'Mummy, I'm coming to find you.' She crept on tiptoes, moving towards the trees. After a couple of minutes looking, she gave up. 'Umm, you're too good at this, Mummy.'

Back in the house, Meagan checked the rooms downstairs, all the places where she and her mother had hidden before.

As she went to go back upstairs, her father came out of his room.

'Where's Mummy? I can't find her anywhere. Have you seen her, Daddy?'

Her father moved to the stairs as Meagan climbed the steps. She had the usual knot in her stomach anytime she was alone with him.

'Go and wash your face, young lady. You look awful.'

'I-I've been looking for Mummy. Can you help me?'

'Don't be ridiculous. I have adult things to deal with. I don't have time to mess around.'

Meagan knew better than to answer back. She went into the bathroom to throw cold water on her face, annoyed that her father dismissed her so casually.

At dinner, they sat in silence. Meagan was unable to lift her head and look at her father. She felt scared. Her mother had never left the house without bringing Meagan or at least letting her know where she was going.

Meagan twirled the pasta with her fork, staring at the food. 'I've had enough now. Can I go and play for a little bit?'

'Eat everything. You know the rules, young lady.'

She looked up briefly, watching her father stare into the distance, his cold impassive glare, his dark eyes. Meagan was certain she saw a smirk appear on his face.

At bedtime, Meagan found her father in his bedroom. She often wondered why he slept in a separate room. Sarah's parents slept together. She pictured Mr and Mrs Tunney, cuddled together in the bed. *Yuk.*

As she knocked and entered, her father was talking quietly on his phone.

'Is Mummy coming back tonight? She reads me a story. We're at the good part of *The Gingerbread Man.* I know how the story ends.'

Her father turned off the phone. He crouched, reaching out. Meagan edged towards him and held her father around the waist, her arms only managing to slide a quarter way around his frame.

'Brush your teeth and then bed. Do you hear me, young lady?'

'Yes, Daddy.'

As she left the room, her father called out, 'Love you, Meggy.'

A queasiness formed in Meagan's stomach and she struggled to control her breathing. Her father never called her Meggy.

Meagan lay in bed, listening to the rain pelting against her window. She eyed the copy of *The Gingerbread Man* lying on her bedside cabinet. She could hear her mother's soft voice reading the story. Meagan remembered how she'd glance at her over her reading glasses and push a hand through her daughter's hair at the scary parts, watching her daughter's wild expressions. Her mother would finish the story, then lie on the bed with her arm wrapped tightly around her daughter, making Meagan feel safe. Her mother would place the book to the side, instructing Meagan to turn the side lamp off after ten minutes.

Then Meagan would listen as her father entered the room next door, saying bad words while her mother cried. Meagan listened to the pitiful sobs, wishing she could go in and comfort her mother.

Tears filled Meagan's eyes as she stepped onto the floor of her bedroom.

Looking out of her window, she watched the rain lashing outside, small droplets of water running down the glass as if the window was crying, hoping her mummy was going to be all right.

～

That night, Meagan had a dream. She was running through a field, her father just in front, pounding the ground in his bare feet, effortlessly sweeping through the long grass in his path.

Meagan looked over her shoulder; her mother was behind and floating through the air. Her mother's dress was colourful with bright spots, and she wore ballet shoes.

Her father was beckoning them to hurry, Meagan reached out a hand and her mother grabbed hold of it. Suddenly they were side by side.

Her father stopped just in front, turning towards his wife and daughter. He crouched, holding his arms out, pulling them both into his embrace, the three of them were so happy, content. Meagan was laughing, a childish giggle as her mother and father danced to soft, old-style music. Her father led, her mother was spinning, then he tucked her under his arms and flipped her over. They were graceful, like swans gliding across the water.

Meagan sat on a nearby haystack, the sky clear, and the air warm.

Her parents held each other tight; she watched them kiss, then her father extended his arm, with her mother rolling outwards, spinning. She stopped, then carried out the same move in reverse until they held each other again.

Sarah had joined them and was sitting beside Meagan. The girls were laughing and excited at the amazing spectacle.

Her father once again extended his arm, Meagan's mother was on tiptoes, lifting her leg outwards, then twisting and whirling like a spinning top.

Meagan stood, suddenly her mother was gone and her father's arms were empty.

Sarah screamed as Meagan leapt off the haystack. Her mother had disappeared.

Meagan opened her eyes. The rain was still pelting against the window, the stream of water dripping down the glass. She cuddled into Arthur and went back to sleep.

## 13

### PRESENT DAY

Meagan took a deep breath as she removed the front door key from her handbag, placed it in the lock and went inside to the communal hall.

She'd never been more nervous, struggling to contain the anticipation.

But the excitement edged her fear, something a dozen coffees couldn't simulate. She walked past the table by the front door; today's post was scattered untidily across the top.

Meagan crossed the communal hall on the ground floor. The lift was still out of service. She listened to her heavy breathing. It was as if she was wearing a mask that emphasised her laboured breaths.

Meagan went up the stairs, watching, listening intently, her mind racing.

She pictured Oliver here earlier. How brave he'd been, doing all this for her. She imagined the emotions racing through his body.

As Meagan reached the second floor, she stood still. *Okay, you can do this. Get a grip and face what you have to face. It's what needed to happen. Remember that. This needed to happen.*

Meagan opened the door of apartment six. Her stomach was somersaulting, spinning in all directions. Sharp pains pulsed through her arms. She felt as if her body would give way any second, and she'd drop in a heap to the floor.

She crouched, then sat in the hall, controlling her breathing, drawing a prolonged, deep intake, then out slowly. Once she regained her composure, Meagan stood, and placed her coat and handbag on the rail.

Meagan called out, 'Rob, are you home?' She had to be sure.

No answer.

Meagan checked the rooms off the hall. They were all empty.

The kitchen was also vacant. She moved to the bathroom. She needed the toilet; she'd had too much coffee, and her nerves were gradually taking over.

After a minute, she flushed the loo, washed her hands and left the room, checking the floor behind for any drops of water.

She made her way slowly along the hall. Now she was at the foot of the stairs, glancing upwards. She went up, one step at a time.

Her heart was racing. She could feel the early stages of a migraine, with the left side of her head pulsating. Her body throbbed. She was weak. She struggled to fight the fatigue that was slowly creeping over her, emanating from her legs.

Near the top of the stairs from sheer force of habit she extended her leg and stepped across the third step from the top.

She stood on the upstairs landing, then went to the bedroom and placed her hand on the door. It creaked as she pushed slowly, causing her to jolt and grind her teeth.

Meagan stood motionless.

The light to the bedroom was off, the bed was empty.

Meagan had to ring Oliver. She thought about the call log, and how easily it could be traced. At that moment, she didn't care. She raced down the stairs, got her phone from her handbag and quickly returned to the bedroom.

She dialled Oliver's number, and he picked up after the third ring.

'Did you do what we planned?' she asked.

Oliver paused. She wondered if he was irritated by her call. 'Meagan. Yes, of course I've done it. Do you know how fucking shit I feel at this second?'

'Look, we'll deal with that later. Come over, now, quickly.' She hung up without waiting for his response.

Oliver arrived thirty minutes later. Meagan was waiting for him in the hall. He watched as she stood, gripping her hair, her frustration evident.

'Where is he, Oliver?'

'He's in the bedroom upstairs.'

Meagan looked at him, watching his fearful expression and the agitation in his body. He was unable to keep still and shuffled from one leg to the other.

'Show me!' Meagan demanded, her voice louder and more shrill than she'd expected.

Oliver led her upstairs. As he opened the bedroom door and flicked on the light, Meagan stood behind him. They both peered across at an empty bed.

Meagan looked at her phone, suddenly seeing a voicemail alert. She played it on loudspeaker. 'Meagan. It's Rob. Look, something's come up, I won't be home this afternoon as planned. It's important I stay for another day. I'll catch a flight in the morning. See you then.'

Meagan spun round, looking at Oliver. 'Who the fuck did you kill?'

## 14

TWENTY YEARS AGO - BEFORE THE
PHONE CALL

Meagan woke, thinking about the dream she'd had the night before.

The curtains in her bedroom were open, the light shining through the window. The rain had cleared, but the sky was overcast, patches of blue trying to push through.

Meagan lifted herself off the bed and listened at the bedroom door. She could hear her father shifting in his room across the landing. She gauged what kind of a mood he was in this morning. Occasionally he'd whistle to himself; that was good. Other times, he raised his voice, talking on the phone, puffing sharp breaths; that wasn't so good and it was best to keep out of his way. This morning his bedroom door was open. Meagan watched as he fixed his brown tie, slipping into a dark jacket, combing cream through his hair.

He looked at Meagan. 'Morning, did you sleep well?'

She wanted to close the door and never open it again. 'Uh huh.'

He sprayed cologne on his hands and rubbed them on his face, fixing his tie again.

'Why do people wear ties, Daddy? They're weird.'

'You need your breakfast. Hurry up now.'

Meagan opened the door wider, passing her mother's room. She was thrilled to find her in the bed, sitting up, propped on a couple of pillows.

'Mummy. Where did you go? I'm so happy you're home.' She raced across the bedroom floor, leaping on the bed.

'Easy now.' Her mother winced. Meagan noticed dirt marks under her nails, like she'd been clawing through mud. Her feet were black, poking out from under the sheet and she had scratch marks on her forearms.

'It's so good to see you, Mummy. I thought you'd gone away forever. I looked all over.'

Tricia reached out, pulling her daughter closer. 'I have a surprise.'

'What is it, Mummy? Tell me.'

'Well, Mr and Mrs Tunney have invited us for a barbecue at Sarah's house. Won't that be nice?'

Meagan peered into her father's room, dropping her voice to a whisper. 'Daddy doesn't like us going there. I thought he hated Sarah.'

'Oh Meagan, don't be silly. Anyway, Daddy's car broke down this morning, so Mr Tunney helped get it going and invited us over.' Tricia laughed. 'He couldn't say no, now could he? Go and wash, then I'll get us something to eat.'

'You need to wash too, Mummy. What happened? Did you sleep in a pit or something?'

Meagan watched her mother turn away as the colour drained from her face. 'Please, Meggy, go and wash. Enough with the questions, young lady.'

Just after midday, Meagan's father returned. He had been out for most of the morning. His mood had become more serious, and his face more troubled.

Meagan and Tricia waited patiently while Sean went upstairs to the bathroom to freshen up. He returned a few minutes later, his face beaming, and Tricia struggled to read his state of mind.

The three of them walked across the road together. Tricia wore a summer dress. Sean had donned a pair of short jeans, trainers and a loose white T-shirt. Meagan wore a plain yellow dress.

Sarah was waiting at the front door, waving overexcitedly.

Meagan glanced at her mother, who nodded in approval and let her daughter run across the road.

Mr Tunney came into view, lifting Sarah and swinging her round at the door. Meagan felt a tad envious, wishing her father would do the same thing to her.

They greeted each other at the front door. Sean thanked Mr Tunney again for fixing his car that morning and the invite. 'God knows I can do with some downtime. It's been pretty hectic lately; work, family. You know how it is.'

Mr Tunney reached out, placing an arm around Sean, greeting Tricia with a kiss on the cheek and a sly eye roll as if to acknowledge the self-centred remark.

The girls hugged awkwardly, then disappeared into the garden to play with the guinea pig.

Although still overcast, the day had significantly brightened. Everyone was in good spirits, drinking, chatting and enjoying being together outside.

Tricia heard Sean talking to Mr Tunney about the horses, explaining how to place a bet, an accumulator, a tenfold and how he often got tips from the stables, claiming he knew someone who knew someone who worked with a trainer. *Yeah, right.*

She watched Mr Tunney, a gentleman as always, listening intently, never moving his eyes from Sean as he spoke, holding his wife's hand and making sure everyone had drinks. His social skills were incredible. He always said the right thing, always cared for the people around him. He reminded Tricia of a head teacher; authoritative, trustworthy and reliable. He also spent time with his daughter and listened to her. That was his most impressive attribute. He listened.

Tricia stared at her husband, watching how well he interacted, how confident he was, and how genuine he seemed. If only they knew.

As Sean opened another bottle of beer, Meagan came racing over. 'Daddy, please can we get a guinea pig? Sarah says they are so easy to look after. Please, Daddy?'

He laughed, assuring his daughter it would never happen. Tricia changed the subject, talking to Mrs Tunney about the school that the girls attended.

Meagan was pulling at her father's arm, pleading for a pet.

Sean spoke over her, sounding embarrassingly loud.

'Daddy. Can I please? Please, Daddy?'

He leant forward and shoved his daughter. Everyone watched her stumble backwards, her right arm breaking her fall.

She was crying. Tricia jumped up, going over to make sure her daughter was okay. She looked towards her husband with venom in her eyes. 'Sean, really, did you have to do that?'

Sarah came over, concerned for her friend, helping her to stand.

Sean stood up abruptly, knocking his chair over. 'Guinea pig! Fucking guinea pig. Is that all you lot can think about for Christ's sake?'

'Sean, watch your language, please,' Tricia instructed.

Mr Tunney intervened. 'Come on, Sean. Forget about it. Drink your beer.' He regretted the proposal instantly.

Sean swung the bottle up, guzzling half the drink and cracking open another one.

Tricia looked on, perplexed. 'Sean, go easy.'

He was mid-sentence, raising his hand, beckoning Mr Tunney to wait. 'What did you say?' directing the question at Tricia.

She went red, feeling her heart race. 'I just said "go easy". It's a long day. Pace yourself is all I'm saying.'

Sean reached forward, grabbing his wife by the hair, pulling her head back. A large vein showed blue against her pale throat. 'Say it again.'

'Sean. You're hurting me. Stop.'

As Sean let go of his wife's hair he clasped her jaw, squeezing tightly. 'Don't get all brave because we're in company. If I have an instruction, you'll hear it regardless of who I'm with.' He let go, pushing her face away.

Mr Tunney and his wife looked away, unsure of how to act.

Sean turned. 'Where was I?'

Mr Tunney stood, instantly clearing the plates, bringing them inside. His wife followed, then Tricia got up, staying close behind them and leaving Sean to think about his actions.

A little later, it started to rain, a light drizzle that forced everyone inside. Tricia sat at the table, deep in conversation with Mrs Tunney. The girls had chosen to position themselves on the floor, lying on their bellies, stuffing their faces with popcorn, watching cartoons.

Mr Tunney stood at the sink washing plates. His wife called out, 'Sarah, can you go and get the guinea pig? He'll perish outside.'

Sarah jumped up and Meagan followed her. The girls ran out to the garden. 'Can I hold him this time?' Meagan asked.

'Okay. But not for long, remember he's my pet.'

As Mr Tunney placed the dishes into a cupboard, he heard Sarah screaming. He looked into the garden from the kitchen window, saw Meagan holding her hands to her mouth. He went to the back door, calling out, 'What is it, girls? What's wrong?'

Mrs Tunney jumped up, Tricia moving with her. They made their way down the garden path. On the ground at the girls' feet the guinea pig lay motionless. Its head had been removed.

Inside Sean was putting on his jacket and heading out the door.

## 15

## PRESENT DAY

Oliver stood over the empty bed.

'It's not the same room. It's not where I broke into.' He was pointing at a tall grey bedside lamp. He turned to view the room layout, the large wardrobe standing behind the bed, the open curtains allowing him to see outside. 'This isn't the same apartment. It's different.'

Meagan watched him. 'It's different?' There was contempt in her voice. This is my apartment, our home. This was the plan, Oliver. What the fuck have you done?'

Oliver held up his hand. 'Wait. Just wait, I need to think.' He played out the scene in his head; getting into the building, finding the store cupboard in the basement, climbing the stairs, standing in the communal hallway on the second floor, the lift to his right, finding apartment six, jimmying the Yale lock with a credit card, opening the front door. He'd acted quickly, not taking any notice. Why would he?

He recalled how disorientated he'd become, stressed from their scheme, the plan that they'd plotted together. He remembered steadying himself, holding onto the hallway wall, but Oliver was struggling to recall what happened.

He moved out of the bedroom, down the stairs and out to the communal hall, Meagan following.

'I need to get this clear. I came up to the second floor. I found number seven at the top of the stairs. I counted down the apartments from the right. I remember finding number six past the lift.' Oliver pointed along the hall. 'That's apartment six, down there. I shone the torch on the door, for fuck's sake. Look and see.' He quickly went past the lift. 'This is number six'.

Oliver shone the torch at the door he was standing in front of, next to the apartment that he and Meagan had just walked out from. The number on the door was clear and visible – apartment seven. 'Wait, that can't be! I remember seeing it clearly when I came here earlier. I was sure this was apartment six. I walked along the hall to the right of the stairs, and past the lift. Number seven was next door, the one we've just come out from. I'm fucking sure, Meagan.'

Oliver pointed to the first apartment to the right of the stairs, the apartment he'd broken into.

Meagan stood dishevelled, numb. Oliver listened to her rapid breathing, saw the tension in her body. He heard the panic in her throat as she tried to talk. She stood back, watching him, staring right through his body.

After a minute, she mustered the strength to speak. 'The apartments go down, not up, not fucking up, Oliver. I'm six, to the right is seven, then eight. How the fuck could you get it wrong? How, Oliver?'

'Keep your voice down; we'll be heard, for Christ's sake. I made a fucking mistake.' Oliver went out to the fire escape, gaining access to the back. 'There, see?' He was pointing to a large window. He guessed it was the kitchen. Oliver and Meagan stood on the flat roof space, surrounded by small cupboards containing the water tanks.

Oliver pointed towards a window at the end of the building. 'Earlier, there was a couple in the kitchen just there; I watched as a woman mixed ingredients in a bowl, her partner pouring them wine. He kept pulling her towards him, showering her with kisses, and she was jokingly pushing him away, holding up a finger to let him know he'd have to wait. I kind of guessed it wasn't you and Rob. I waited. A light came on in the room to the right of the kitchen, the same guy moving across the floor, setting out plates. I remember he lit candles. I watched them sit and eat, knowing I wouldn't get disturbed.'

Meagan looked up at the window; the lights were now off. 'Yeah, that's Jen and Paul. They moved into apartment eight a couple of months back. What did you do then?'

Oliver paused, thinking, trying to recall his exact movements. 'Okay. So I looked to the left of where I saw the couple, to the one I thought was your apartment where I'd find Rob. I had to be sure I had it right. I looked in at the windows, keeping hidden. I made sure Rob wasn't downstairs walking around. The lights were off as I looked across the kitchen into the hall. Then I made my way back to the communal hall and got inside the apartment.' Oliver looked towards Meagan, fear in his eyes. 'For fuck's sake, what have I done?'

They stood in the hall, staring, blank expressions on both their faces, thinking what to do.

Meagan broke the silence. 'Look, did anybody see you?'

'No. I'm pretty sure of it.'

'Pretty sure isn't good enough, Oliver. Why did you go out onto the roof? The instructions were clear. You've just killed an innocent man. How are we going to deal with it?'

He dropped to his knees, holding his head with both hands, pulling his hair. 'I don't fucking know. It's your mistake, Meagan. You said apartment six was on the second floor, to the right.'

Meagan raised her voice. 'Left. I fucking said left. I know

what I bloody said. Top of the stairs to the left. Don't go blaming me, Oliver.'

Oliver stood. 'We need to deal with it – both of us. It's our mess now. We're in it together.'

Meagan turned, rubbing her face hard, swinging her head back, facing away towards the back of the communal hall. 'We need to get rid of the body.' She turned back round. 'Do you hear me?'

Oliver contemplated the idea, mulling it over. 'How, exactly?'

'You broke in earlier. Do it again. You get your car, then we lift the body downstairs, load it into the boot, drive and dump it somewhere, that's how.'

'You're crazy. We'll never get away with it. We'll be seen. You know it.'

'Not if we're quick. The hardest part will be getting it outside; the rest should be straightforward.'

Oliver thought. He could run, get out now and never return. Leave Meagan to deal with the shit. He could disappear and she'd never find him.

'Oliver. Are you hearing me?'

'Yes. I hear you. Let's do it then.'

Oliver removed from his wallet the card that he'd used to gain entry earlier. Placing it into the side of the door, he slid it, pulling up and down, forcing the lock.

'Hurry up,' Meagan demanded.

'I'm doing my best here.'

He wriggled the card, pushing it hard against the Yale. 'Come on.'

'Where did you learn to do this?'

'My granddad was a locksmith. When I was younger, he took

me out on Saturdays. I carried his tools mostly, but every so often he let me have a go. I guess it's like riding a bike.'

The door opened. Oliver entered and Meagan followed. 'Hello. Is anyone here?'

'Oliver, for Christ's sake. What are you doing?'

'I have to be sure. What if he has a visitor, or someone else lives here with him?'

Meagan suddenly had a flashback to when she'd called Oliver. 'Shit, the girl in the bath. This is gloved-man's apartment.'

Oliver climbed the stairs, trying to ignore what Meagan had said. He couldn't deal with this now.

Using his phone torch to light the path, he went upstairs to the bedroom. Meagan shut the front door and followed him.

They looked at the body, the guy lying on his stomach, motionless.

'There's not much time,' Oliver announced. 'We need to get him out of here.'

'And how do you envisage doing that? We can't just walk out of here with him, wandering around in the hall with a stiff and risk being seen. Use your bloody head, Oliver.'

'I'm thinking. How can you expect me to do anything when you're shouting? You're making me panic. This isn't my fucking fault.'

Meagan stared across, wanting to shake him, make him realise the seriousness of the shit that had gone down and what he'd done. Now wasn't the time to curl up in a ball and pass the blame back and forth. They had to act fast, hide the corpse, move it out of there to somewhere safe – someplace it would never be found.

'Wait.' Meagan had a plan. 'Here's what we'll do, Oliver. It might just work.'

Oliver watched as she paced around the bedroom of apartment seven, her brain working overtime.

'Rob has a travel trunk; a large leather container where he keeps his paperwork, all sorts of shit from the club he owns. He hasn't opened it for ages. It's lying in the spare room downstairs under the bed. He shouldn't miss it. Come and help me get it, and if anyone sees us, we can make out we're helping a friend move, storing junk, anything, but it won't look suspicious.'

They found the trunk exactly where Meagan had said it was. Oliver lifted the bed while Meagan slid it out into view.

Oliver crouched beside it, feeling the top, blowing off the dust and sizing up the container. 'It's perfect. Quick, let's get it out and move the body. We haven't got much time.' He opened the leather flap while Meagan ran to the kitchen, returning with a handful of carrier bags.

Oliver lifted the paperwork out in bundles, flicking through the contents.

'What are you doing? We're on a fucking deadline here. Dump everything into the bags and let's go. Jesus, Oliver.'

Once everything was neatly bagged, Meagan slid the contents under the bed. There were four carrier bags that Meagan would have to explain the next time Rob came looking for the trunk. But she didn't care to think about that at this moment.

Oliver felt the weight of the trunk, thankful it wasn't as heavy as it looked.

Meagan came out from under the bed. 'Okay. Let's bring the trunk next door, get the body into it and go.'

Oliver lifted the trunk, trying to balance it while Meagan guided him, making sure it was safe. He struggled, unable to see in front, because the large trunk was pushed against his face. He was trying to get a grip, his arms wrapped around it in a bear hug, and he was banging into the walls on the way out.

'You need to be careful, Oliver, someone will hear. That's it, move along, no, no, back up a little. There you go, that's it.'

Oliver struggled to squeeze the trunk through the front door and out into the communal hallway.

Once inside apartment seven, he laid the trunk on the ground and Meagan moved around the side, gripping the handle. They pushed it awkwardly up the stairs. It was much easier to move now that the two of them had a hold of it.

'Okay. You lift him, I'll grab his legs. On three.' Meagan was standing in the bedroom, with Oliver just in front of her. They were staring at the body.

'I don't think I can.'

'What are you talking about? Hold him, Oliver. This is ridiculous. Or shall we leave him here? Is that a better plan?' Meagan asked with a hint of sarcasm.

'What if he moves? He might jolt or something. What then?'

'Oliver, you've been watching too much shit on the telly, just carry him.'

He moved forward, his arms placed in front, steadying himself in case gloved-man shifted suddenly. He slowly edged forward, his head aching with stress, wanting to be anywhere but here. He began humming a tune in his head as a coping mechanism. He counted backwards from 100 but was unable to get the numbers in order. He saw a haze of digits as he struggled to think straight; a mass of confusion which steered his thoughts away from what he was doing.

Once at the bed, he grasped the body under its belly with both hands, then lifted. Meagan took the legs. Oliver was struggling to move the blanket which was coming away from the bed, aware he could be leaving fingerprints, saliva, DNA.

As he moved the body to the end of the bed, Meagan pushed the trunk across the carpet and Oliver dropped the body inside. She quickly shut the flap, securing the leather straps.

Meagan had a plan. 'Here's what we do, Oliver. Go and get the car. The straps of this trunk are too flimsy and we can't risk it opening while we move it. Rob has a strong chain in a drawer in the kitchen. He used to cycle occasionally and used it to lock his bike. He sold the bike recently so he won't miss it. We can wrap it tightly around the trunk.'

Oliver took gloved-man's phone from the bedside cabinet.

'We need to dump this as well.' He went out onto the street, leaving Meagan to clear up his dirty work.

～

While Oliver was gone, Meagan went into apartment six, frantically opening cupboards and pulling out drawers in the kitchen, scrabbling through the junk and tipping all the contents onto the floor. She found the chain under a pile of papers, checking its strength by pulling it tightly, pleased to see the key was still in the lock of the barrel.

It was sturdy enough and would definitely be secure.

She quickly placed everything back as neatly as possible, turned out the kitchen light and returned to apartment seven and the trunk with the body.

～

Oliver returned to apartment seven forty minutes later. He'd parked around the back of the building.

Meagan had managed to secure the trunk with the chain. Her face was flushed, her breathing heavy. She looked exhausted. 'Let's just get him out,' she commanded.

'Go and open the door, Meagan. Make sure the hall outside is empty.'

Meagan stood by the front door of apartment seven, keeping a lookout, making sure the communal hall was deserted. 'Come on. It's clear.' She looked inside. Oliver was struggling to pull the trunk, crouching low. One end of it was trapped at the bottom of the stairs.

'Push him back. He's stuck. Take the angle wider.' Meagan went back inside the hall, forcing the edge of the trunk away from the skirting board.

Oliver looked up; his face was bright red, sweat dripping

down his forehead. He wiped it away with his sleeve. 'What's the plan?'

Meagan was outside, again checking the communal hall. 'I know a reservoir in north west London. I remember passing it a few times. It's quiet. No one goes there much. It's at the back of the main road, the A406 if I remember correctly. It's perfect as it's deep and we can drop him off from the edge.'

Oliver looked down at the trunk, wondering how he had got in this mess, how he had let Meagan talk him into it. 'Fine. Let's do it then.'

They reached the ground floor, Oliver struggling to pull the trunk, Meagan keeping watch. The trunk bashed along every step, the noise echoing through the hallway. He thought that any minute someone would come out from one of the doorways. How would they explain what was going on?

*Hey, what are you doing? It looks like you're dragging a dead body?*

*Oh, he's had too much to drink. Yeah, he's dead. But I'd rather he was dead outside your property. I can't deal with the flies, my friend. I'm joking of course, it's a blow-up doll – my partner's kinky like that.*

Oliver's thoughts were interrupted; Meagan was calling out. 'Oliver, quick, someone's coming.'

He stood still, feeling his heart racing, panic flooding his body.

Meagan watched the front door of the building as they stood in the communal hall. Someone was moving a key, flicking it left and right, grunting, puffing out deep breaths. The door opened. Meagan turned to Oliver, who was standing behind her. 'Quick, the lift. Go.'

Oliver glanced behind him then pulled the trunk backwards, sliding it along the wooden floor, racing to the lift doors. He placed it inside and joined Meagan.

'Mrs Sheehan! You're out late,' Meagan commented.

Meagan had startled her. The old lady from the fourth floor gazed at the couple, watching them. 'I could say the same for you. Hello, Rob.'

Oliver thought it better to play along; it was too confusing to introduce himself.

'We're popping out. Speak soon, okay?' Meagan stood, waiting for the lady to pass and go on her way up the stairs.

'I'm going to see if the lift is working,' Mrs Sheehan announced.

'No. I mean, it's still down. I think they're coming next week. Didn't you get the letter?' Meagan asked.

Mrs Sheehan paused. 'Letter? I didn't get a letter. I'd like to check anyway. You never know, do you?'

'I can assure you the lift is still broken. We were upstairs a minute ago. I had a look. Definitely out, isn't it, Rob?' Meagan turned to Oliver.

'Huh. Yeah, it's still broken all right. Damn lift. You can never rely on them.'

Meagan was looking past Oliver at the trunk sticking out of the lift door.

The old lady advanced, staring. 'You look different, young man. Have you lost weight?'

Oliver froze, struggling to hide his shocked expression, thinking what to say to the curious neighbour. 'Well, that would be the lift, you know. All that walking up and down the stairs. Bound to be good for you. At least there's a plus side.'

Meagan was still staring at the part of the trunk that was poking out of the lift. Any second now, Mrs Sheehan would see it and ask what was inside. How would they explain away this one? Thankfully, the hall was dark.

'Look, why don't I walk you up? I'll take your trolley. You must be tired.' Meagan linked Mrs Sheehan's arm, leading her to the stairs. 'Did you hear about the burglaries? Shocking isn't it?' Meagan's voice became distant.

Oliver listened to Mrs Sheehan's concerned voice as it drifted from where he stood.

'No. When was this? It's getting worse, isn't it? What's wrong with some people? You just don't know with young folk these days, do you?'

Oliver listened to the conversation as the ladies disappeared up the stairs.

Oliver was wondering what to do now he had the body in the lift, when he heard a phone ringing. Gloved-man's mobile had been inside the front pocket of his jeans. He debated whether to answer. If he didn't, whoever was calling would likely get suspicious. But what would he say if he answered? It stopped, and Oliver let out a sigh of relief. Moving over to the stairs, he listened for Meagan. The phone rang again. Oliver decided he had to answer as it would draw unnecessary attention if the phone continued ringing. He reached into his pocket, wishing he had dumped the phone earlier. Pulling the mobile out, he slid his finger across the screen. Oliver listened to the voice on the other end. He kept quiet, as still as possible, listening.

'Tony, where are you? I've been calling all evening. We have another job. This one owes money big time. She needs threatening. Don't go heavy yet. Hello. Hello?'

Oliver ended the call. 'Shit.'

It rang a second later.

'What the fuck is wrong with you? Do I need to call over? You fucking know how much it aggravates me when you hang up.'

Oliver dropped the phone. They had to get out of here, fast.

## 16

## TWENTY YEARS AGO - BEFORE THE PHONE CALL

Meagan lay in bed, listening to the loud voices coming from downstairs. Her father shouting, her mother crying, asking him questions. She could hear them clearly; her mother was pleading with him.

'Why did you do it? How could you? What were you thinking? She's just a little girl! You know how much Meagan and Sarah loved the pet.'

Meagan worked out it had something to do with the guinea pig and its missing head. She thought maybe her father had tried to fix it but just made things worse. She clutched her grey toy bunny, worrying that his head would also fall off.

Loud crashes were coming from the kitchen. Her mother walked to the living room, her father shouting after her, ordering her not to walk away while he spoke.

Meagan pulled the covers over her face, trying to drown out the noise from downstairs. She placed the cloth bunny on the pillow, kissing it goodnight. 'Nothing's going to happen to you, don't worry. I'll look after you, I promise.'

She knelt on the floor beside the bed, saying her prayers. 'Please, God, protect Mummy. Look after her and don't let anything happen. I love her very much. Also, please help my daddy to not be so angry. Mummy says that when you're loved by your family, nothing else matters. We love Daddy, so he doesn't need to worry about anything else. Please, God, make him also stop shouting at Mummy and making her cry. Amen.'

She climbed back into bed, tucking her cloth bunny in, placing the blanket around its chest to keep it warm.

An hour later, Meagan woke. The room was dark. A noise had startled her; the front door banging shut. She looked over at her toy, still in the same place, and suddenly felt calmer. Her bedroom door was slightly ajar. The light from the outside hall provided enough glow to see out.

Meagan stepped out of bed, placing her feet on the cold wooden floorboards. As she went out to the hallway, the cold air hit her: a window was open further down the landing.

Meagan listened from the top of the stairs. Total silence. She crept over to her father's room, tapping the door with her knuckles and waiting for him to tell her to enter. Nothing came.

She edged backwards to her mother's room. The door was open, the bed empty. Meagan wanted to go downstairs, making up an excuse that she couldn't sleep, she could hear noises, her tummy hurt. But her father had heard it all, and he'd only send her back to her room.

She went to the open window. The wind howled through the gap, the high-pitched whistle piercing Meagan's ears. As she reached the glass, she went up on her tiptoes, looking out.

A full moon shone in the sky and sprinkles of tiny stars were dotted everywhere. Meagan thought how wonderful it looked. The field behind their house was black. Dark shadows waved from the trees. Meagan often thought there were people in the hills, calling her to come over and join them.

She stood on the skirting board so she could look out. Suddenly a spotlight came on. She saw a figure walking away from the house, across the back garden and heading towards the fields. Meagan was unsure if it was a person or an animal. As she leaned her face closer to the glass, she could make out the shape of her father. He had something slumped over his shoulder.

Her mother.

Meagan watched in horror, wanting to shout out the window at him to bring her mother back and not leave her alone in the house. She panicked, trying to open the window wider, but the handle was jammed. Meagan forced it upwards and then down. It was no use.

She ran into the bedroom, making sure her bunny was warm, then put on her white slippers and her pink Tom and Jerry dressing gown and went downstairs.

Meagan struggled to push the back door open against the force of the wind. She watched the blades of grass swaying hard in the breeze, small trees with overgrown branches pounding against the side wall.

There was no sign of her father. Meagan walked along the path across the lawn, stepping into the middle of each paving stone, counting them out loud. Reaching the end, she jumped onto the grass bank, forcing herself upwards.

She looked further into the distance. Her father was down by the water, moving across to the caves which were cut into the hill.

Meagan ran towards him, making sure to keep out of sight: she'd be in so much trouble if he saw her. She waited, the wind beating against her face, her body numb with the cold and her bones aching. She watched the cave below, wondering what her parents were doing.

Meagan was shivering, fighting off the cold, stamping her feet. Her teeth began to chatter, vibrating behind her lips, and her mouth was dry with the taste of salt in the air.

In the distance she watched the glare from the lighthouse, wishing she could swim over, stay the night, and keep watch for the ships.

After another couple of minutes, her father resurfaced, coming into view, moving fast. He was on his own.

Meagan stepped backwards, terrified he'd catch her out here. She ran as fast as she could back to the house and up to her room, shutting her bedroom door tight.

The following morning, Meagan got out of bed and headed into her mother's room. It was empty. The covers were made, and the room was spotless, as if she hadn't been here for a while.

Meagan listened from the upstairs hall, her father talking in his room. His occasional laughter, then whispers.

Suddenly, there were footsteps coming towards her. Meagan stepped back into her room, shutting the door.

Her father called out. 'Meagan. Are you awake? I'm popping out; I'll be back in a while. Don't open the front door to anyone. I'll be as quick as I can.'

She heard him move down the stairs and leave the house a minute later. The smell of his aftershave made her sneeze.

'Okay. You wait here, bunny, I'm going to find Mummy. Daddy told me not to open the front door. He didn't say anything about the back door.'

Meagan walked through the kitchen, still in her night clothes.

She remembered her father had walked down by the water, going into the caves with her mother slumped over his shoulder. That's where she wanted to go.

Meagan stood in the back garden, pleased to feel the warmth from the sun, which finally pushed through the clouds, making everything much brighter. In the distance, she saw a boat far out, and the lighthouse was clearer. Its light was just a dim glow in the distance.

She looked above at the scattered clouds moving fast across the sky. The shapes amazed her; she could see sheep. Another one seemed to form the picture of a genie.

Meagan reached the hill, peering underneath at the caves. They reminded her of a dark grey cauldron from a story her mother had read to her. She watched the clear water flowing, rolling back and forth, like a baker kneading dough, pushing it away, pulling it, rolling it outwards.

She removed her slippers, placing them to the side to make sure they didn't get wet. She pulled her dressing gown tight, adjusting the belt.

From the mouth of the cave, she called out. 'Mummy. Where are you? Are you still here?' The echo made her jump, and imagine that there were more people inside. Meagan crouched, pushing her way inside. She could hear the shriek of bats hanging overhead.

Meagan suddenly heard a whining sound in the distance, underneath where she stood. 'Mummy. Is that you?' Quickly, she went further inside the cave. She found steps towards the back that led below.

Once at the bottom, the cave became wider, the ceiling higher. A large wooden container like a coffin lay on the floor at the back. Meagan opened the heavy lid.

She fell backwards with the fright of seeing her mother, a gag placed around her mouth, rope holding her hands behind her back. Tricia was lying down on her stomach, her head resting to the side, struggling to manoeuvre onto her back.

Meagan panicked, stood up and helped release the gag from her mother's mouth. She wriggled the rope until Tricia's hands were free. 'I'd never have found you Mummy, only I peeked. I saw you both last night. That's a great place to hide.'

Tricia burst into tears, clutching her daughter harder than she ever had before.

Once back at the house, Tricia asked Meagan to pack a small case with the clothes she wore the most.

'Are we going away, Mummy?'

'Quickly, Meagan. Just do as I say.'

'Is Daddy coming too? Can I pack Arthur the bunny?'

'Meagan. We don't have much time. We need to leave. Now.'

'Are we hiding from Daddy?'

'Yes, you could say that. It's why you need to go and pack, so stop with the questions. Hurry now.' Tricia hoped that where they were going, she and Meagan could hide from Sean for the rest of their lives.

She raced frantically, pulling clothes from the washing line outside, emptying her belongings from the bedside drawer upstairs, grabbing a few items from the bathroom, placing them in a case, struggling with the zip. 'Come on, close for crying out loud. Meagan, are you done?'

'Nearly. I'm leaving a note for Daddy telling him we're hiding.'

'No. Don't do that. It will ruin the game. Give me the piece of paper, quickly.'

Tricia glanced at the huge writing in felt tip.

*Daddy. It is yor tern. You hav to find us. I hop you don find it hard.*

Tricia folded the note, struggling to stem the lump in her throat, fighting back the tears. 'Okay. Let's go. You ready?'

Meagan nodded, holding Arthur the toy bunny under her arm and the small holdall in the other. Tricia closed the back door and led Meagan across the vast green behind the house.

## 17

PRESENT DAY

Oliver was standing by the lift, watching over the dead body in the trunk. He'd placed the phone on silent, pushing the side switch to mute the calls. The phone had been ringing continuously.

Meagan had been gone ten minutes and Oliver was panicking. Any minute now the guy on the other end of the phone could turn up, find the body, and they'd be another two stiffs joining gloved-man in the lift.

Sweat trickled along the side of his face. His arms were numb from dragging the body from the second floor.

Suddenly, he heard footsteps coming towards him, moving down the stairs. He stepped into the lift, pulling the body closer to the back.

'Right. You ready?' Meagan asked. She was puffing, struggling to take breaths, her hands placed on her hips.

'You took your bloody time. Let's move. We haven't got long.' Oliver explained the phone calls as he watched the horror on Meagan's face. She spun towards the front door, expecting it to open any second.

'Give me the keys to your car; I'll bring it to the fire escape.

Wait a minute and if you don't hear from me, presume it's safe and come out.'

'A minute? It's not the bloody egg and spoon race, Meagan. Do you know how heavy this guy is?' He tossed her the keys, telling her where the car was parked.

She disappeared along the communal hall. Oliver heard the fire door open at the back of the building, then slowly close. He checked gloved-man's phone. The last call was two minutes ago. Whoever was ringing was possibly on their way over.

He waited a few minutes, then went to the back door and held it open. He was pleased to see the barrier rise, and Meagan driving to the back of the building.

He could hear the car running, pumping out fumes from the exhaust. Meagan was sitting high on the driver's seat; her body pushed forward, frantically wiping condensation from the windscreen. The screech of the wiper blades grated through his head.

He checked once more, moving to the front of the building past the lift on his right side. He then returned, got a firm grip on the trunk and dragged it to the car.

Meagan was standing outside with the boot open. 'Quick, lower the seats, chuck him in and let's go.'

She stood by the passenger door, keeping watch as Oliver fought to lift the leather trunk. Oliver used his legs, keeping low, crouching, then turned his body and heaved, pushing the trunk into the back of the car.

Then he jumped into the driver's seat, opened the passenger door so Meagan could get in, and they drove away from the building and towards Kensington High Street.

Oliver and Meagan were quiet; the events of the last couple of hours had justified the silence. Oliver's brain felt like it was about to explode. *How could this happen?* He was sure Meagan had said the top of the stairs and turn right.

Who the hell was the guy they'd killed and how would they get away with it? He was confused. The pressure had got to him, and he struggled to think clearly. He panicked, wanting to open the car door and jump out. But he couldn't leave Meagan to clear up his shit: it wasn't fair. This was their mess; they had to sort it.

He watched Meagan as he drove, the way she concentrated on the road, her beautiful face, the shit she'd been through and now this.

'I'm sorry.'

Meagan seemed pleased that the ice had finally broken. 'We just need to get rid of the body. Move on, but we can never talk about it to anyone, you understand?' She placed her hand on Oliver's arm, gripping it gently.

'Goes without saying. It's not something I do regularly, I can assure you.'

Meagan turned. 'I'm glad to hear it.'

Oliver saw a sign for Brent Cross Shopping Centre in north west London. He'd tried to focus his eyes, seeing images of gloved-man flashing through his mind.

'It's just up here towards Hendon,' Meagan announced. She pointed at the dual carriageway as Oliver used the indicator and moved the car to the left side of the road.

'Are you sure it's safe?' he asked.

'Yeah. I can't imagine anyone comes out here at night.'

Oliver turned left down a quiet side road and through an open gate at the bottom, spotting the sign, *Reservoir*.

'This is the place,' Meagan announced, as they pulled into the car park. The tyres rolled over the gravel, causing a loud crunching sound.

Oliver looked out at the long grass and the calm water, which glistened with the light from the street lamps.

They got out of the car, leaving their doors open. Oliver went to the boot and eyed the trunk.

Then Oliver walked to a concrete ledge and looked into the water, hoping it would be deep enough to swallow the trunk and gloved-man. Meagan came behind him and gripped him around his waist. He could feel her shaking.

They waited for a couple of minutes, holding each other, immersed in the peaceful surroundings, the distant sounds of vehicles moving along the dual carriageway; the drivers oblivious to what Oliver and Meagan were about to do.

Oliver shifted from Meagan's hold, then walked to the boot of the car. He gripped the flimsy handle of the leather trunk and pulling it to the ground, watched it crash with the weight, aware of the indents it would leave in the earth.

He looked across the water. Rings appeared in several places like stones dropping from above, and midges hovered over the reservoir. The glint from the moon reflected on the water, glistening in their faces.

Meagan said, 'Are you ready?'

Oliver had let go of the trunk and was spreading his fingers, opening and closing them to allow the blood to circulate. 'Let's get it over with.'

Oliver pushed the trunk while Meagan kept her distance, watching Oliver step to the end of the ledge. Oliver crouched, placing his hands under the trunk, flipping it over into the water and getting soaked with the splash-back.

They stood for a few moments, watching the bubbles rising as if the trunk was sinking into a hot cauldron, rather than a reservoir.

They realised the water wasn't deep enough. The trunk was still visible.

Oliver turned. 'Shit. Someone's going to find it. We can't leave it here! What if someone pulls him out? Opens the trunk? Sees what we've done?' He moved forward, pressing his hands against the trunk, pushing hard, urging it to vanish to the bottom. 'It's too fucking shallow, Meagan. Look, we may as well have dumped him in a bloody bath.'

'Get a grip, will you. How many people do you know that would just pull a trunk from a reservoir, huh? I know I wouldn't. Would you? Besides, it's pretty desolate here; no one comes to this place. Why would they? It's London for God's sake. The water is probably contaminated anyway.'

'Well, if it wasn't before, it sure as hell is now, Meagan. I can't believe this shit, really. I can't.'

Meagan made her way to the car, pissed off with the way Oliver was shouting at her.

He watched her, moving his eyes between Meagan and the trunk in the water. 'Where are you going? Meagan, I'm talking to you. Hello.'

She was already halfway between the reservoir and the car park. He got up, brushing the mud from his knees, watching the trunk, knowing just how easily it could be found.

Oliver pulled into the car park at the back of Albuquerque House, killing the lights and the engine. As Meagan got out, she crouched over towards him, brushing the back of her right hand along his face. 'Will you come up? I don't want to be alone just yet.'

Oliver's heart raced as he struggled to contain the excitement of being in her company.

'Park the car in that space there,' she said, getting out of the car.

He watched as Meagan crossed the car park and did as he had been told.

She let him in through the fire escape. 'Thank you. We need to talk about earlier, and what happens now. I'm frightened, Oliver.'

They were standing alone in the communal hall, worried they'd be caught.

Oliver's heart raced, his face flushed with anticipation and his body shook with adrenaline. Meagan drove him wild. He struggled to understand how he'd feel like this after earlier: the break-in, the body in the trunk, what they both did. It all seemed to add fuel to his already raging fire.

He seized her hand, pushing her against the wall, the light from the lift showing the passion on his face. Oliver turned, drawing his hands through her hair, moving her head back, planting kisses on her neck and chest, then guiding his leg to her crotch, pushing between her thighs.

She lifted her finger, placing it on his wet lips. 'Not here.'

In the kitchen. Oliver pushed a heap of papers from the counter onto the floor. The crash caused Meagan to jump.

He gripped her around the waist, lifting her onto the edge of the table. They looked into each other's eyes, driven by overwhelming passion, holding each other's gaze. Oliver leant forward, pushing his lips on hers, both their mouths open, intense short breaths, hard kissing, biting. He moved towards her ear, breathing deeper, causing her to lose control. She was quivering, goose pimples covering her arms as he gently blew warm air onto her lobes, sucked on them.

Oliver pulled her towards him, pushing himself between her legs, gently kissing the top of her arms, caressing her shoulders, tracing his fingers to her breasts, ripping open her blouse, buttons hitting the floor as he pulled her closer.

Oliver removed his T-shirt. Meagan glimpsed his firm chest, tight stomach and broad shoulders.

He lifted her dress, at the same time removing his jeans, kicking them to the side and entering Meagan for the first time.

They sat in the kitchen, wrapped around each other, both naked and feeling immense satisfaction. The passion between them was electric, an overwhelming release for what they'd been through together.

After a few minutes, Meagan broke the silence. 'What now?'

'How do you mean?'

'Will I see you again? Rob's back tomorrow. I can't bear the thought of him returning.'

Oliver stood. The worry concerning her husband returning was too much. He couldn't be here. 'I have to go, Meagan. I'll call you.'

She threw on a bathrobe and walked him to the door, peeping out to make sure the communal hall was empty.

As Oliver stepped out of the apartment and stood at the top of the stairs, he noticed the front door to apartment seven was open. 'Meagan, I shut the door when I dragged the trunk out here earlier. I made sure of it. I pulled it hard and tested it. It was closed.'

Meagan moved to where Oliver was standing. 'What's going on? How can it be open?'

Oliver pictured the scene earlier. They had moved gloved-man out to the communal hall and he was certain he closed the door before manoeuvring the body downstairs. He was sure. He pushed the door open with the sleeve of his jacket. The hall was dark; the lights switched off, just how they'd left it earlier.

Oliver stepped inside apartment seven while Meagan waited in the hall. He came out a few minutes later. 'I don't get it, Meagan. I must have left it open. That's all I can think.'

Oliver pulled the door to apartment seven, making sure it was closed.

A deathly silence fell over the two of them as they listened to footsteps charging up the stairs, moving at a great pace, heading towards where they were standing.

'Quick, Meagan. Go inside, lock the door, I'll hide in the lift. Go now.'

Oliver raced along the hall, listening to the person making their way to the second floor. The doors to the lift were open, and Oliver stepped inside, jamming them as close together as possible with his foot so he could keep hidden.

The front door to apartment six was shut, and Meagan was dipping her hand furiously into the pocket of the bathrobe, fishing for the keys. The footsteps were at the top of the stairs. Oliver watched between the lift doors.

The guy stood in front of her. She turned slightly, watching from the corner of her eye as he frantically looked up and down the corridor. He was over six foot, well built, with cropped black hair and wore a leather jacket and dark blue jeans. Oliver could see his desperation and sense his overbearing demeanour.

The man pointed along the hall. 'You know a guy called Tony? He lives here. I think it's this one.' He pointed to apartment seven.

Meagan turned, facing him. 'I don't know. There's a guy who lives in seven. I don't see him much. He keeps himself to himself, you know.'

The guy stood against the door of apartment seven, rapping it with his knuckles. 'Tony. Open up.'

Oliver listened from the lift, running the scene from earlier in his head, hoping they hadn't left any evidence inside the apartment.

'Who would have the key for this place?'

'Key?'

The man turned, moving closer. 'That's what I asked.'

Meagan took a deep breath. 'There are no skeleton keys. We have our own.'

He moved away from Meagan, heading to the lift.

'Where are you going?' she asked. Her legs were shaking, her voice cracking. Oliver was standing inside the lift, hearing the heavy footsteps moving towards him.

'Is there a back entrance? I'm going to see if a window is open,' snapped the visitor.

'You're going the wrong way. It's back here.' Meagan pointed to the other side of the hall as the guy stopped, turned and headed to where Meagan was pointing. Oliver let out a deep breath, edging further against the lift wall.

'Come with me, show me how to get out there,' the guy instructed.

Oliver listened to Meagan and the guy as they walked along the hall, pushing open the fire escape which led out to the second-floor roof. He could hear voices; the guy was shouting, Meagan was stuttering, fearful of what this guy was going to do. Oliver edged out of the lift, watching the door as Meagan held it open, stood against it. The guy continued shouting, swinging his arms like a large oaf.

Oliver kept as quiet as possible, his heart racing as the guy moved into the communal hall and charged down the other side past apartment six to the lift.

'No!' Meagan shouted.

He stopped suddenly, and Meagan raced towards him. As she reached where the guy stood, she looked into the empty lift.

The guy turned to Meagan, shouting at the top of his voice. 'If I don't get answers, I'm coming back tomorrow.'

She watched him move to the stairs and go down onto the street.

## 18

## TWENTY YEARS AGO - BEFORE THE PHONE CALL

'Mummy, I'm tired. When will we be there?'

They were heading to Tricia's sister, who lived around seventy miles from them in a beautiful cottage on the outskirts of Exeter.

Although Tricia and Anne hadn't kept in regular contact over the last few years, they were extremely close with one another. Life had gotten in the way, and it was hard to keep in touch. Besides, Sean would never let Anne stay for more than a night if she visited them.

Tricia knew her sister would be there for her and insist they stay for as long as they needed. She didn't bother calling ahead, as it was difficult to explain on the phone. Although Anne had an idea of what Sean was like, she didn't know the depth of his cruelty.

'We need to get to the station, Meggy. It's not far when we get to the other side. A short bus ride.'

They were walking along a deserted country lane, fields either side of them. The wind had picked up, and a faint howl screeched through the trees.

Tricia glanced at Meagan, thinking she could have waited and asked Mr Tunney for a lift, but she couldn't trust him not to slip up and tell Sean where they were going. Besides, it wasn't fair on him to keep a secret like this. She was on edge. Sean had no reason to drive out here, but there was always a slight chance.

'Are you thirsty, Meggy?' Tricia dipped into her bag, pulled out a small bottle of water and handed it to Meagan. 'It shouldn't be too far now. Are you okay?'

Meagan looked up at her mother; her large brown eyes were wet from the cold, and her top lip was dry from wiping it on her sleeve. Tricia admired the determination in Meagan's face to keep going, watching her daughter as she swung Arthur the bunny in her right hand.

How Tricia wished life was different, that she could bring up their girl in a stable family environment, a happy home. There was no denying Sean loved Meagan; he was even a good father and occasionally spent time with his daughter. As far as Tricia could tell – and she questioned Meagan several times – he had never hit Meagan, ever.

The abuse was all directed at Tricia; that's what broke her heart the most. Meagan was seeing the cruelty every day, as if it were the norm. She was learning that it's the way it is, for husbands to beat their wives if rules were broken. With Sean, there didn't have to be a reason. His *rules*, as he called them, were arbitrary. Ordinary families didn't make laws that had to be followed. They didn't write long lists and make orders that needed obeying. Meagan had to see how life was without him. Tricia felt guilty, but it was the only way to deal with this.

They reached a corner in the road where it veered to the right. Tricia stopped by a tree, dropping the bag. The tips of her fingers were a red glow, and a numb ache had developed along her hand.

Meagan was sipping from the bottle of water. 'Is this where we're hiding, Mummy?' Meagan was pointing. 'Behind the tree?'

'No, Meggy. I told you we're going to Aunty Anne.'

Meagan placed her bag down, sitting Arthur on top of it, setting his legs out to make him more comfortable. Tricia watched as her daughter placed the bottle of water to Arthur's lips. Then she went to a large oak tree, putting her hand on the bark. 'This is how you can tell how old a tree is, Mummy, by counting the marks on the bark. Mrs Lester told us at school.' Meagan walked over to her mother. 'You only have one line on your forehead. That means you're ten.'

'Oh, Meggy, you are a sweetheart, I only wish it were true.'

Meagan was facing the road they'd just walked along. 'The game's over, Mummy.'

Tricia was looking out at a field, watching a small herd of cows that were sitting close by. 'What do you mean, Meggy?'

Her daughter was pointing at the road. 'There's Daddy's car.'

Tricia watched in horror as her daughter went racing towards the road.

'No, Meggy, stop. Please, Meagan.' Her mind raced, images playing out from the past, hoping they'd become distant memories. The cruelty at the hands of Sean, keeping her locked up, the beatings. If he found them he'd most certainly kill her, and she couldn't take that chance.

Tricia reached her daughter and pulled her to the ground. They kept low, watching the car speed past, Sean driving.

'Is he still looking for us, Mummy?'

Tricia struggled to communicate. Her body ached, she was tired, feeling she couldn't go on, but they had to. Tricia had to do it for Meagan.

'Yes, Meggy. He's still looking. We need to make tracks; the station is just a little further. You okay to keep going?' Tricia crouched beside her daughter, stroking her hand through Meagan's hair.

'Yes, Mummy. If you're okay, then I am too. Arthur is sick. He has a cold, but I'll look after him.'

Tricia made sure the car had passed, and her husband was out of sight, then they gathered their belongings and headed to the station.

The car park was quiet. A couple of taxis were waiting patiently at the side rank, the drivers reading newspapers. A young couple were embracing outside the main doors, and Tricia wondered if one of them had arrived or was just leaving. She hated goodbyes. It broke her heart when she had visited the west of Ireland as a child, and she had watched her uncle's tear-soaked face as the train pulled out, heading to Dublin.

As they walked through the main doors, Tricia worried if they'd brought enough clothes with them; if the trains were running; if her sister was home.

She glanced up at the departures board, while Meagan stood beside her. They watched the letters flapping and forming the destination names.

An announcement came over the tannoy. 'The next train to Exeter will arrive on platform nine in ten minutes. Please make sure you keep your belongings with you.'

Tricia looked at her daughter. 'That's us, Meggy. Quick, we need to get tickets. We haven't got long. You ready?'

Meagan smiled at her mother, and the two of them went to the kiosk.

Sean had driven for half an hour and spotted no sign of his wife. His body was pumping with aggression, anger and fear. Fear of what he'd do when he found Tricia. He frantically rubbed his face, pulling down hard on the skin of his cheek, forcing the gearstick, pumping the clutch, gripping the steering wheel and squeezing it in his hands.

'What the fuck is she doing? Running out on me, taking my daughter!' Sean screamed out, punching the side window. He pulled into the train station, parked up and raced inside, checking the toilets, shops, looking along the platforms and questioning the taxi drivers outside as he darted back and forth.

One of the guys gave a quick response. 'You want to take care of your family a little better, mate.'

Sean squared up to him, and another driver stepped in the middle to calm the situation.

Sean was back in the car and driving along a country road, slowing up, peering into the fields either side. It was like looking for a sand grain on a pebbled beach.

He pulled up, parking beside a field, traipsing across the long grass, calling his daughter's name.

After a few minutes, he got back into the car and decided to head back to the station and take another look.

Tricia collected the tickets, paying in cash, then led her daughter to platform nine.

She flashed the tickets to a woman dressed in a smart black uniform, who smiled and wished them a pleasant journey.

'Wow, Mummy, the train is ginormous. Look, Arthur. We're going for a ride on that. Poor Daddy will never find us. It's not fair on him.'

Meagan was climbing the steps, looking at the tracks underneath. Tricia followed close behind.

The train was busier than Tricia had expected. People were hoisting luggage onto the racks overhead and the corridor was full of people with red, frustrated faces, pushing past commuters hogging the aisle as they tried to settle.

Tricia instantly felt claustrophobic and had to fight the tightness in her chest.

Once seated, Meagan placed Arthur on her lap, while Tricia waited anxiously for the train to pull out. She watched a family to her left; a mother and father with their teenage son. They had a newspaper spread out on the table and were sharing a crossword, the three of them contributing. The woman got one of the clues and her partner looked proud, applauding her, praising her effort. The woman laughed, basking in her glory. Tricia watched them holding hands, relaxed, so content in each other's company. The guy stood, asking what they'd like from the buffet car.

How Tricia wished that her life was like this.

A loud piercing whistle sounded from the platform, the doors closed, a beeping noise echoed through the carriage.

Tricia's heart pounded. She fought back the tears as she watched the excitement on her daughter's face, her eyes wild with anticipation.

They were sat in the first carriage, Tricia facing the platform, watching as the train pulled out slowly.

Suddenly there was a commotion by the ticket barrier, someone running to the platform, racing towards them, with two people in uniform giving chase. Tricia rose in her seat to see what was going on. The guy was jumping wildly, frantically waving his hands for the train to stop. He reached their window, pounding his fist on the glass.

'Mummy. It's Daddy. Wow, I knew he'd find us. He's so good at this game, isn't he? Can I open the door for him?'

Tricia sat in sheer terror. Her face was frozen, numb and expressionless. She watched as her husband became a distant figure, the train gathering speed, leaving the platform and station behind until it was surrounded by miles of fields and empty country lanes.

'Get the fuck off me. That's my wife and child, you arsehole.'

A security guard was holding Sean to the ground, asking him to calm down, telling him the train had already left and there was no way he was getting on. Sean was fighting to get the guy off him. A lady in a smart black uniform stood behind, saying something into the walkie-talkie that was clipped to her jacket.

As Sean cooled off, they let him stand, watching him brush himself down, wiping his shirt.

'Where is the train going?'

The staff looked at each other, then the guy answered. 'Exeter.'

Sean raced from the platform, out to the car park and into his car. He knew the roads to Exeter; it wouldn't take long. *Tricia will be so pleased to see me.*

## 19

PRESENT DAY

Meagan stood in the hall of apartment six. She reached into her handbag, removed her mobile phone, dialled Oliver's number and waited.

A minute later, she heard his voice. 'You're through to Oliver. Leave a message, and I'll return the call when I can.' A long beep sounded.

'It's me, I know I'm not supposed to call you, Rob doesn't know I have a spare phone so don't worry, but I need to talk. Can you ring me back? Urgently.' She hung up and went into the kitchen, placing the phone on the table, pacing up and down the floor like a caged animal.

A few seconds later, she picked up the phone and dialled the number again. After Oliver's message, she spoke, desperation in her voice. 'Oliver. You need to call. I have to talk to you. I need to know if you're okay. Call me, please.'

She waited, thinking about the guy who'd been here, her husband Rob and the dumped trunk in the reservoir.

Suddenly she heard a hammering on the front door. Meagan froze, panic now setting in. She feared someone had seen them;

her head started pounding. If the buzzer had rung, she'd feel safer, knowing whoever was calling was standing outside the building. *Could it be a neighbour?* No, it was too late for a friendly call, even for the old lady upstairs who never seemed to sleep.

In the hall Meagan listened for conversation, a voice she recognised. She deliberated on whether she should shout for the caller to go away and leave her alone. But they'd know she was inside, alone, a sitting duck. She waited in the hall of apartment six, isolated, frightened.

Meagan listened. Had they gone? She jumped at hearing another knock on the door, this time louder; three bangs. The person was getting more agitated and impatient.

'Who is it?' she called out, her voice breaking.

'It's Oliver. Open the door.'

Meagan raced to the door, her anxiety temporarily evaporating, removing the security chain, pulling it open. 'Oliver. You frightened the shit out of me. Why didn't you answer your phone? I've been calling.'

'I turned it off when I hid in the lift. Is he gone?'

'For now. Yes.'

Oliver rubbed his chin, bringing his hand to his forehead and pulling it downwards along his face. 'What are we going to do? We're in the shit.'

Meagan opened the door wider. 'You want to come inside?'

'For a minute. I need to get home. It's not safe.'

Oliver moved through to the kitchen, watching as Meagan made some coffee. 'Where is Rob anyway?'

Meagan placed two cups on the breakfast bar. 'He's in Spain. Madrid. He owns a sleazy bar over here, someplace in the East End. Strippers and the likes. It's how he gets his liberation. He has a poker room and gambles heavily. Calls it his release. He's looking at opening another one over there. I hate him, Oliver. I hate him with every ounce of my being.'

Oliver stood, moving towards Meagan, placing his arms around her, comforting the lady he'd fallen in love with, the person he'd do anything for.

She stood, pulling him closer, removing the belt of her dressing gown, dropping it to the floor and lifting his T-shirt over his head.

They made love for a second time that evening.

It was gone midnight when Oliver finally left apartment six. He'd wanted to stay, but it was too risky. There was always the slight possibility that Rob could arrive home early.

He stood outside the building, looking up at the second floor from the street, his head racing with the events that had unfolded earlier. He was freezing, swinging his arms and gripping himself to get warm. He stood in the car park, digesting the events that had taken place.

After a minute he got into his car, aware of the possibility of being seen. He started the engine and pulled slowly out of the car park, watching, being attentive.

He realised he needed a coffee to keep him awake. He found an all-night garage with a coffee bar. The woman who served him attempted to make conversation.

'You been working tonight?' she asked.

'You could say that, yeah.'

'How was it?'

'Murder,' Oliver replied.

Oliver woke the following morning with a thumping headache and cold sweats. He hadn't slept much, unable to push the thoughts out of his head; gloved-man, the body in the reservoir. He'd decided it was best to keep his distance from Meagan, lie low for a while in the hope it would blow over. He was frightened, unsure how things would pan out. The more he tried to forget, the more it ran through his head like a circling conveyor belt.

He peered at the alarm clock and realised he was late for work. He couldn't go in feeling like this.

Oliver stood in front of the mirror in the bathroom, staring hard at himself, his dishevelled reflection staring back. His hair was tousled and there were heavy bags under his eyes, deep lines across his forehead and his complexion was pale and deathly. How had he let this happen? He was a guy who was always on top of things, in control.

He turned on the shower, watching the steam from the hot water rise above the shower curtain. Removing his underwear, Oliver stepped inside. Standing naked, the stress seeped from his body, the water pelting against him, the strain of the last twenty-four hours momentarily leaving and disappearing down the plughole.

Once he'd finished and dried himself, he got dressed, putting on a fresh pair of jeans and a black T-shirt. He again eyed himself in the mirror. He was looking a little more alive and presentable.

He called the office, making out he had a migraine and needed rest. His boss told him to take it easy and come back when he was ready. That was all Oliver needed to hear. He didn't like to take advantage, but he needed time out.

He filled the coffee machine with water and turned it on. Standing at the window he watched Chelsea Bridge and the Shard in the distance. He needed fresh air, to get out of this place. His apartment suddenly felt claustrophobic. The walls seemed like they were moving, edging towards him, closing in. He breathed deeply, trying to gain control. His head was aching and trickles of sweat were rolling down his forehead. Oliver caught the metal handle on the oven door, steadying himself because the room was suddenly spinning. He breathed deeper, forcing himself to slow down.

How had he let Meagan talk him into murder?

His phone rang, making him jump. Peering down, Oliver checked the screen. No caller ID. His hands were shaking as he sent the call to voicemail. The phone rang a second later.

'Oh, for heaven's sake.' He hated impatience, but he realised it may be his boss. He answered aggressively, 'Hello.'

'And how are you this morning?'

Oliver was numb, unable to believe who was on the other end of the line, bold as you like, calling him when he was so vulnerable. 'Meagan. Why? How? I thought we agreed not to speak on our mobiles?'

There was a short pause. 'I thought you could come over. I'm making coffee; I have croissants too.'

'I don't think it's a good idea, do you?'

He could hear the disappointment in her voice, that telling sigh, the sure giveaway of how she was feeling, what she was thinking.

'Okay. I understand. I do. It's for the best, I suppose. I just miss you. You can't blame me for trying.'

'Meagan. There's nothing more I'd like; you know that, but it's too dangerous, and Rob's back today.'

'Shit. I forgot about that. Oh, God. What are we going to do?'

Oliver waited a moment, gaining the courage to say what he was thinking. 'Look. You know what you need to do. Leave him. Pack your bags and go. Just get out.'

'I can't, Oliver. He'll never allow it; there's no way he'd let me walk. It's impossible.'

Oliver was disappointed, let down. He expected Meagan to be more assertive and courageous. He was knocked back, shocked by her response. 'Well, I don't know what to say. I've told you what needs to happen. There's no other way, Meagan. You have to leave him.'

The line went quiet. Oliver thought she'd hung up, then he heard her, taking a deep breath, lowering her voice. 'There is another way. Finish what you started.'

## 20

### TWENTY YEARS AGO - BEFORE THE PHONE CALL

Tricia glanced at her watch. The train was twenty minutes from Exeter station. She knew there was a slim chance her husband would be waiting. Fortunately, the country roads were narrow and not built for speeding. The train they were on was direct, one-stop, one destination, but if her husband did make it before them, they'd have to hide. The train toilets were their best bet, either that, or run for it. Tricia had to get away; she had little choice. She would have to convince Meagan to keep going, ignore her father and find someone to help them.

She watched as her daughter sat in front of her, colouring a picture of Noddy with a crayon set that another girl sitting nearby had kindly shared.

The couple, who Tricia assumed were her parents, had tried to make conversation, but Tricia didn't have the strength to talk. She'd never been so alone. She wondered how it all went wrong. 'You okay, Meggy? We'll be there soon. You can see Aunty Anne. You're looking forward to that, aren't you?'

Meagan continued colouring, scribbling outside the lines and trying to rub the marks out, making more smudges. 'I'm scared Daddy won't find us. What if he never does?'

'Oh, Meagan. Maybe he will.' Tricia quickly changed the subject. 'Do you want Daddy to find us?'

Meagan paused, then looked up. 'Only if he's kinder to you, Mummy and stops making you cry.'

A voice came over the tannoy. 'The next stop is Exeter. Please take your belongings with you. We will be arriving at Exeter station in approximately five minutes. We thank you for travelling with us today and wish you a safe onward journey.'

Tricia looked at the country lane on her left side, leading to the station, praying she wouldn't see Sean's car.

～

Sean had his right foot to the floor, pumping the accelerator. 'Come on. I need to be there. Move, you piece of shit.'

He'd just passed a sign. Ten miles to Exeter. The roads were narrow, clear, with little obstruction. He knew Tricia had a sister and presumed that's where she was going with Meagan. The only problem was he hadn't a clue where she lived. They didn't speak much; Sean couldn't even recall what she looked like.

He slowed at a crossroad, making sure it was clear left and right, seeing more narrow country roads ahead. He couldn't wait to surprise Tricia.

～

'Come on, Meggy. This is us, let's go.'

As they stepped off the train, Tricia searched for a bus timetable, aware they needed to move quickly. 'Excuse me, where can I get a bus to Adlington?' A member of staff was standing by the barrier, beckoning people to move forward. Tricia was losing patience. 'Hello. We need to get to Adlington.'

As the uniformed woman turned to her, an arm reached out,

grabbing Tricia from behind. Meagan looked on in horror. Tricia spun round.

'I'm going there too. Follow my wife and me; it's just outside. Sorry if I startled you.'

The guy was tall, middle-aged and dressed in a smart black suit. His wife was much smaller and was dressed in a dark red dress and a long brown jacket.

Tricia pushed out a deep breath, noticing how weak her legs felt. She was on edge, which was exacerbated by being in a confined space, and she was dizzy from the crowd of people who had spilt from the train.

The guy reached forward. 'I'm Danny. This is my wife, Bev. So, who do you know in Adlington? I grew up there. We've come down for the weekend. It's so quiet and peaceful this time of year. I can't wait to just kick back and relax. We love it, don't we, Bev? We live up north now, Birmingham, but how we miss this place, isn't that right, Bev?'

Tricia watched as his wife kept nodding, wondering if she ever actually spoke.

He continued, 'So, how long are you down for? Is it just a couple of days or longer?' We've spent a bit of time in Devon, haven't we Bev?'

Tricia went to speak but was cut off before the words could leave her mouth with another bombardment of questions.

As they stepped outside, Danny pointed over to the bus. 'That's us.'

The engine was running and the driver was stacking away paperwork. He opened the main doors.

Tricia scanned the car park looking for her husband's car. Although Danny was annoying (she hadn't had a chance to speak to Bev), she was pleased with their company and remembered how her mother had always said there was safety in numbers.

Tricia lifted Meagan up the steps. Her daughter was yawning

and asking if she could sleep. 'We'll be there soon, Meggy. You can sleep all you want then. Sound good?'

Meagan looked at her mother as they sat towards the back of the bus. Her mother crouched, bringing her elbows up and shielding her face, keeping low and turning away from the window. 'How do you know Danny, Mummy?'

Tricia laughed. 'Oh, Meggy. I don't know him, darling. He's just being friendly. That's what people do.'

'Well, he's awfully nosey. Why does he want to know so much about you?'

'That's just him making conversation.'

'I thought we weren't supposed to speak to strangers?'

Tricia gently pinched the end of her daughter's nose. 'It's okay for adults. You're asking too many questions now, young lady.'

They laughed together, watching Danny and Bev move towards them and sit down. Tricia struggled to drag her eyes from the car park as the bus pulled out, heading for Adlington.

Sean was a mile or so from Exeter station when a tractor pulled out in front of him from a nearby field. The road was tight, with just one lane.

He honked the horn, watching the young lad driving, sitting high on the seat, swerving left and right. He pulled the machine into a ditch to the left side of the road and Sean went to overtake, but saw a car coming the other way at the last second and pulled back behind the tractor.

Sean again steered to his right in the hope of overtaking, but the tractor driver looked over his shoulder and pulled the large machine back onto the road in front of him.

'You're not serious for Christ's sake? Pull over, you arsehole. Can you believe this guy?' Sean hammered the horn. But the tractor driver ignored him.

By the time he reached Exeter station, the bus had already pulled out and was halfway to Adlington.

## 2 1

PRESENT DAY

Oliver stood in the kitchen, holding his mobile phone at arm's length like it had suddenly become boiling hot, poisoned with radiation and could burn a hole through his head.

He was unable to believe the question Meagan had just asked. He ran it over and over in his head.

*There is another way. Finish what you started.*

*How could she think I'd do it again? What the fuck is wrong with her?*

He was panicking, realising he had to cut loose from this predicament. He'd have to tell her. He ran the conversation through his mind, rehearsing what he'd say. *Meagan. I've fallen for you much harder than I could ever have imagined. What you see is what you get, but I've got to be honest, you're the first partner I've had who asked me to kill their husband.*

His phone rang again. No caller ID showed on the screen. Oliver flipped it, sending it to voicemail. He waited a few seconds to see if a message had been left. No alert. No beeping sound. He decided to switch the phone off and get some air.

Outside, the streets were crowded, people with their heads

down, banging against him, standing in his way like skittles lined up on a bowling alley just waiting to be knocked over.

To his left was a group of teenage girls standing in line. A passer-by had been persuaded to take their photo as they lifted their arms and loudly shouted how much they loved London. The passer-by then handed the phone back to one of the girls and was struggling to push past them, clearly agitated that his time had been taken up. There were small crowds of people lining the pavement, families mostly. And youngsters were stepping out in front of cars so drivers sounded their horns and swerved.

Oliver stood for a moment, composing himself, imagining a beach, the rolling waves, soft sand and a large beer. He closed his eyes, taking deep breaths, fighting the dread which engulfed his body like flames rising in the pit of his stomach.

Oliver was struggling to deal with the chaos. He needed to get away, to move from where he stood. He stepped onto the road, narrowly avoiding a car himself. Edging along the path, he spotted a café and decided to go for a much-needed caffeine fix.

Oliver walked inside and as far from the front window as possible. He couldn't face seeing anyone he knew. Conversation seemed like the hardest thing in the world at the moment.

He called his order to a guy behind the counter, asking for the largest cup of coffee possible. Then he turned on his phone and waited anxiously. There were no new messages, no emails. No one wanted him.

A figure appeared at the table, causing Oliver to jolt. 'Coffee, mate? You look like you need it.'

Oliver thanked him, ignoring the sarcasm.

The morning dragged, as if he had taken the wrong train, one that stopped at every station. Oliver settled down; his breathing going back to a steadier pace. Oliver felt comfortable here; hidden, obscure, oblivious to the damaging world outside.

While on his third cup of coffee and feeling the buzz of the caffeine, his phone beeped loudly. A message had come through. He lifted it from the table, squinting, then read the words.

You know what you have to do so we can be together. I'm counting on you, Oliver.

He dropped the phone on the table, his arm suddenly losing strength. The shock left him unable to hold the device. A pain ran through his chest and his heart started racing. Oliver needed to go home, get into bed and brush all this under the carpet, hoping time would help him forget about the trunk, gloved-man, Meagan, his life.

He stood, holding the back of his chair, edging towards the counter.

'You okay, mate? You don't look so good.'

'I'm fine, it's just the coffee. It's strong, you know.'

The guy finished wiping the shelf behind him then removed a piece of paper that had been pinned above him and handed it to Oliver, who paid with cash.

In the street the cars were louder. It seemed like there were even more people, spewing out from every corner. The streets were hectic, too busy for Oliver. He felt crammed in, compressed with no escape. His heart pounded, racing under his T-shirt, palpitations off the scale. He needed two hearts to deal with the sudden rush.

Oliver edged past the blurry stationary figures that were wavering in front of his vision, shouting for people to move out of his way.

Once inside his apartment, he locked the door. He removed his T-shirt and jeans and in the bathroom doused his hot face, letting the cold water relieve the stress he was feeling.

He had to cut all contact with Meagan. It was no good; she was asking too much. They'd already fucked up, killing a man, taking his life, dumping him in the reservoir. Yeah, the guy was a piece of shit, the lowest of the low, but it didn't ease the feeling. He'd killed someone. He couldn't and wouldn't do it again, no matter how many times Meagan asked.

He drew the curtains, turned off the light and got into bed, lying in silence. Now he had a migraine. Karma. It was his turn. He was lying to his boss, pretending he was ill, and now he really was sick. His head was pounding, his heartbeat resounding through his ears. His forehead ached. His eyes were heavy, his mouth dry.

Oliver lay on the bed and tried to relax. Breathe in for five, then out. Controlled long breaths. He jolted, the type of spasm you make when your body switches off, and you're almost at the point when you're out, unconscious, drifting, but not quite there yet.

He glanced at the alarm clock next to him. 1.52pm. His colleagues would be returning from their lunch break. His boss would be placing a pile of paperwork on the table, asking for the new client's details to be logged, contacted, added to the database and emailed relentlessly with any old shit about the company's plans for the future. *'Come with us on our journey. We are so glad you're on board. We value your custom more than you could ever imagine. Blah, blah, bloody blah. We're with you for the journey... Travel with us... We'll help you finish what you started'*

~

Oliver woke in a cold sweat, his body aching. He was shocked to see the alarm clock showing 6.02pm. *Shit, I slept – just over four hours. This is good – rest is what I need.* He lifted himself, propping a pillow behind his back for support and reaching for his phone, pleased to find no one had contacted him for a while.

Oliver stepped out of bed, running a hand through his hair,

focusing on his surroundings. He pulled on a clean pair of track-suit bottoms and a fresh T-shirt.

*God, I could get used to this.*

In the kitchen he drew the blinds, unable to display himself to the outside world. He'd stay here forever, hidden, protected by the four walls; he could do this, fuck the world out there.

He thought about food, how great a takeaway would be now – pizza or Indian. He and Claire had usually saved the junk nights for Saturday, but he was sick, unwell and needed a stodge fix.

He stood in the kitchen, enjoying the silence. *I'll take Monday off, too. They'll understand. Who gets sick for just a day? I can draw it out; it will give me time to get myself together, re-group as they say. Maybe I'll never go back. I have savings, enough to last for a year or two, maybe more. I need to deal with this shit, let it all blow over, then I'll feel better and I can move on.* Oliver penny-pinched. He liked to compare prices; he'd saved drastically over the years and watched his bank account grow. He knew he wasn't in a position where he'd end up penniless. He was wealthy, comfortable.

Oliver was distracted by a sharp pinging beep from the bedroom. His mobile. He chose to ignore it, not wanting to distract himself, now he was enjoying his own company.

The phone pinged twice more; three messages in total. *It must be urgent. Maybe it's work.* He took the device from the drawer. He screwed up his eyes, half closing them, thinking he may need glasses. He could just about read the blurry writing – twelve words.

You know what you have to do so we can be together.

The other two messages were exactly the same.

Oliver yelled out, louder than he'd intended, covering his mouth, banging his forehead with the palm of his hand. 'Fuck you, Meagan. What the hell is wrong with you?' He felt faint. He wanted to throw the phone to the ground and crush it into a hundred pieces.

He was struggling to comprehend her words, her thoughts. *Why would she do this? Calling me? Asking me to finish a fucking job I shouldn't have started in the first place? I helped her, goddammit. I fucking helped her. Well now it's her mess, she can deal with it. She can leave her husband. It's not my problem anymore.*

As Oliver stared at the message, he was sure someone was in the apartment. He had that intense feeling you get when you're not alone. He stood, motionless, aware of his breathing, listening intently. He froze. *Something moved in the hall, I'm sure. There was a bang, like a knock against the wall.*

He eased his way to the door, slowly opening it, firstly pushing his head out, then the rest of his body, stepping into the hallway. 'Hello.'

He didn't expect anyone to answer back.

'Is someone here? Hello.'

He opened the door of the bathroom, found it empty and looked over his shoulder. He worried that the guy who showed up last night at apartment six, Albuquerque House, could have followed him, found where he'd lived. He was being paranoid, surely. Oliver was certain no one had tailed him. He remembered the café, sitting alone, coming back home. He'd been dizzy, unaware of his surroundings, but he'd know if someone followed him. Wouldn't he?

He pulled the shower curtain sideways, with images of *Psycho* (mad Norman and the crazed mother) filling his head. He looked at the small window above. It was slightly ajar, held open on a rod, and impossible for someone to squeeze through. *Get it together, Oliver.*

Back in the hallway he peered through the spyhole in the front door and assembled the security chain, before going along the hall to the kitchen.

He glanced at the large clock, the window towards the back with the blind down, the shelf on the wall containing boy's toys, old comics, pictures, memories. Once he'd composed himself, he tapped a message back to Meagan, not wanting to get too heavy.

So do you, Meagan. Leave him before he kills you. I'm not doing this anymore. Please don't contact me again. Goodbye.

Rob placed his key into the front door of apartment six, lifting his small sports bag over his shoulder, shouting his wife's name. He stood in the hall, closing the door and listening. 'Meagan. Where are you?'

He was instantly agitated, in need of sleep, hungry and frustrated.

He'd met with complete idiots in Madrid, builders who promised the world but knew sod all. He had spent so much time going over drawings, plans and ideas for his new gentlemen's club. The building he'd looked at buying was in dire need of upgrading. Plumbing, air conditioning, decorating, and the roof needed a complete refurbishment.

Rob had made up for it, though, meeting with the owner of another club, moonlighting, pretending he was there for a couple of beers and a private show and taking the hottest dancer in the club back to his hotel with the promise of making her extremely rich when his seedy joint opened.

Now he reached into his jacket pocket, screwed up the piece of paper with her details into a tiny ball before dumping it into the kitchen bin.

Rob called Meagan's number a couple of times, refusing to leave a message. He decided to go and have a rest. He could wait for his dinner until she returned.

Rob woke a couple of hours later. The bedroom was pitch black. He was confused and disorientated. He reached to the other side of the bed, pawing for his wife, circling his arm and calling her name. When she didn't answer, he grabbed his phone, switching on the torch.

'Meagan.' He scanned the room, gliding the torch through the darkness. 'Where the fuck is she?' Rob was shouting, his voice loud, echoing through the walls. He knew something was wrong; she'd never leave him to sleep without bringing him coffee, food, checking he was okay, making her presence known.

He phoned her again, waiting, listening. It went straight to voicemail.

He left a brief message. 'Meagan. Don't make me come looking for you, do you understand? Call me.'

He hung up, groaning with tiredness. 'Worthless piece of shit.' Rob lay back down in the bed, turning off the torch, shaking with anger.

*Meagan is going to get it this time. No excuses. She's going to get hurt.*

The door to apartment six was closed, the communal hall empty. Down the corridor, the lift doors kept trying to close, the bell sounding every time they attempted to meet. The light at the back of the hall had begun flickering again. Now it was buzzing. It sounded like an electric chair ready to fry its next culprit.

Even from his bedroom Rob heard the impatient fist landing on his apartment door.

As Rob reached the bottom of the stairs, the thumping continued. 'All right. For Christ's sake, I'm coming.' He opened the door. 'Meagan. Where the fu–?'

Rob was pulled by his jumper out to the corridor, then hoisted against the communal wall. He was struggling to catch his breath, watching the menacing figure in front of him, the smirk on the guy's face.

'Who the fuck are you?' the guy asked, looking along the communal hall. He was agitated.

Rob was on tiptoes; the guy had lifted him partially off the ground, squeezing his neck. He tried to answer, but it felt like his head was going to burst. 'I live here,' Rob spluttered. 'What's this about?'

The guy let go of Rob, watching him drop to the floor. 'I'll just ask this once. Where's Tony?'

Rob was disorientated, trying to push himself off the floor, crawling like a baby to escape along the corridor. 'I don't know who you're talking about. I swear. I've been away. Tony who?' He watched as the guy removed a large machete from the back of his jeans. The tip was glistening and razor sharp. He slashed Rob across the face, causing blood to spill onto the carpet.

'Wrong answer, you prick.'

Then he lifted the weapon and continued slicing.

Soft music played in the background, the lights were dim, and the blinds were still drawn. A single plate lay on the table, empty metallic cartons were stacked on top of each other, and three beer cans with the contents finished.

Oliver lay on the sofa with his feet up, enjoying his own company. This is how life would be from now on; plain and simple. It was less aggravation, less complicated.

He stood, went to the fridge, took out another beer, cracked it open, slugged half of it and returned to the sofa.

There was a knock at the door. Not just a tap, a pounding, someone's fist thumping in agitation.

He sat motionless, wondering who could be calling so late. He flicked a look at his watch – almost 10pm. That was too late for a visitor. His mind raced, trying to figure out who was at the door. He didn't want to budge from the sofa, not now, not ever. He was content, comfortable.

The door banged again, louder this time. Oliver stood slowly, moving to the kitchen, past the breakfast bar, the electric oven, the American-style fridge. He reached forward to turn off the radio. He was breathing faster, panic was setting in, his body aching and his head fuzzy from the alcohol.

Three more bangs caused him to freeze. He had to answer, had to go and see who it was.

At the front door he stepped up on his tiptoes, his eye to the spyhole. Outside seemed blurred and cloudy, like looking at the world through binoculars that were the wrong way round.

He gently raised his left hand, removing the chain, pulling the door open, edging it towards him, then stepping into the corridor. 'Hello. Who's there?'

He listened intently – the couple next door to his right were arguing; an intense debate, raised voices. Something slammed from inside their apartment, a saucepan or kettle. He'd only seen them a few times, a middle-aged couple, usually quiet.

Oliver looked to the left. He could make out a faint shadow; someone was standing on the stairs leading down to the main communal doors.

He wanted to shut the door, fasten the chain, return to the sofa. *Why have they knocked on my door? Are they drunk? In need of help?*

As he stepped back into his apartment, feeling behind him for the door to move inside, he heard a groan, a gasp for breath. 'Hello. Who's there? Can I help you?'

Another groan. Louder this time.

Oliver let go of the front door, edging to the communal stairs, looking behind him, peering along the hall. 'Who's there? Hello.'

He froze in shock, his head spinning, feeling like he was about to heave up all the food he'd eaten earlier.

In front of him, attached to the wooden balcony with thick rope around her neck, was Meagan, dangling over the staircase. Her legs were kicking like a fish that had just been taken out of water.

## 2 2

TWENTY YEARS AGO - BEFORE THE
PHONE CALL

The bus pulled away, out onto the country lane. Tricia and Meagan were standing in the cold alone, waving to Danny and Bev who were leaning over the back seat as the bus pulled out of sight.

'They were friendly, weren't they?' Tricia stated, looking around to get her bearings.

Meagan nodded. 'Are we here, Mummy?'

'Yes, Meggy. See the large white house on the corner? That's Aunty Anne's place.'

Tricia picked up her bag, holding her daughter's hand as they made their way together, side by side.

'It's very quiet here, Mummy. It's scary.'

'Oh, Meggy. There's nothing to worry about.'

As they reached the house, Tricia opened the black wooden gate, and they walked up the cobbled path. They noticed a light towards the back of the house coming from the kitchen; the curtains were drawn in the front living room to their right side.

It was an old-style farmhouse, Tricia recalled. Although she hadn't been here for quite a while, she still remembered the layout. She searched for a bell, finding a long pole hanging from the wooden porch at the front.

'Can I do it, Mummy?'

Tricia lifted her daughter, who reached out and pulled the pole towards her. A loud sound came from inside, the tune of Big Ben's chimes.

They waited patiently, Tricia cupping her hands and looking through the glass of the front door. *No, please be inside. Don't do this to me now. She has to be inside.*

Tricia pulled the pole again and a window opened above. 'Who's there?'

Tricia immediately recognised the hoarse, croaky voice. She realised her sister must have been asleep. 'Anne. It's me. Open the door.'

'Tricia. Is that you? Oh, my lord. Is everything okay? Give me a second.'

The window closed, and a light went on in the upstairs hall, a shadow moving down the stairs towards them. Anne unlocked the front door. She was wearing a dark brown dressing gown and had a sleep mask resting over her forehead. 'Well, look here.' Anne reached out, pulling her sister close, leaning back, taking her in. 'And look at you. You've grown, young lady,' directing her comment at Meagan.

'What do you say, Meggy?' nudged Tricia.

'It's so good to see you.'

Anne leant forward, moving towards Meagan. 'It's so good to see you too.' She beckoned them inside. 'Where's Sean. Is he with you?'

'No. We're hiding on him,' Meagan said.

Tricia looked at her sister. 'It's a long story.'

Anne crouched down, holding Meagan close. 'Why don't you come with me and I'll show you your room? Then your mother and I can have a catch-up.'

Once Meagan was tucked into bed, she went straight to sleep, with Arthur lying beside her.

~

In the kitchen Anne found Tricia bent forward on a wooden chair, staring at the ground, rocking backwards and forwards. She went over to her sister, crouching by her side. 'Tricia, love. Talk to me, tell me what's going on.'

Tricia looked up, mascara running down her pale face. Her eyes were bloodshot and she looked beaten, like someone who'd given up and couldn't carry on. She gripped her sister's arm, pulling her towards her and embracing hard. 'You have to help me. I'm begging you.'

Anne placed her arm around her sister's back, rubbing gently, comforting the broken woman who sat in front of her.

As Anne held her sister, Tricia completely broke down, sobbing uncontrollably and telling her about Sean, the terrible things he did to her, how he treated her, finishing with her being locked in the wooden container and Meagan finding her, the two of them making their escape, running to freedom.

Anne listened in shock, shaking with hatred for the man Tricia had married.

When Tricia had finished, Anne took a bottle of whisky from the kitchen unit and half-filled two glasses. Tricia reluctantly downed the alcohol and watched as Anne tipped the bottle for a refill.

'You did the right thing coming here. You can't live like that, Tricia. He'll kill you, and Meagan. Why didn't you do it sooner?'

Anne watched her sister, whose face was red from the cold and the sudden hit from the whisky. Her hands were shaking as she struggled to spill the words out. She was trembling, softly humming to herself to blank out the terror of the last few weeks.

Anne stood, wanting, needing to show authority. It was the only way she knew to deal with this situation. 'I'm going to run you a bath. Take as much time as you need. You're staying here now; this is your home for as long as you like. Do you hear me, Tricia?'

Tricia nodded, reaching for the bottle and pouring another shot.

Anne went upstairs, turned on the taps and started filling the bath with warm water.

Tricia leant back on the chair, finally pulling herself together. She rarely drank but could now easily finish the bottle. Her tears had stopped, the shaking temporarily ceased, and she was calm.

She thought about Meagan, how all of this was affecting her; the nightmares, the questions she'd asked, how she worried about her mother. Meagan was such an innocent, beautiful girl who didn't deserve to witness such horrific episodes. How she loved to hide, it was her favourite game. Tricia just hoped they could keep hiding forever and never be found.

An hour later, Tricia returned to the kitchen after her bath, wearing a dressing gown that Anne had found for her. Anne had emptied her holdall and put Tricia and Meagan's clothes into the washing machine to freshen them up a little.

Tricia was feeling a little lightheaded from the effects of the whisky, and wanted coffee.

Anne boiled a kettle of water on the stove. It started whistling, a high-pitched screech that grated through Tricia's body.

'How are you feeling, or is that a stupid question?' Anne asked.

Tricia looked up, clinging to the dressing gown, wrapping the belt tighter around her waist. 'What are we going to do, Anne? Meagan and I can't stay here forever.' Tricia looked beyond her sister, to a large window behind her, the blackness outside, so cold, so bleak and uninviting.

'I've told you, you can stay here for as long as you need.' Anne placed two cups onto the table, watching as Tricia gripped hers, appreciating the warmth and lightly blowing the drink to cool it down.

'We can't stay forever. I don't know what we're going to do, Anne.'

Suddenly the lights went out. Anne stood as Tricia gripped the side of her chair.

'What's going on?' Tricia asked. Her body was pulsating with nervous energy. She wanted to run to Meagan.

'It's fine. We get power cuts frequently. It's a regular occurrence. Wait there. I'll go and check it out.'

'I'll come as well.'

'Honestly. There's no need. Drink your coffee. I'll be back in a second.'

Tricia sat in the darkness, looking out of the window from her seat. A tree branch tapped the glass, like a claw trying to muster the strength to get inside and work its way around her neck. She listened to the wind howling, echoing through her head. The branch stopped as Tricia froze. Again, it slapped against the glass. Tricia screamed out, jumping up, standing alone in the kitchen, sure that someone was outside, looking at her, watching. She jolted as the lights came back on, and Anne walked into the kitchen.

'See, nothing to worry about,' Anne stated.

'I'm going to check on Meagan.' Tricia relaxed slightly, stood and went upstairs. She found her daughter in the back bedroom, fast asleep, with her arm around Arthur the bunny who was wrapped in the blanket beside her. She listened to the light breaths, watching her daughter at peace.

'I wish it could be different, Meggy. Honestly, I do. I love you so much. Always remember that, baby.' She kissed her daughter on the head and left the room.

As Tricia moved along the upstairs hall, the floorboards bowed underneath her feet, dipping and creaking like a moored boat in a marina. She was thankful for her sister, but also guilty that they hadn't kept in regular contact.

It was going to change; her life was going to change. It would get better. Tricia owed it to Meagan; her and her daughter's happiness was everything. She'd have to talk with her, tell her how it is, that her father couldn't be a part of their life anymore. It was time to stand up to the bastard the only way she knew.

Hide and stay hiding.

## 23

Rob was lying on the floor of the communal hall outside apartment six. He had squealed like a pig, now he was turned on his side, crying, his body jolting, his shoulders scrunched towards his neck, and his face bloody.

Phil Cavanagh had just kicked the shit out of him, after asking about his partner Tony. Phil told him he lived in apartment seven and that Tony was missing. He wanted answers.

'See, we run a debt collection, a recovery business as we like to call it these days. People borrow money for all sorts of reasons: a small gambling habit, money for a dirty weekend away, a new bike for their kid. But the debt needs paying on time. It gets vicious – we're underhanded, old school. People have been hurt, houses ransacked. You don't fuck with us, especially with Tony.'

He held the machete high in the air. 'See, this bitch that Tony went after owes us a lot of money. Now she's gone and I can't get hold of Tony. So I'm thinking that maybe there's something going on, underhand if you like. It doesn't look good. So I need to find him. I want you to realise I'm the calmer one. You get my fucking drift?'

Rob knew nothing about the neighbour who lived in apart-

165

ment seven. Why would he? He kept himself to himself. Other people's lives didn't interest him. He couldn't care less about them; they were below him, inadequate, a nuisance.

Phil grabbed Rob by his legs, moving him into apartment six. Pushing his hand inside his jacket he removed a length of rope and pulled on it, as if testing its durability. 'This will do nicely.'

He crouched beside Rob, tying him securely to a radiator pipe in the downstairs hall. Then he dipped his hand back into the same pocket and removed a piece of cloth that he rammed into Rob's mouth. Then he wrapped the rope several times around his lips.

Rob was trying to speak; muffled sounds were coming from his mouth, beads of sweat dripping from his forehead, blood stains on his hands. His eyes and face were sore, stinging as he tried to blink and focus. He had a metallic taste in his mouth from the blood, and was struggling to swallow. He gagged with the cloth, fighting to breathe, trying to empty the contents of his nose so he could push air into his lungs.

Once Phil was confident Rob was securely tied, he stood, checking the communal hall. Then he returned to the apartment and watched the fear on Rob's face.

'I'm going now. If I find out you, or the girl I saw here last night had anything to do with Tony's disappearance, I'll come back, and the next time you won't be in such a fit state. That's a promise.'

Rob watched him walk casually out the door, zipping up his jacket.

Oliver struggled to lift Meagan's feet. The more he heaved, the harder she gagged. Her face had turned a dark purple, veins spreading on her forehead like a cracked window. She twitched as Oliver struggled to support her.

'For fuck's sake, Meagan, hold still. I'm going to get you down, okay. Help me out here.' He watched her face; her eyes were rolling upwards, flickering, resembling white marbles, her mouth opening wider as she gasped for air. Her arms fell limp by her sides. Oliver was losing her. He wanted to shout for help, but he couldn't let go.

In desperation, he pushed her body, watching her swing out to the right. As she came back towards him, he caught her legs, anchoring her body onto the side rail. Meagan was balancing as Oliver held her body against the railing with his shoulder, managing to quickly remove the rope from around her neck.

He laid her down on the hallway floor by the stairs, desperately rubbing her neck, hoping it may clear her airways. He lifted her head, pleading for her to move, jolt, anything to say she was still alive.

'Don't do this, Meagan. Hold on. You're not going on me, please, Meagan. Stay with me.' Oliver pushed on her chest, unsure if it would make a difference. He'd seen it many times in films, but only if someone was drowning, or having a heart attack. He didn't know if it made a difference to someone who had just tried to hang themselves. After a few chest pumps, his hands placed on top of each other, pushing as hard as he could muster, he tried rubbing her throat. Meagan suddenly spasmed, like she'd just had an electric shock, her eyes opened, and she focused on Oliver.

'Oh, thank you, God. Thank you. Can you hear me, Meagan?' He waited for an answer, a movement, anything to indicate she was okay.

As Oliver lifted her head, she turned on her side, vomiting onto the carpet. When she'd finished, she slowly turned back over. She whispered, 'What happened?' She pushed herself up, trying to get to her feet.

Oliver helped to lift her. 'Are you okay to stand?'

She glanced around, as if unsure where she was. 'Rob. Where's Rob?'

'Shhh, Meagan. Don't worry about Rob. I'm calling an ambulance.'

'No, you don't understand. I need to be there. He's back. I have to get to him now.'

'You're not going anywhere until you rest. Come on. You're in no state to go home.' As Meagan lifted herself off the floor, Oliver saw the deep mark across her neck, wondering how her head hadn't come away from her body.

He slowly helped her into his apartment, one arm guiding her as she walked, flicking the lights on in the hallway with his free arm.

He sat Meagan down in the kitchen and went to make two strong coffees.

He picked up his phone. 'We're going to get you checked over. I'm calling 999.'

Meagan pleaded with Oliver. 'If you call an ambulance, you may as well sign my death warrant. Don't do it, Oliver. I'm begging you. Rob will kill me.'

Oliver cancelled the phone call, then lifted the blinds. Light filled the room as he looked out over London, watching the stillness, the bright lights gleaming on the Thames. He gazed out from his apartment on the fourth floor, thinking about his situation. He couldn't carry on like this. His life had turned upside down in the last few weeks. This woman in his apartment, the trouble she brought with her! She'd blown in like a breeze – correction, a hurricane, a tornado that had lifted him to a place far stranger than Oz. This wasn't him. He'd had a simple life before he met her; him and Claire watching the same programmes night after night, a takeaway at the weekend, a commute together, great conversation. He craved this now. The plain, dull, easy life he had had before didn't seem so wrong. At the time he wanted something different; excitement, a break from the dull world he seemed to be drawn into. He found himself wishing at this moment that Meagan and Claire would swap places. He couldn't be with this woman who was sitting in his kitchen. She fucked with his head more than she'd ever know.

Meagan had to go.

Oliver turned, bringing the coffee towards her. 'There you go. Drink this. It will make you feel better. Nothing like a caffeine hit.'

Meagan reached for one of the mugs. 'Thank you. I don't know what I'd do if I hadn't met you, Oliver. Please, don't ever leave me, do you hear? I can't be without you; you understand what I'm saying? I can't.'

*No. Please. Don't start this shit again. Don't play with my emotions. You're drinking this, then going. That's it. Out, out, out.* 'It's no problem. I'm glad the colour has returned to your face. Jesus, Meagan, what were you thinking?'

She placed the mug on the table, then she broke down, sobbing uncontrollably, her shoulders jerking, streams of tears spilling from her eyes.

He placed his arms around her, kissing her damp forehead, pulling her closer, needing to be there for her until she gained control.

～

Oliver glanced at the clock on the wall in the kitchen, not wanting Meagan to catch him. She had just finished her second coffee. He mustered the strength and took a deep breath. 'Okay. Come on, I'll drive you home.'

She looked at him, through him, her calm, dull expression, the emptiness which filled her eyes, the broken woman struggling to assemble her thoughts, gather herself together, make sense of everything, the life she was sucked into through no choice of her own. Oliver could see it all, an open book, like he could read her mind, connect with her thoughts.

He needed her to leave. 'Are you ready?'

Meagan simply answered, 'Fine.'

As they reached Albuquerque House, Meagan stopped, watching above her. It was a place she'd never get used to; a nightmare gateway to another dimension, a dark, mysterious building with supernatural powers, a place where once you set foot inside, you are never the same again.

She turned to Oliver. 'I can't do it.'

'You can. It's your home, Meagan. It's where you live.' Oliver fought the lump in his throat as he kissed her on the cheek. 'This is where it ends. I can't do this anymore. I'm so sorry, but you need to leave him before it's too late. You know what you have to do. Make a better life for yourself before it's too late.'

Meagan looked at Oliver. It seemed her confidence had momentarily returned. 'I won't contact you again. If that's what you really want.'

'I think it's best. Take care, Meagan.'

With that, she stood on the street, watching him disappear along the road until his car was a speck.

Meagan placed her key in the door, twisting it slowly, pushing the door, the creak, a slow screech that grated through her head.

She had a plan. Rob would ask where she'd been, why she hadn't been here to greet him, coffee in hand, his robe, his fucking slippers, a red carpet rolled out for him to glide down, so he could parade himself and announce his return from Spain. God, she hated him with every fibre of her being. Every breath she took was resentment and bitterness towards her bastard of a husband.

She rehearsed it in her head while climbing the steps. *I was attacked on the way home. Hijacked*– Wait, maybe hijacked is too strong a word. Mugged, yes. *Two guys in masks grabbed me from the street. They took my handbag.*

She glanced downwards. Her bag was dangling by her hip, the strap placed loosely over her left shoulder. *That won't work now Meagan, will it? Fuck it. I've taken a lover. We planned your death while we were together. How mad is that? We both came up with the sickest way possible to top you off. Only it went a little pear-shaped. We have a neighbour at number seven. No, of course, you wouldn't know, how could you? Self-indulgent prick. Well, the poor unfortunate bastard is no longer with us. Coffee?*

Meagan decided to tell Rob she'd been jumped, and her handbag had been lifted off her shoulder. One guy ripped it from her, causing the burn mark on her neck and a passer-by came to her aid. It was the best she could think of at that moment.

'Rob?' Meagan whispered as she stepped inside apartment six. How she hoped he hadn't come home.

Suddenly, her anxiety lifted, fear turning to shock. She glanced on the hallway floor, looking at her husband, a gag strapped to his mouth, hands tied firmly to the radiator pipe.

He mumbled, squealing something she couldn't make out. Suddenly her nurturing side went into overdrive. She temporarily forgot it was her fucker of a husband on the floor. It was someone who needed help. Her help.

'Oh my God, Rob. What happened?' It was pointless asking until she had removed the gag. Meagan leaned forward, struggling to untie the knot, pulling the cloth and yanking Rob's head forward, feeling sorry for him for the briefest of moments. She needed to help him, untie the rope and cut her husband loose.

Once freed, he leant forward, clasping his wife, sobbing onto her shoulders. 'Oh, Meagan. I'm so sorry. I'm so very sorry.'

She crouched, moving further into his grasp, and among all the craziness of the last few days, she found herself suddenly feeling like a normal person again.

Once Rob had composed himself, he explained what had happened. He held his ribs, struggling to move, patting his scarred face with the back of his hand.

Meagan dabbed her husband's face with antiseptic wipes, cleaning the blood, aiding her partner.

He winced as she firmly wiped under his eyes. His cheeks were severely cut and there was a gash along the right side of his forehead. He was a complete mess. Those cuts would scar. Her husband would bear the remnants of this attack for the rest of his life.

They stood in the hall and Rob was shaking, struggling to keep his legs still.

Meagan felt like the one in control. She stood back, the blood-stained wipe in her hand. 'Here, let me look at you. Oh, Rob, what have they done? You're a mess.'

She watched the pathetic look in his eyes, his slumped figure, his sudden vulnerability. She liked this. This newly-formed person, so needy, destitute, wallowing in self-pity. She could do this. She suddenly realised her husband was human – with a heart, feelings, emotions.

Meagan instantly regretted how she'd felt about him, the anger, the fear. She had doubted her husband could ever change, but here it was, proof that people can change, people are good. They are good after all, aren't they?

Aren't they?

## 24

TWENTY YEARS AGO - BEFORE THE
PHONE CALL

'Good morning. Did you sleep well?' Anne was placing three plates with poached eggs on the kitchen table.

'Oh wow. You're amazing.' Tricia glanced at the wall clock above the fridge. 'You should have woken us. I can't believe the time. It's nearly midday.'

'You obviously needed the rest.' Anne pulled out a chair from under the table and motioned for her sister to take her place and eat.

Meagan came down the stairs, slightly disorientated, happy to see both her aunty and mother together.

'Good morning, young lady. How are you today?' Anne asked.

Meagan looked at the food, scrunching her face. 'I'm good, Aunty Anne.'

'Glad to hear it.'

Meagan sat at the table; her chair was unstable as it balanced on a cracked floor tile. Tricia and Anne laughed together as Meagan grew more frustrated, trying to steady herself.

They ate, Tricia watching a ray of light shining through the window where the clawed hand had been the night before. The tree was now still.

Anne refilled the kettle with hot water from the urn.

The women kept quiet regarding any future plans. Tricia wanted to let Meagan know what was happening, but it was too early, she needed to pick the right moment.

After they'd eaten, Anne announced she'd go to town and thought it would be good for both Tricia and Meagan to join her.

Tricia was adamant she'd stay and tidy the place a little, stating it would make her feel better, but Anne persuaded her to go. 'The fresh air will clear your head, Tricia.'

The three of them spent the day at the market which seemed to sell everything from old books, to antiques to food. To Meagan's delight there was a pick-and-mix stall. She asked her mother if she could have something. Tricia quickly declined, but was then overruled by her sister.

'Go on, Tricia. Let her have some fun. We scoffed our faces with sweets most days as kids. What harm did it do to us?'

Tricia gave in, and Meagan quickly filled a brown paper bag with everything from white mice to cola cubes. The guy behind the stall seemed to take a shine to the young girl and also filled both her coat pockets to the brim, adding a peanut brittle bar as an extra treat. He winked. 'Don't tell your mother, sweetheart.'

Meagan smiled. 'I have a carrier bag as well.'

The guy laughed. 'You'll get me shot.'

After they'd looked at more stalls, Anne brought them to a small bakery for coffee. She knew the old lady behind the counter who allowed Meagan to join her and make sugar dough-nuts, much to Tricia's dismay.

'She's a kid. Leave her be for heaven's sake, Tricia.'

'Oh, Anne. It's not that I'm worried about. Today has been wonderful, more joyous than I can ever say. I've never felt so happy, nor has Meagan. That poor girl has witnessed so much shit. I feel guilty.'

Anne stretched across the table and placed her hand on

Tricia's shoulder. 'Guilty for what, exactly? You're an amazing mother. Anyone can see that.'

Tricia sipped her coffee, looking out at the market through the bakery window. People were dismantling frames, folding them up for the day, placing items into the back of vans, shouting over to each other. A young lad fired a potato across the road, narrowly missing his mate from another stall.

'It can't be like this though, can it?'

Anne stared at her sister, taking in her glum face and disorientated features. She noticed the heavy bags under her eyes, her brow furrowed with deep marks from years of frowning.

'Who says? You? Is that how life should be, Tricia? Living in fear? Worried that the next time you're together will be your last? Sean is a complete bastard. Do you hear me? You deserve happiness. You are going to be happy. I'll make sure.'

Tricia broke down and sobbed into her sister's chest.

Meagan was distracted, pouring sugar into a bowl to make the doughnuts, impatiently waiting for the fix and unaware of how pitiful her mother was feeling.

She joined Tricia and her aunt a few minutes later, wiping the sugar from her mouth onto her coat sleeve. She eyed the doughnuts, offering them out, both women declining.

'Ohh, Meggy, they look delicious but I can't have them because the lady makes cakes with nuts in her kitchen, and remember even a tiny piece of nut can make Mummy very ill. You'll get sick if you eat all those. Just a couple, okay.'

Her daughter looked up. 'This is the best day of my life.'

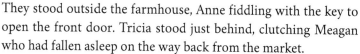

They stood outside the farmhouse, Anne fiddling with the key to open the front door. Tricia stood just behind, clutching Meagan who had fallen asleep on the way back from the market.

'Okay, I'll get dinner prepared. Bring her upstairs. Poor love has had an exhausting day,' Anne said.

'Yeah, too much excitement.' Tricia climbed the stairs, balancing her daughter around her hip with her left hand, holding onto the rail with the other. She placed Meagan down on the bed, pulling the blanket over her and tucking Arthur the bunny under her arm. Tricia whispered, 'Hey, baby. You had a good day. Life is going to get better, I promise, this is only the beginning: you, me, Aunty Anne. You wait and see. I love you so much. Get some sleep.'

She leant down and kissed her daughter's forehead, and found the sweet taste of sugar on her own lips.

Downstairs, Anne poured pasta into a pan of boiling water. She added tomatoes to another pot for the sauce, sprinkling the contents with salt. She heard Tricia returning. 'She's out, I'm guessing?'

'Like a light, as they say.' Tricia moved towards her sister. 'I can't thank you enough. Really, Anne. How can I repay your kindness?'

Anne turned, facing her sister. 'Tricia, you deserve better, don't play the victim, please. We're going to toughen you up. You'll see, life is going to get so much b--'

The lights went out; the kitchen was in complete darkness.

Tricia pushed her hands forward, reaching for her sister. 'Anne. What's happening?' She listened for her voice, pawing, jabbing the space where Anne had stood. 'Anne? Is it a power cut? You said this happens frequently. Anne?'

Tricia listened to her own heavy breaths, trying to gain control, struggling to stem the anxiety that had shot through her body.

Her first thought was Meagan. She had to get to her, make sure she was okay.

Tricia moved forward, arms in front, swiping left and right. The water was spilling over the pan and the lid rattled sharply. 'Anne. Turn the stove off, you're scaring me. This isn't funny, do you hear?' Tricia reached forward, moving her fingers along the knobs of the cooker, turning everything anticlockwise and making sure the gas was turned off. The water stopped bubbling.

*What the hell is going on? If this is a joke, it's cruel.* Suddenly the power returned and the kitchen was drenched in light. Tricia was standing next to the cooker alone. She could feel her heart beating hard. She felt faint, worried she'd collapse. Tricia was too frightened to move, but she had to get to Meagan. As she forced her legs forward, she screamed out, 'Anne! What's going on? Where are you? Please, Anne. Why are you d–?'

Again, the lights went out. Tricia was standing alone in the kitchen of a strange house with her daughter upstairs.

Tricia spun round, looking out the side window. The branch had started tapping, lightly knocking against the glass, its fingers beckoning her outside. She listened intently. The clock was ticking behind her as the second hand pounded around the large face, getting louder, sounding like a hammer crashing against the wall. She jumped as a shadow passed the window. Tricia couldn't be clear, but from the corner of her eye she saw someone or something move. She stepped back, tripping over an object on the floor. She broke her fall by placing her hand down, dropping to the side and rolling onto her stomach.

She crawled slowly towards the kitchen door, her hands pawing on the floor in front of her. She was sure she could hear the front door creak open. As Tricia paused, listening, she was certain. The front door to the cottage was banging against the hallway wall. Every few seconds, she heard the wooden door swinging, crunching, getting more intense. She could feel the wind hard in her ears. She looked behind and up at the side window. The branch was crashing against the glass. Tricia manoeuvred herself upwards, getting onto her hands and knees and crawling towards the kitchen door. Once she reached it, she grabbed for the handle and twisted, opening the door to the hallway.

The front door was open. Trees swung outside, the branches like pendulums, viciously swinging left and right. Tricia stood, raced to the door and forced it shut, using her body weight.

She pictured Meagan asleep upstairs. She needed to go to her now, get her out to safety. Whatever was going on, her sister had vanished. She'd stood beside Tricia only a few moments ago, cooking, chatting, telling Tricia everything would be okay and that she was safe. 'Anne. Where are you? Please answer me.'

Tricia eyed the stairs; the lights were on above her. She raced up the steps, taking them two at a time, barging the door open. Meagan was still sleeping.

'Oh, thank God. Sweetie, sweetie, wake up quickly. Something's wrong.'

Meagan sat up, clutching her bunny. 'Don't worry, Mummy. I'll protect you.'

Tricia lifted her from the bed, glad to see her daughter was still wearing the clothes from earlier.

'Okay, listen, something is happening. I'll explain in a minute, but you need to come now, hurry. We need to find Aunty Anne. Something isn't right. Okay?'

'Is she hiding too, Mummy?'

'Maybe, I'm not sure. I hope so.' Tricia placed her hands over her face, pulling down hard in frustration. 'Quickly. We need to go.'

Tricia headed out towards the hall, looking over the steps to the darkness below. She needed to get out to the street, ask someone for help. She stood on top of the stairs, listening, trying to figure out what had happened. There one minute, gone the next. *Surely Anne wouldn't play a trick; she knows the situation I'm in.*

Meagan was at the top of the stairs. 'Mummy, did you find Aunty Anne yet?'

'Meggy, keep your voice down. We need to keep very quiet, okay?'

'Why, Mummy?'

Tricia took a deep breath, held it for a second and steadied herself. 'We just do, Meggy. Remember when we're looking for someone? It's much easier to catch them if they don't hear us coming.'

'Okay. I got it, Mummy. I won't make a peep. Nor will Arthur. He's very tired, Mummy, he's had a long day too.'

Tricia reached the front door. The house was still plunged in darkness, and suddenly so still. 'Okay, Meggy, when I open the door, we run. Got it?'

Tricia looked up the stairs, watching Meagan nodding, her finger covering her lips. 'Good girl. That's great. Keep as quiet as possible.'

Tricia turned the handle. The front door was jammed. 'Come on, you piece of shit, why won't you open?' She took the handle with both hands, placing her leg on the side wall, yanking, twisting the handle, pulling until her hands were numb. 'What is going on? Come on.'

Meagan had joined her. 'Don't worry, Mummy, I'll help you. I can pull hard. I'm strong. Miss Lester said I'm as strong as some of the boys in my class. One day I–'

Tricia cut her off. 'Quick. Move with me to the kitchen. I'm going to try and open the back door. Hurry, Meggy, we don't have time.'

Tricia placed her hands in front, moving as fast as she could towards the kitchen door, swiping at the space in front of her, with Meagan following, listening to her mother's voice.

They made their way to the centre of the room, guided by a light close by, giving a small glow where they stood.

'Wait here, Meggy. Don't move. I'm going to try and open the back door. I need to check if it's safe. You hear me now? Don't move. Stay here with Arthur. You got it?'

'I got it, Mummy. Stay here with Arthur. I'm not going to move.'

'Good girl.' Tricia felt for the back door, tapping the glass, feeling below for the handle, touching a key placed in the lock. She turned it, opening the back door. 'Oh, thank God.'

She stood outside. The wind had eased slightly, but the chill in the air was icy cold. She glanced upwards. The sky was almost transparent, covered with tiny specks of light. She needed to be sure it was safe for them to run. Tricia was worried about where her sister had gone. She hadn't time to look for her. The main concern was getting Meagan to safety, out of the house and unharmed. Something had obviously stirred with Anne's emotions. Maybe she was having a panic attack, feeling sick. Whatever was happening, Tricia would get help and find her later.

As Tricia went from the side of the house to the street, she looked along the road. There was no one in sight. The street was clear; empty and desolate. She stepped back inside the cottage. 'Okay, Meggy. It's clear. Are you ready to run?'

'Yes, Mummy.'

'Okay, let's go. Take my hand.' Tricia reached out, searching for her daughter. She heard her voice, tiny and soft.

'Mummy?'

'Yes, Meggy. Come on. Take my hand, we need to go.'

Tricia could just about make out a shadow in front, standing close to her. 'Please, Meggy. Where are you?' Suddenly she felt a sleeve. 'Got ya. Okay, move. We need to go.'

Tricia tugged on the sleeve, trying to let her daughter know the sense of urgency.

'Meggy, please baby. Why aren't you moving? Come on, will you? I've got your arm; you're safe now.'

'I'm here, Mummy. I'm behind you. That isn't my arm.'

Suddenly a light came on. Sean was standing in front of Tricia, holding a bright torch, his other hand clasped around Tricia's wrist. She saw the familiar smirk, the smug look, the evil expression.

'You found us, Daddy. I knew you would. Oh, Mummy, you must be so happy.'

Sean looked at his daughter. 'Oh yes, Meagan, she must be.'

## 25

Oliver hadn't seen or heard from Meagan for over a week. It was best this way. Both of them had to move on. Yes, it had been great while it lasted. Oliver had fallen for this woman hard. He'd never had feelings or known as much emotion and passion as he had for Meagan. She blew into his life like a hurricane, turned it upside down and left like a cool breeze, calmly saying goodbye as she prepared to face her husband.

Oliver was in the process of moving. The flat in Chelsea was too expensive. He'd spoken with an estate agent, who assured him he'd be placed on their priority list. He'd just had a call from Darren, head of property management. 'Good morning Oliver, it must be your lucky day.'

Darren told him about a small flat that had just come onto the market in Kilburn. Newly refurbished, cosy, quaint, great views, affordable. All the usual shit they throw at you to try and coax you into falling in love with the place, with an offer too good to be true. A drop everything, take a deep breath, humdinger of a once in a lifetime opportunity.

'Oh great, excellent, that's news I've been waiting to hear.' Oliver went on to explain his sudden split with Claire, his ex, the lady who calmly kissed his forehead before pissing off without a thought about how he'd feel. 'But she still wants to be friends,' he added bitterly. *Oh yes, that would work now, wouldn't it? I've ploughed all my time into honing my skills as a partner, just to share the odd pizza and a glass of wine every few weeks. Thank you, Claire, how very thoughtful. Am I pissed off? No, why would you think that?*

He scribbled the address down on a piece of paper that was lying on a side unit in the kitchen, marking it as urgent at the top of the page.

When the call had finished, Oliver looked out of the window over West London. He'd grown attached to this place, the amazing views, the well-insulated apartment, quiet neighbours and vibrant life outside on the streets, although maybe he wouldn't miss the crowds as much.

He'd get to know people in his new place, that was for sure. It wouldn't take long. Oliver had a good feeling about the future. *I just need to get Meagan out of my head.*

He stood in the kitchen. Everything was in its place; tidy, neatly arranged. The thick white shelf to his left, stretching halfway along the kitchen wall, was furnished with souvenirs and memorabilia. The bag he'd bought as a kid on a family trip to Margate; Banksy pictures; photos of nights out with his parents, cousins, sister, all placed in large frames; mementos displayed along the shelf; spice pots; empty wine bottles he'd collected from trips abroad, their red-stained corks attached to a large board.

In the living room, he eyed the black sofa, the Marvel comics piled knee-high and perfectly in line, the statue of a ballerina which doubled up as a lamp. Everything in its place, a place for everything. He was a collector; hoarder was too strong a word.

Once he'd checked over the apartment, Oliver left, deciding to get something to eat at the café a few doors down.

'Have you seen my white shirt?' asked Rob. 'I'm sure it was hanging in the wardrobe. I must be going mad.'

Meagan was still in bed, watching her husband hunt for his clothes. She had forgotten life could be like this. It was 10.30am and she was resting, relaxed, calm.

They'd been out the night before at a steak house on the Old Kent Road. As they left apartment six, Rob placed Meagan's red coat over her shoulders, helping her into it. He opened the front door, holding her hand as they walked out onto the street. He sat beside her in the taxi on the way there, let her choose a meal and drink, as much as she wanted. He paid the bill himself, making conversation, taking an interest in what she had to say. When they returned home, she fell asleep in his arms. No sexual demands, no pawing and mauling.

This was good. Too good. Meagan thought she didn't deserve this; her new life, new husband, it wasn't her. It wasn't them, Rob and her. But it was, and it felt so bloody good.

'I may have washed it. Let me go and check.'

Rob reassured her. 'Don't worry, I'll check. I'll bring a coffee back up. Stay where you are.'

Rob left the room, returning a few minutes later wearing the ironed shirt tucked into his black trousers, her latte in hand. He placed the drink on the bedside unit. 'Thanks, Meagan. I appreciate you doing this.' He was fixing his collar in the mirror, standing back, eyeing the deep scars across his face, too embarrassed to mention them.

'No problem. Good luck today, by the way. I hope it goes well for you.'

Rob had a meeting with a buyer for the strip bar he owned; it was too much hassle, too much stress, the cause of his continued anger. He was dealing with it. He was going to get help and get better. He said he owed her that much.

He leant forward, kissing her cheek. 'I love you. I need you to know that.'

Meagan didn't respond; it was too early, so she couldn't say it back, not yet.

She lay in bed for another half hour. It was Saturday morning. The sun shone through the small window facing over the roof platform, illuminating the room. Meagan was immersed in the comfortable heat which penetrated the blankets.

She needed to get up, make a start, clean the kitchen, wipe down the worktops, mop the floor. It was her way of feeling normal. This new-found happiness was great, really great, but the couple of years she'd been married to Rob had taken its toll. She knew she'd struggle to deal with the sudden change, but she'd have to find a way.

As Meagan entered the kitchen, she thought about Oliver. She missed him, but maybe this was normal. Meagan had taken a lover behind her husband's back. It wasn't guilt she felt, she couldn't. Rob had forced her to seek refuge, to get help. Now it seemed her husband was different, but she couldn't forget her lust when she and Oliver made love in this kitchen.

She thought about how Oliver had made her feel, how she had been unable to control her lust. Oliver was willing to do anything for her. He was the guy she'd met on the train, the hapless gentleman who was there to help pick up the pieces. She wanted him in her kitchen, right this second.

*No, don't think like this. I can't. I simply can't.*

Meagan picked up the phone she kept hidden, scanning through her recent contacts for Oliver's name. It was next to Sarah's, who had called during the week to check in.

She suddenly felt alone, isolated; Sarah hadn't called for a while, it was as if she didn't care.

Usually, your social media is filled with comments, love hearts, smiling emojis and thumbs up, approving of family pictures, photos of food you're preparing, days out, weekend breaks. People asking how you are. How your day has been.

Wishing you a great evening, or asking what you're up to. Meagan had nothing. *It's like I never existed*, she thought.

Rob never allowed her on social media.

She needed to occupy her mind. She got a J-cloth from the cupboard under the sink, damped it with warm water and wiped down the worktop. Then she filled a bucket with water, jabbed the mop inside and circled it across the floor. She had the radio on, listening to Heart London, turned up loud, too loud, but this was her now: a new, confident Meagan. This was good.

Maybe she could even fall in love with her husband all over again.

She laughed.

*Yeah, right.*

It was early afternoon. Meagan's hands ached, throbbing from the hard work she'd just put into cleaning the place. She stood in the kitchen, taking in the smell of detergent. The windows behind were open, a light breeze pushing forward. She shivered and went to shut the window.

She debated whether to make a start on the bathroom, to hose out the shower, wipe down the cubicle, when she got distracted by the key in the front door.

Rob was standing in the hallway, his black jacket hanging over his shoulder. She noticed his shirt was ruffled. It looked inside out. As he entered the kitchen, the waft of Chanel hit her. His hair was slightly tousled, falling forward.

Meagan stepped forward, hoping for a compliment. *Wow, the place looks amazing. Sit hun, let me get you something to eat. You should rest more. Stop being so busy all the time. It will get done.*

Rob stood, motionless, oblivious to the hard work his wife had been doing.

'How did it go?' Meagan was instantly aware of the break in her voice.

'What? How did what go, Meagan?'

She filled the kettle with water. 'Here, let me hang up your jacket. You must be tired.' Meagan walked towards her husband, reaching for his coat, taking it from his hands. She went out to the hall and placed it on the stand. When she turned, Rob was behind her. She jumped.

'Wow, Rob, you startled me.' She watched the menacing look on his face, the sudden change of expression.

'I'm going for a lie-down. Bring me something to eat. A sandwich or something. Ham, cheese, no mayonnaise.'

Meagan reached her arm forward, running the back of her hand down his face. 'Okay, it'll be a few minutes. Go up Rob, take a rest.'

As he walked away, she clearly saw the label of his shirt, the tag that should have been on the inside.

Meagan was balancing the coffee in one hand, the plate with her husband's sandwich in the other. She knocked on the bedroom door with her foot, struggling to push the handle down.

The room was darkened, the curtains drawn. Meagan placed the items on the bedside unit and then went back to the door. As her eyes adjusted, she saw the empty bed.

Meagan called out, 'Rob, I've made food. I've left it by the bed.'

As she turned, his large figure was standing behind her, close to the door.

'Jesus, Rob. You scared the life out of me. I've left your fo–'

He grabbed her around the throat, squeezing so hard Meagan thought she'd pass out. With his other hand, he pulled her hair, ripping her head backwards.

'Rob. Stop, what's got into you?'

'I lost the fucking contract. The buyer pulled out.'

She struggled to talk, to make any sound. Meagan was gagging, pulling desperately at her husband's arms, trying to get free.

Once he'd loosened his grip, she managed to talk. 'Okay, it's not the end of the world. There'll be others. Rob, please, you're choking me.'

He let go, moving forward, ripping her blouse open. Buttons fell on the ground, bouncing on the wooden floor.

'Rob, not now. Don't do this.'

'Shut your fucking mouth. If you speak again, so help me.' He grabbed her by the waist, throwing her on the bed, removing his belt and dropping his trousers.

Meagan struggled, reaching for the side of the bed, desperately trying to escape. Rob pulled her by her legs. One of her shoes came away and he stumbled back. She kicked out, catching the side of his face. He instantly clasped his cheek. 'Don't make this difficult, you fucking bitch.'

He jumped on the bed, trousers hanging by his ankles, and punched the side of Meagan's face, forcing her down. His eyes were wild, saliva dripping from his mouth. Rob held her neck with one hand, slapping her face with the other. He reached her skirt, pulling hard, breaking the zip and trying to pull it down her legs.

Meagan was desperate. *There's no way this is happening. The week had been amazing. One of the best of my life. How had it come to this?*

She was convinced he'd changed. Her husband was a good man. The best.

*This can't be happening. No, please. I thought he'd changed. He told me he loved me.*

As Rob removed Meagan's skirt, she lay in her knickers, struggling to turn. Suddenly, she mustered the strength, kneeing him hard in the groin. It was like a brick dropping from the second floor to the ground below. Bang. She shocked herself with the strength she'd gathered. Rob screamed out, and he spasmed, holding himself. Meagan jumped off the bed, racing towards the bedroom door, slamming it behind her and charging down the stairs.

She reached the front door, desperately pulling the security chain, watching it drop. As she pulled the handle, Rob was standing at the top of the stairs. 'Meagan. I'm coming for you, do you hear? There's no escape. I've told you time and time again. You can't leave; I'll never allow it.'

She heard him wince. Meagan dropped to her knees with fright and exhaustion. Her body was weak, but she had to summon the strength to hide, to get away from him.

Now on the floor, she crawled on her hands and knees, trying to stem the fear, the panic in her breaths, the desperation to get away from this man, her husband, her so-called life companion who should care for her and protect her.

She reached the store cupboard under the stairs, managing to hoist herself upwards, pulling the handle and crawling behind a wooden rack. The light came on, and as she moved to the back of the small room, the door closed, terminating the brightness.

She stayed crouched down, hiding, concealing herself from the brute she was married to. This was it. Enough. Whatever it took, Meagan was leaving.

Lying on the cold floor, curled up like a scared child, she was suddenly reminded of the past, her poor mother and the years of abuse she had taken at the hands of Meagan's father. She started having flashbacks; the time she found her mother locked in a box at the bottom of a cave, the terrible beatings she had witnessed as a child, the night her father came for both of them while they stayed at Aunty Anne's. The events that followed.

Meagan tried to push the thoughts away, but they were there; so real, even now, after all these years. That horrible night when her father brought the two of them back home. How could she ever forget?

Meagan jumped as she heard Rob screaming her name, pacing up and down the hallway, then going out, the front door slamming behind him.

She dipped into the pocket of her ripped blouse, pleased to find her mobile was still there, then messaged the only person she knew would help.

## 26

## TWENTY YEARS AGO - BEFORE THE PHONE CALL

'Daddy, are you angry? Me and Mummy picked a good place to hide. I knew you'd find us. I'm so pleased. Aunty Anne is pretty, isn't she? She looks like a princess. Aunty Anne and Mummy talk lots. We had fun. I made doughnuts. I'll make them when we go home if you like?'

Muffled screams were coming from behind them. Meagan sat in the back, trying to lift the seat of her father's car to see what her mother was doing in the boot. Her father was sweating, his cheeks flushed. He was driving faster than usual, talking to himself. Meagan leant forward, trying to hear what he was saying.

'Daddy, why is Mummy in the boot?' Meagan leant back, listening to the panic in her mother's voice. She'd never heard these sounds before. Yes, she'd listened to her mother crying frequently, shouting out, even the odd swear word, but this was a deathly squeal, a noise Meagan would never forget.

'Daddy, please let Mummy out.'

Her father turned, watching his daughter. 'Meagan, keep quiet. This is adult stuff which you don't understand, okay? I'm teaching Mummy a lesson for running away. This is how she learns.'

He turned back, narrowly missing a lorry on the other side of the road. He swerved, causing Meagan to grip the seat rest.

'But she didn't.'

'Didn't what, Meagan?'

Meagan looked out the window, then checked under the seat, hoping she could hold her mother's hand. 'Mummy didn't run away. She was hiding, at Aunty Anne's. We both were, Daddy, but you found us. I thought you wouldn't find Mummy and me, but you did.'

Sean kept quiet and concentrated on the road ahead. Rain had started spilling on the windscreen. He wiped the glass ferociously with the back of his hand, leaning forward to see more clearly. The whimpering cries from his wife caused his head to ache as he gripped the steering wheel harder, trying to ease his stress.

Meagan had been quiet in the back of the car, too worried to speak, distressed about her mother and wanting to find a way into the boot.

She glanced down at Arthur, making sure he was comfortable, whispering in his ear and telling him she loved him. She was pleased that her father hadn't put him in the boot as well. She couldn't have coped without her toy for comfort.

Meagan had fallen asleep. She woke as her father steered the car into their drive, rolling the vehicle towards the front wall of the house.

Sean opened the door for his daughter then went to the house.

'Daddy, let Mummy out now.' Meagan was stomping her right foot on the ground, Arthur in her left hand.

Sean fiddled with the key, opened the front door and beckoned Meagan inside.

She slowly moved past him, nervous about his demeanour, checking his face to see a sign that her father was relenting, his mood loosening. She saw little to confirm this.

Once inside, Meagan went up the stairs, into her father's bedroom and watched through the window. She saw her father open the boot and pull her mother out. Tricia was kicking and screaming. He placed his hand over her mouth, frantically moving his head left and right, making sure no one could see him.

A minute later, the front door closed with a loud thud.

Meagan quickly placed her toy bunny onto the bed and walked along the upstairs hallway.

She listened to her father shouting in the hall, telling her mother she'd never do it again, that she'd never have the opportunity, he was going to ruin her. He stated over and over that her life was finished. She'd pay for what happened in the last couple of days, and he'd see to it.

*Pay? What does Daddy mean? How much would it cost Mummy? She shouldn't have to give Daddy money: he has his own. Mummy wears the same clothes and her shoes are broken. Daddy always has nice clothes. He always looks smart.*

As she listened, Meagan heard her mother. She was talking and crying simultaneously. 'I've had it with you. I'm going to kill myself, I swear. You'll be on your own, you bastard, do you hear me? I fucking despise you, every ounce of my body has hatred towards you, what you represent, how you treat me, and your own daughter. She's your flesh and blood and she's witnessing the heartless, calculating bastard of a father that you are. How do you think she feels about relationships? Husbands and wives? How can you do it, Sean? How?'

'Tricia, lessons need to be learned. I love you, you know that. But I'm doing this for your own good. God, I do everything around the house while holding down a full-time job. You should show me the respect I deserve; it's not difficult. Just show me some fucking respect.'

Meagan looked down through the bannister and saw her father remove his belt. Tricia sobbed, 'Go on, just fucking kill me, I'm no good to anyone. Do it, kill me. I beg you. Anything is better than the hell you put me through.'

Sean lifted the belt over her head, stretching it out, holding it at each end. He held the leather strap above his wife's head, bringing it down hard, catching the side of her face with the metal buckle. Tricia screamed out.

Sean was sweating, a red flush moving from his neck, spreading across his face. His cheeks were bloated with air, his eyes wild. As his wife winced in pain on the floor, he lifted the belt again, bringing it down hard on the side of Tricia's neck. 'You'll pay, you bitch. It's another simple lesson for those who betray me.'

Sean continued lifting the belt, holding it in the air like a prized trophy and bringing it down hard onto his wife's body.

Meagan listened from the hallway upstairs, covering her mouth with her hand, unable to believe what her father was doing. She needed to act fast. A sentence went over and over in her head like a loop, an ongoing conveyor belt. As hard as she tried, Meagan couldn't shake it from her mind.

She raced into her bedroom, making sure her bunny was safe, then she quickly grabbed what she needed from her coat pocket and made her way downstairs.

Meagan listened as she passed the living room; the moans from her mother, the cracking sound every minute or so, echoing through the house. Her father repeating the words, 'You'll learn, lady. It's for your own good, you hear?'

Meagan stayed hidden in the kitchen, waiting. She could hear her father had stopped; he was breathing heavily, sounding tired and worn out. Her mother was crying. The living room door swung open, and her father went upstairs. Meagan held her breath, hoping he wouldn't notice she was out of bed, listening, praying for him to go into his bedroom. *Please don't find me down here, Daddy. I know you're mad with Mummy. I don't want you to be mad at me too.*

A second later, she heard his door close. Meagan waited. Fear had seized her body as she stepped forward, her heart racing, her body flooded with adrenaline.

She slowly tiptoed along the hallway towards the living room door, listening intently. Her father was talking in his bedroom, mumbling. Meagan struggled to hear what he was saying.

She moved the door handle slowly downwards, hoping her father wouldn't hear. The door opened, and Meagan eased it away from her, slowly pushing it until her mother was visible.

Meagan saw her, lying on her back, holding her face, cowering on the floor.

Slowly, Meagan came closer. The sentence was repeating in her head, over and over – a stuck record with the arm jumping continuously, jamming on those same words.

She crouched down beside the dishevelled shape. Her mother hadn't noticed Meagan entering the room.

'Mummy. Are you okay?' Meagan whispered in the darkness. She waited patiently for an answer which didn't come. She put her hand to her mother's face, feeling the indents, the cuts from the beating she'd taken.

Meagan held the treat she'd been given by the guy at the market, a small packet which she tore open with her teeth, placing a piece of the bar into her hand and then forcing it into her mother's mouth.

She watched as her mother opened her eyes, gazing at her daughter – the smile of unequivocal love. Tricia chewed hard, pleased to be alive, seeing her daughter's face. Her husband was gone, which was an immediate relief.

Meagan broke off another piece, feeding her mother first, then herself.

Suddenly her mother spasmed, coughing hard, her face turning red. Tricia felt nauseous; her face was swelling, her immune system in overdrive, launching a violent response. Meagan held her mother's hand as she watched her gasping for breath, struggling to muster the strength to inhale. Tricia grabbed her own throat, rubbing her neck to clear the airways, begging for Meagan's help, asking for water, but unable to form any words.

'It's okay, Mummy. It's what you wanted, isn't it? I heard you telling Daddy you want to die.'

Tricia was foaming at the mouth, her breaths became harder, her face a bright purple colour. She was slamming her hands on the wooden floor.

Meagan listened, hearing her father's bedroom door open, footsteps pounding down the stairs.

The door burst open; her father was standing under the wooden frame.

'Meagan, what's going on? Get away from her now.'

'She wants to die, Daddy. I heard her.'

'What have you done, Meagan? What the fuck have you done?' He slapped his hand against the light switch, suddenly seeing his wife more clearly. She'd stopped breathing, her body now still, her hands neatly by her sides.

'I gave her some of my bar to help her die, Daddy. It's what Mummy wanted.'

Meagan listened to her father scream. She watched him drop to his knees, desperately trying to pump his wife's stomach, wiping the mucous from her mouth.

'Get help Meagan, quickly. Get Mummy's phone, dial 999. Oh my God, don't do this Tricia please, I'm here. You're not going to die on us, do you hear?'

Meagan watched as her father raced to the kitchen. Drawers

slid open and banged shut. He returned a minute later. Meagan glanced at the EpiPen in his hand. He knelt over his wife, ramming the syringe into her thigh, hoping it wasn't too late.

'No, Daddy, she wants to die?'

'You don't get it, Meagan, you don't fucking get it.' Sean recalled the many times he'd heard Tricia explaining death to his daughter. She'd asked numerous times, kids had spoken about it at school, one of her classmates, Mary Darcy, had lost her father to a massive heart attack. Mary hadn't been at school for over a week and her friends were concerned. When she returned, they questioned her. She'd told them her father wouldn't be around anymore. When Meagan had questioned this, Tricia told her he'd only gone to sleep until the bad times had passed and Mary would see him again when life was better.

In a panic, Sean rose to his feet; his head spun, the living room now resembling a fun house. The walls were closing in on him, turning, mirrors capturing his reflection. His head was confused. He saw half a peanut brittle bar on the floor.

'Where did you get these?'

'Mummy has a nut problem. You've both told me before. I remember you said if she eats them, it could make her sleep, like Mary's dad.'

Sean struggled to compose himself; he was deep in shock, panic racing through his body like a charging bull struggling to overbear a matador.

'You fed her nuts? You know they can kill her. What the fuck have you done? You know she can't go anywhere near them. She has an allergy, Meagan. A fucking life-threatening allergy. Why?' He was shouting, running back and forth over the living room floor. Sean panicked, dragging Tricia's body to the bottom of the stairs. His daughter followed.

Meagan calmly looked up towards her father. 'It's what she wanted, Daddy.'

Sean stood in the downstairs hallway, watching his wife's

limp body, needing to get her into the car and to a hospital, he had to get help. In a panic, he turned and raced upstairs, needing to douse water on his face, to calm himself. He shouted at his daughter to call 999. He was unable to process what had happened, and his mind had shut down. Outside his bedroom door, Sean dropped to his knees.

Meagan picked up her mother's phone, doing as her father had asked.

~

'999, what's your emergency? Hello, 999, what's your–?'

'Hello.'

'Hello. What's your emergency?'

'It's my mummy.'

## 27

PRESENT DAY

'What can I get you? The usual, or shall I read the specials?' The waiter stood beside Oliver.

It was too early in the day for anything fancy. 'I'll just have the number two breakfast, extra sausage.'

'Very good, sir. Tea, coffee?'

'Er, tea is good.'

'Very well, sir.' Then the waiter turned to another table, welcoming the family that had just arrived.

Oliver suddenly felt alone, vacant. He found himself thinking about Claire. *God, it had been great while it lasted. We had fun. We were good together.* A sudden rush of anger raced through his body, followed by panic. Oliver had no friends because he mostly kept himself to himself. His family were up in the north of England, his parents separated. He hadn't spoken to either his parents or sister for months. They got on with their lives, he with his.

A large mug of tea was placed in front of him, causing Oliver to retreat from his thoughts. 'Thanks.'

'Very good, sir.'

*Wow, the guy's polite. He sounds like a butler serving a large mansion.* As Oliver gripped the mug, blowing on its contents, his phone on the table in front of him beeped. Opening the screen and tapping the message icon, he read the contents.

Can we speak?

It was Meagan. A whirl of emotions surged through his body. Repeating the words in his head, he felt excitement, fear and dread all at once.

He looked around the café. The family had ordered and were deep in conversation. He watched the couple to his right. The guy leaned forward, removed his wallet from the back pocket of his jeans and tapped the card machine. Then he stood and pulled the seat out for his partner. God, how Oliver wanted this. It shouldn't be this difficult. Maybe he was attracted to the wrong women.

He brushed a hand through his hair, pushing his neck backwards, stretching his throat out, thinking what he should do. He wanted to ignore the message, block Meagan's number, disregard her plea.

He placed the phone in front of him to the left, straightening it out, touching it nervously.

'Okay, sir, here's your order.'

Oliver looked at the waiter; he was short, middle-aged and wore a stained white apron. A thick moustache ran along the length of his top lip and curled upwards at each end.

*Bloody hell, just take it off already, it doesn't become you, mate.*

It resembled a giant caterpillar that had been hit with a mallet. Oliver kept the sarcasm to himself.

He glanced at the food, choosing to push it to the side. Picking up the phone, he reread the message. Meagan would know he'd seen it, and would be waiting for a response. He pictured her, pacing up and down the hallway, the phone held at arm's length, waiting for a reply.

*Shit, what am I doing? Be strong, Oliver, brave it up, lad.* He started tapping.

It's not a good idea.

He clicked send, then watched the phone, waiting for a reply. The word *delivered* appeared in the bottom right corner of the screen.

He pictured her, broken-hearted, placing the phone in her handbag, dejected, crushed. The last thing Oliver wanted to do was upset Meagan. However hard he tried, he couldn't get her out of his head.

He kept the phone in front of his face. His food was getting cold and the steam had ceased rising from the mug of tea. He waited. Part of him wanted another message, another part hoped this was the end.

Suddenly, jumping bubbles appeared on his phone screen, letting him know that Meagan had started writing. Oliver waited; it looked like a long one. Then it stopped. He waited a few minutes, apprehensive, looking for a sign of her response. He closed the phone, then opened it, swiping upwards on the screen to refresh the app, just in case something had been sent and got caught in the cogs of the virtual world.

After another couple of minutes, he placed the phone back on the table. His heart rate had slowed to a more reasonable speed, and the anxious knot in his stomach dispersed.

He tucked into his food, sipping his cold tea, beckoning to moustache-man for a refill.

The phone beeped and vibrated slightly. Oliver's eyes instantly directed to it.

It was Meagan. Oliver placed the cutlery down in front of him, holding the phone six inches from his face, wondering when the messages would stop, if she'd ever quit.

You need to finish what you started.

He stared at the message, trying to make sense of it all, wondering why she kept asking the same question, making demands. He needed to be strong, polite, but forceful. He needed to show authority, let her know he wouldn't give in to her sick demands. He'd done it once, a stupid mistake, and he was determined not to go back down that path. He started typing.

Meagan, we're done. I'm sorry. Please stop with the messages. I've moved on. You need to do the same.

He reread the message a couple of times, then tapped the send button.

He watched the phone, balancing in his left hand, imagining how she'd feel when opening the message. He pictured her hanging from the rafter outside his apartment a week ago. Oliver fought to shed the image from his mind. He thought it was goodbye, a final farewell when he kissed her on the cheek outside Albuquerque House and told her not to contact him. Now this, out of the blue. He suddenly felt suffocated, like he would never be released from her claws.

The phone beeped almost instantly. He was losing patience. As he opened the message, he read the one-line sentence across the screen.

I need to show you something.

*Show me something. What's she talking about? Has her husband beaten her again? Maybe it's a picture of her, slit wrists, lying in the bath, about to drown and she wants me to be the last person to see her alive.*

He tapped, just a quick one-line response, trying to stop the intrusion into his new-found happiness and contentment.

Show me what? I don't want you to keep messaging.

He hit the send button and waited impatiently, aching to know what she wanted.

After a minute or so, Oliver placed the phone down, but it beeped when he reached for his knife and fork. Again, he opened the message; it was the same as before.

You need to finish what you started.

*This is fucking ridiculous. That's it, I've had enough of this bullshit,* thought Oliver. He tapped back:

Meagan, you need to listen very closely. I fell for you hard; obsessed is maybe too strong a word, but from the first time I saw you on the train, you had a certain vulnerability about you. I reached out, offering a helping hand. But you chose to ignore my pleas to leave your husband, and it seems the only way you will ever abandon this selfish lowlife is when you're carried out of your apartment in a box. I've tried, God knows how hard, but I can do no more. Please stop with the fucking messages. I will ignore anything else after this. You deserve so much happiness, which I doubt you will ever find with that prick. Leave him before it's too late. Do it, Meagan, do it for yourself. Goodbye.

Oliver placed the phone on the table, satisfied he'd said what he needed without being rude.

He sipped his tea, leaning back in the chair, his body suddenly lighter, a weight lifting from his shoulders. He eyed the family in front of him, watching how they conversed, confident with each other. It's what he needed: security, comfort, stability.

He leant forward, cutting one of the sausages in half, dipping it into the middle of his egg, watching the thick yolk spread across the plate.

The phone beeped, causing Oliver to jump. His eyes were wild with fear and trepidation, the excitement had gone.

As he brought the phone towards his face, he opened the message.

The word *Meagan* appeared on the front of the screen. He read the text, the same as before.

I need to show you something.

There was a video attached. Oliver clicked it with his thumb.

It was him in a field, trampling on long grass, dragging something, struggling with the weight of what he was hauling.

Oliver pinched the screen to zoom in. He had been unaware he was being filmed. It was a clear image; the water was so still behind him, silent. Oliver was talking, asking for help from the person taking the recording. When Oliver reached the water, he flipped the trunk over, dumping it in the reservoir.

'Fuck.' Oliver realised he'd said the words louder than expected. He dropped the phone, causing a loud crash. Now people were looking at him; he watched as a father cuddled his small child, holding him close as if offering protection. The guy's partner was staring over at him, her face grimacing in disapproval.

Oliver lifted his arm. 'I'm sorry.' Suddenly feeling embarrassed, he dropped his head, waiting for the moment to pass.

Oliver's appetite had suddenly diminished. As he glanced at the food, his stomach started swirling around like the drum of a washing machine. There was a painful throbbing in the side of his temple. He was hot, sweat appearing on his forehead and his face itching. His T-shirt was damp with perspiration.

He eyed moustache-man who was standing by the kitchen, looking out over the café. He appeared to be swaying and blurred. Oliver was sure he heard him laughing. He leant forward, squinting, trying to focus his eyes on the peculiar little figure.

'Are you okay, sir? You don't look well.'

Oliver peered upwards. 'Huh?

'The food. Is it no good, sir?'

'I need to leave. I'm sorry.' Oliver placed a twenty-pound note on the table in front of him, picked up his phone and left, welcoming the cold air outside.

He stood for a moment, watching the traffic as people rushing along the street weaved around him. He felt barricaded, like the walls of the buildings opposite were closing in on him. He had to run, get away from here, anywhere, just go. His mind raced. Panic was taking over his body and making him weak. *How could she do this? Meagan, the person I trusted more than anyone.*

He ran along Kensington High Street towards his apartment, fighting the fatigue that had developed in his legs as nausea moved quickly through his body.

He twisted his key in the lock and opened the main door, shoving it against the wall. Oliver raced along the ground floor and took the stairs two at a time, charging forward to his apartment. He slammed the door behind him.

He paused in the hall; the lights were out, the place silent. He listened to the stillness, unsure whether to go and lie down, or open a beer and slump on the sofa.

*How could she do this to me? Meagan, the woman who was so afraid, frightened, vulnerable, detached from normality.*

The video she had sent him ran through his head, the vision of him rolling the trunk into the reservoir. *Caught, hook, line and fucking sinker. How could I let this happen? Shit, I'm usually so careful, distrusting even the most trustworthy. She's got me; she's got me good and proper. You're fucked now, Oli, done up like a kipper.*

He pulled out a chair that had been set neatly under the breakfast island, kicked off his shoes and removed his phone from the front pocket of his jeans. He opened the message Meagan had sent, clicking on the video in the hope he'd imagined the whole thing.

As he sat, watching the recording of him again, dragging the trunk through the grass, rolling it into the reservoir, he deliberated. Meagan was the only person who'd seen this, the only one who knew. Maybe he could go to the reservoir tonight to the same spot, remove the body himself, drag it back to the car, dump it in the boot and hide it somewhere. How would anyone be able to prove what he'd done if there wasn't a body? It was her word against his. He'd deny everything if Meagan tried to blackmail him. *After all, it's what she's doing; using something against me to get something she wants herself.*

Oliver had to do it, there was no choice. He'd wait until tonight, go to the spot where they'd dumped gloved-man and get the body out. *It's my only option,* he thought. *And this time I'm on my own.*

Oliver spent the day battling his anxiety, struggling to stem the sick feeling of dread in his stomach, which was churning like butterflies on speed. His mind raced, recalling Meagan and him returning to apartment six.

How was it only a week ago? He remembered the guy turning up, so aggressive, looking for his partner, making threats. *What if he found out? What if he knows what I did? I'd be next, lying motionless at the bottom of the lake.*

He had to get to the trunk.

These men were obviously involved in illegal activity. They were criminals, the lowest of the low, people who didn't give a shit how things were done, who was hurt, or how they made a living and God help anyone who got in their way.

Oliver didn't need to find out what they were capable of, what they'd do to him if they knew about the trunk in the reservoir. *Aren't I the same? What Meagan and I have done, what does that make us? We're just as bad.*

Oliver struggled to understand what had happened, reasoning with himself. *The guy deserved it, he was a lowlife and if I didn't do it, someone else would. It was just a matter of time.*

But then he found himself arguing back. *Wait, it doesn't make it right. I broke into his apartment and poisoned him! It's first-degree murder, and I'll never get away with it, never. No matter how evil this fucker was, it's still murder. I broke in, killed him in his bed and dumped his body.*

Then later he found himself thinking that he had got away with it after all. *Maybe it'll blow over. We've heard nothing for a week, so I'll continue to lie low, off the radar. No one knows.*

Oliver fought to understand why Meagan would record him dumping the body and send it to him. *What the fuck is she thinking?* He wondered if she would leave him alone if he killed Rob. *I could break into apartment six and end the life of another complete scum-bucket.* But where would it stop? How many people would he have to kill? Would Meagan finish with the demands?

The sentence replayed over and over in his head: *"You need to finish what you started."* *Maybe that's it, kill Rob, be done with it, then move on.*

~

He woke just after 7pm. The room was dark, the curtain blowing from the slight breeze pushing its way inside. A chill ran through his body; his legs were numb with the cold air, his heart racing.

He glanced over at the bedroom door. The glow from the hallway seeped through to his room. He'd shut the bedroom door, he was sure. It was cracked open three inches or so. Oliver pushed the blanket back and turned on the lights. The cold air from outside caused an icy chill to race through his body.

He closed the window tight. A noise from the kitchen startled him. Was that a light? A voice? Two voices?

He carefully opened the closet door, reaching for something, anything, to protect himself with. The first thing he found was an old slipper. *Oh great, beat whoever had broken into the apartment with this.* To the left side of the cupboard, he felt a long rubber handle resting against the shelf. It was a nine iron; strong and robust. He gripped it, holding it by his side, then walked towards the kitchen.

The voice was more evident; someone discussing a political matter. Oliver turned on the light, relieved at seeing the small radio on the shelf close to the fridge.

He backed out into the hall. He was uncertain if he'd put the radio on earlier. He stood in the empty hall, eyeing the locked front door. The security chain was still in place. He felt relief, satisfied he was alone.

He needed to take a quick shower and get ready to go to the reservoir.

~

The drive had taken him around forty minutes. He struggled to concentrate on the road because he couldn't stop thinking about the past week's events.

He was running the scene through his head: meeting this stranger, agreeing to join her for a drink, stunned by her beauty and vulnerability, then equally stunned by her demands. Oliver had been brainwashed, hypnotised, possibly both. What was it about her? The grasp she seemed to have over him?

As he drove, he fought the bitter taste in his mouth, wishing he could be more assertive and positive. Why did he take instructions? Why did he agree to things so easily? Was he incapable of putting up a fight?

*No is no; I'm not doing it. Why should I? If only I could say what I need without worrying who I might offend.*

Now he had no choice: he had to get the body out of the water.

He steered the car into the grounds of the reservoir, cutting the lights and rolling the vehicle into the far corner of the car park. As he stepped out, he could see his breath; a dim, hazy fog with every gasp he let out.

Oliver was shaking; he struggled to curb the anxiety. He stood for a moment, peering into the stillness. The grounds were quiet. At any other time, Oliver would appreciate the isolation. It would be a place he'd visit, to rest, recharge, and contemplate life. Now, it was sombre, formidable and lonely.

He locked the car, placing his keys into the back pocket of his jeans, then went through the long, wet grass to the spot where they'd dumped gloved-man. The leather trunk wouldn't be hard to find: he could recall the outline as it sat in the water. He just hoped no one had been down here since. The area was overgrown with nettles and shrubs. It was littered with dumped mattresses, wine bottles and empty condom wrappers. It wasn't a place you'd go for a romantic walk.

He approached the water, swiping his torch to help navigate through the darkness. He thought he could hear someone behind him. He glanced back. Fear took over his body, making his legs weak. Oliver paused, slowly turning, looking behind at the grass he'd trampled seconds ago. He could see a shadow. *Is that someone watching?*

The sky was almost pellucid, the moon hidden by a haze of cloud. He shone the torch, aiming it at the shadow in the distance, wishing now that he'd brought the nine iron from his cupboard.

'Hello. Is someone there?' Oliver waited for a response, unsure if the darkness was playing tricks. 'Is someone there?'

He moved back slightly, edging to his left. *Pull it together, Oliver. Get the job done. End this.*

Oliver waited in the same spot for a few seconds, then went to the shore of the reservoir. The water was still.

He looked into the water, preparing himself for the freezing plunge. Oliver took one more glance behind him, removed his trainers and socks, then emptied his pockets, placing the contents on the muddy bank.

He stood on the edge, then jumped off the concrete ledge, landing into the water, the bottom half of his body immersed. It was colder than he'd expected, the water was muddy, the bottom thick and congealed. Oliver went under the water, trying to open his eyes, pawing around him, then coming up, gasping for breath, pleased to find he could stand.

He ducked his head under again, swiping the water with both arms, holding his breath for what felt like minutes. He grabbed clumps of mud, dirt and weeds. He came back up, spitting out the taste of oil and rotten plant life.

Oliver waited, standing in the icy reservoir. His body was numb, his hands ached and his face stung from the severe cold. The water seemed stained, soiled.

He counted to ten, then went back under. His lungs were heavy, like they were going to explode, his eyes were itchy, his arms weak from pushing against the weight of the water. Finally, he felt something underneath where he stood. He reached for the object as he struggled to keep himself under the water. He felt the rough leather, the thick chain, the straps.

It was the trunk, lying on the bottom of the reservoir.

## 2 8

PRESENT DAY

It had taken Oliver almost an hour to heave the trunk out of the water, onto the bank and through the woodland to the boot of his car. He'd stopped numerous times, struggling to drag his soaking wet burden. The weight was enormous. His hands were raw, his biceps throbbed and his legs were sluggish as he stumbled over himself several times.

Oliver opened the boot of his car then hoisted the trunk upwards. He shut the boot as quickly as possible.

He had another look around, got into the driver's side and headed out of the woodland.

He checked the time. 9.30pm. He needed to keep driving, away from the reservoir, possibly to the coast, a quiet place where he could dump the body and forget about this shit. There wasn't enough time this evening, as removing the body had taken longer than he'd expected.

He drove along the A406, heading towards Hanger Lane. The road was practically empty. Oliver kept below the speed limit, driving on the inside lane to avoid attention.

His head was fogged, addled with the image of gloved-man lying motionless in his boot. He thought about dumping the body outside apartment six, letting Meagan clean up the shit. *See how she likes it.* He could text her over and over, *"You need to finish what you started."*

Oliver found himself missing her, wanting to be with her now, their arms around each other, planning their future, a future without Rob, without the shit he put her through day in, day out. He thought about the first time he met her at the station as he caught a glimpse of her bruised face, so troubled and disorientated. God, she was beautiful.

He needed to be strong. She was messed up and the baggage she came with would fill a jumbo jet.

It was better this way; do what he had to do, then move on. Simple.

He glanced in the rear-view mirror. He was still on his own, the road empty behind him. A couple of lorries hauling long, heavy trailers passed on the other side of the central reservation, keeping to fifty-five miles an hour. He pictured the drivers, stamping their feet in the cab to keep themselves awake, opening the window for fresh air and blasting old-school rock music.

As he turned left, heading towards the centre of London, Oliver noticed a car on his tail, hanging back slightly. The road was clear ahead, and the vehicle made no attempt to overtake. He jabbed his foot on the brake slightly, making it awkward for whoever was driving to stay behind. As Oliver slowed, so did the car behind. *Go on then, go around me. What's your problem?*

The vehicle was difficult to make out in the darkness, but Oliver could see the guy's face in the rear-view mirror. He looked young, twenty-something and was wearing headgear of some kind.

Suddenly, Oliver hit the accelerator, pushing his speed to over fifty. The car behind also increased its speed, tailgating, almost touching Oliver's bumper. *This is ridiculous. What's with this prick?* Again, Oliver hit the brakes, causing the car behind to slow. He spotted a parking bay to his left and decided to pull over. As he did, the vehicle behind moved in; flashing blue lights appearing and a siren blasting noise.

*Shit. I don't believe this.*

Oliver watched the uniformed officer move along the road towards him. His first thought was to pull out, drive like the clappers and get away from here. Oliver felt nauseous, panic racing through his body. He was unable to see clearly and realised he was fighting an anxiety attack.

A tap on the window swiftly brought him back from his thoughts of the guy in the boot, the dead body.

'Hi officer, how can I help?'

'Do you know why I pulled you over?'

*Oh yes, you saw me down at the reservoir earlier, trampling through the grass, pulling the dead body from the reservoir. It's amazing what you find while fishing. He's a big one, officer. Check him out; he's in the back as we speak.*

'No, officer. I don't think I was speeding.'

'Can I see your driving licence, sir?'

Oliver rooted in the glove compartment, found the small folder and handed it to the officer through the passenger window. He watched as the guy looked over the document, called in the registration plate and waited for the response.

Oliver could feel his heart racing, a thumping through his eardrums. Any second now he'd pass out. Then what? Surely the body would be found. The end of the road. He would be locked up with no chance of release.

Oliver listened to the voice on the radio. The officer repeated his name and gave a brief description.

*Sad little bastard who follows instructions and becomes obsessed with beautiful women, gets talked into murdering their partners and is then lumbered with the bodies.*

Oliver watched the officer moving around the car, kicking tyres and looking into the back seats. *Please, just go, I can't deal with this. I can't take it.*

The officer moved to the passenger window, shining his torch into Oliver's face. 'Okay, looks good. You have a cracked tail light. Get it fixed. You won't be so lucky next time.'

Oliver let out a huge sigh as the officer walked back to his car. He waited for a few seconds before pulling back onto the dual carriageway; the officer remained behind but had dropped back a hundred feet or so. After a minute, he watched the car take a left and vanish out of sight.

Twenty minutes later, Oliver opened the glove compartment, fishing for the fob to the car park barrier around the back of his apartment block. He watched the white pole rise slowly, then moved forward into his parking space. The car park was quiet, a couple of work vans, a dark-coloured jeep, a moped to his left. No one in sight.

He decided to leave the body in the boot of his car for the night. It was too risky dragging it upstairs; there was always a danger he'd be seen. He glanced over at the security camera fitted to the wall by the side entrance which pointed away and towards the far side of the grounds.

He sat in the driver's seat, his mind racing, again thinking how he got in this shit. He'd done stupid things in his life, things he wasn't proud of. He found himself in chaotic situations due to his lack of social skills and his unwillingness to say no.

He pictured dumping gloved-man down a toilet pan, flushing and ramming the guy's legs harder into the bowl, pushing his shoes until he disappeared around the U-bend.

Oliver glanced across the car park, thinking maybe he could dump the body next to the wall, then run, leaving it behind and hope it didn't come back to bite him on the arse. *There'd be finger-prints, DNA; I wouldn't have a hope of getting away.*

As he slowly opened the driver's door, he was aware of

someone approaching from the right side of the car park. He could hear footsteps, high heels clicking on the concrete floor. He watched as the figure approached.

Oliver contemplated getting back inside his vehicle, locking the doors and driving out of the car park. There wasn't enough time. He stood completely still. His legs were frozen to the ground. He was unable to command his body to move.

The woman was right beside him; he could make out her features, her long hair, tall, slim figure, oozing confidence. 'Hello, Oliver. Fancy seeing you out here.'

'Claire. Wow, this is a surprise.' The blood returned to his body. He breathed a sigh of relief. 'What are you doing here?'

Claire stood for a moment, struggling to explain why she'd turned up out of the blue, here, now. As Oliver watched her face, he suddenly remembered what he was hiding. He wondered if the body was giving off an odour which would prompt her to ask unwanted questions.

He walked away from the parked car, standing in the glow of a lamppost. The security camera was still facing towards the back.

Claire said, 'I-I wanted to see you. Can I come up?'

Oliver glanced towards the front window of his apartment on the fourth floor, then back to the parked car. He didn't need this. Talk about timing. 'Yes, of course. It's good to see you, Claire.'

They walked up the stairs to the apartment. There was little communication between them and long gaps of awkward silence.

Once inside, Oliver made coffee. He'd offered Claire something stronger, but she declined. He watched her remove her coat and hang it on the back of a chair, which she pulled closer to the breakfast bar.

Oliver struggled to control his shaking hands as he placed the two cups in front of his ex. He lifted his cup, blowing on the contents, waiting for an explanation.

Claire took a deep breath, straightening her back. 'I'm sorry, okay. God, do you know how difficult this is? I'm an idiot. I miss you. I miss us. I had shit going on myself, and I needed space.'

Oliver watched her talking, the awkwardness in her body as she spoke, her voice breaking and weak. 'I want what I've lost, what we had. Tell me you feel the same.'

'I miss you too, Claire. Believe me, I've tried to understand why you just got up and walked out. I thought we were good together.'

She reached forward, holding his hand, rubbing the top of his fingers. 'We were. We can be again. I'm sorry, Oliver.'

'So, how have you been? What's going on in your life?' Oliver was making small talk, directing questions at his ex-girlfriend to steer the spotlight from himself. Too much had happened to him over the last few weeks, Claire wouldn't understand. There wasn't time to get into it all now.

'Oh, you know, work, home, work, like a never-ending, depressing conveyor belt of boringness. I've lost my spirit; I thought I wanted something else, if I'm honest. I needed to find myself, understand my thoughts, how I felt about life. About us,' Claire said.

Oliver watched her, the way she moved her hands, the flush of embarrassment when she spoke, the struggle to hold her head up and look him in the eyes. He'd never seen this side of Claire before. Oliver was confused by his feelings. They'd had great times together, shared intimate secrets, laughed, cried together. The memories came rushing back, like a dam split open, and the two of them drowned in emotion. He wanted to stand, pull her close, hold her and never let go.

A relationship with Meagan was out of the question, a no-go zone, a dip your hand in a bowl of piranha fish, a drive to the centre of a cyclone. He knew this. Claire was his future, his life.

As she sat in front of him, telling him how she felt, he was more confident than ever.

After she finished her coffee, Claire stood, fighting the buzz of the caffeine and struggling to stem the adrenaline rush. 'Wow, that's strong coffee. I need to go. Will you walk me to the car?'

Oliver stood, and helped Claire into her coat, then he walked her down to the car park and out onto the street.

At her car, Claire turned towards him. 'Look, it's your call. I've said what I needed to say. It's up to you what happens next.'

Oliver reached forward, pulling his ex into him, holding her close, not wanting to let go. 'I'll call you, okay.'

She smiled, pleased with his response.

Oliver waved as her car pulled onto the road; unaware that Meagan was watching.

Meagan had stayed hidden in the cupboard under the stairs, praying Rob wouldn't find her. She listened to the front door open and Rob leaving apartment six. She pulled her phone out and tapped a message to Oliver. She stared at the screen until her eyes became blurry, waiting for a reply. A few minutes later, she repeated the message.

Please, Oliver. You need to help me. Rob's attacked me again.
I have no one else to turn to.

She slowly opened the cupboard door, crawling on her hands and knees, wincing in pain. A stream of blood was running along the right side of her face and dripping onto the floor.

Meagan held onto the door handle, pulling herself upwards so she stood, bent over. She quickly checked the front door, moving towards it, making sure it was closed, pushing her face to the spyhole.

Her phone beeped, the screen lit up with a new message.

Meagan wiped the side of her face with the back of her hand, inspecting the red liquid. 'Shit.'

She thought about the last week, how great her husband had been, how he'd changed, becoming a caring, loving partner, looking out for her. Now this. Meagan read the message.

Hey babe, going to the club, then a game of poker with the guys. I won't be back until early tomorrow. Rob.

She read the message a second time, unable to make him out.

Once she'd cleaned herself up, Meagan took her jacket from the coat stand, turned off the lights and headed out onto the street.

Meagan needed fresh air to clear her head and think about her next move so she started walking to Oliver's apartment.

Meagan decided she needed to seduce him again, make him want her so badly he'd have no choice but to try again to kill Rob.

As Meagan approached the tall building, she saw a couple holding each other on the street to her right side. The woman pulled away slowly from the clinch, lust in her eyes, moving her right hand forward, caressing the guy's face. He was like a puppy, indulged and drowning in the glory of self-worth.

Meagan watched as the woman kissed him gently on the cheek, asking him to call her, then she stepped into the car, her long legs majestically sweeping into the vehicle, her stare sultry as she casually closed the window, smiling, beaming, oozing sex appeal.

As the car pulled away, Meagan stumbled backwards, pushing her arms out to break the fall. She crouched, watching Oliver standing, a grin on his face, bouncing his door keys in his hand like a juggler practising for a first performance.

He looked upwards muttering something, an act of thankfulness, then went inside.

Meagan stood watching long after Oliver had left, wondering why he'd do this now.

Slowly, Meagan crossed the street, crouching below the car park barrier, moving around to the back of the building, keeping out of sight. On the fourth floor the light came on. She saw a figure standing by the glass, wiping condensation, sipping on a drink, turning away, the light going off and the blind dropping.

Meagan waited for what felt like hours, drowned in emotion, her life in turmoil, unsure of her next step, but she had to do something.

If Oliver had changed his mind, it was up to her to change it back.

## 29

PRESENT DAY

Meagan lay in bed with the window slightly ajar, welcoming the fresh breeze entering the room. She turned over slowly onto her side. The sheet was stained with her blood and she could feel the sticky blotch which had formed on her cheek.

The bed on Rob's side was made and pulled up. He hadn't been home. She glanced at the alarm clock: 8.27am.

As she heaved herself upwards, she heard footsteps on the stairs, moving towards her. Meagan wanted to hide, but there wasn't enough time.

Rob appeared at the door a couple of seconds later as Meagan pretended to sleep. He stepped inside, balancing on one leg as he removed his boots, sniffing and muttering to himself.

He ripped the blanket back forcefully and got in beside Meagan, still in his shirt and pants. Rob placed his arm around his wife, and a few seconds later he was out cold, sleeping off the effects of his long night.

Meagan waited a few minutes, easing the blanket back, hoisting her frame upwards and out of bed.

She took her clothes from the chair by the dresser and crept downstairs, through the kitchen towards the bathroom at the back of the apartment. She turned on the shower, removed her underwear and closed the door behind her, twisting the lock. As she stood under the steaming hot water, letting it splash on her skin, pushing her hands through her long black hair, she thought about her childhood, the death of her mother. She thought about her father thrown to the ground and cuffed, taken from the house and after the trial, locked away in a cell for the rest of his days. He'd taken the blame, shouldered the responsibility, shielding his young child to protect her.

Meagan had been too young to really understand what happened that night. She had poisoned her mother to help her sleep, to ease the pain she suffered, day in, day out. The little girl had watched her mother fight this beast of a man she'd chosen to spend her life with until it'd broken her.

Neighbours had found her aunty in a cupboard at the back of the farmhouse, bound and gagged, a quivering, neurotic wreck, asking over and over again where her sister and niece were. After a handful of sessions with a psychiatrist, Anne stepped up to the mark, taking Meagan in, looking after her.

Meagan had to change her life. She was unable to take the abuse anymore. She was determined not to end up like her mother.

The bathroom was full of steam. Condensation formed a dense fog on the glass. Meagan's body was raw where she had scrubbed her skin with a flannel and from the extreme heat of the water.

She turned off the shower, reaching for a towel which hung over the door, drying herself, shaking her legs to rid them of excess water. She stepped onto the mat, inspecting for water-marks or footprints. Everything was dry.

Meagan stepped into her fresh clothes and gently unlocked the bathroom door.

She picked up her phone, which had been charging on the

side of the kitchen unit, then filled the kettle with cold water and switched it on, covering it with a towel to stem the noise.

Meagan looked at her messages: an ad from a mobile company, a one-month free trial for a local gym, and a restaurant offering half-price food for collection. There was nothing from Oliver. She pictured the two of them last night; him and the other woman, holding each other, embracing, unable to let go, her pulling away, then Oliver standing, watching her get into the car.

*This can't happen. I won't let it; he's with me now, that's how it goes, I'm afraid. We have plans; you're not going to ruin it. He's started something and needs to finish it. You can't crouch on the block, eyeing your opponents, listening for the gun, then walk off halfway up the track. It doesn't fucking work like that, Oliver.*

As the kettle came to a boil, the cloth began to drip with the steam. Droplets of hot water fell onto the worktop. Drip... drip... drip... counting down the seconds as time ran out.

There were two things on Oliver Simmonds' mind as he woke, three if you count the sickie he had to pull again. He made the call to his boss, telling him he had a stomach bug, putting on a croaky voice. He was dangling on a string himself and didn't know how much more his boss would take. It wasn't Oliver's fault, none of this was. He had to deal with it, then move on.

Next, he remembered gloved-man, the rotting corpse lying in the boot of his car; that was a priority. He had to deal with it straight away. Then, he thought about Claire. The unexpected visit. She wanted him back. She had looked beautiful, captivating, and Oliver needed her now more than ever. Fine, she'd made a mistake, God knows Oliver had made a few of those lately. Once the body had been dumped, he'd get back with Claire.

Meagan would eventually give up. She would either learn to

deal with her husband or run. It was her choice and nothing to do with him anymore.

Oliver threw the sheet back, manoeuvred his body out of bed and made his way out to the kitchen. He eyed the two coffee cups still on the breakfast bar, the chairs pushed back.

At the window he pulled the cord, summoning the light from outside and instantly brightening the kitchen. There was a stale smell of alcohol, a musty odour. Oliver reached up to the window handle and pushed, letting in some much-needed fresh air. The sound of Monday morning traffic hit him, causing instant anxiety.

He looked down towards the car park, seeing his vehicle parked alone. People were already in suits, dresses, scurrying like a box of ants that had been turned upside down, embracing the morning. He suddenly felt nauseous and raced to the toilet, heaving. He crouched over the bowl until his stomach was empty.

Once he'd showered, Oliver switched off the lights and went to the car park. He kept low, inconspicuous, holding back and making sure it was safe to move into the open. He couldn't be seen this morning. Claire had almost blown his cover last night. God knows how he'd explain pulling the body out of the boot and his ex standing there.

*What ya got there, Oliver? Looks like a dead body.*

*Oh no. Just a work colleague who's had too much to drink, you know. He'll be fine, he just needs to sleep it off.*

*You sure he's not dead, Oliver? He looks dead to me.*

*Quick, get his head, help me get him out of the boot. The stench is a little overwhelming, Claire. I'll explain it later.*

He needed to move quickly, get the job done.

Oliver got into his car, checking over his shoulder, then pulled slowly out of the car park.

He would keep driving, find someplace quiet, dump and run. The body had to disappear. And then he'd move on to a life with Claire and forget about this.

Oliver was heading towards Tilford, Surrey. As good a place as anywhere to dump a body, as it was relatively quiet, suburban. On a good day, Surrey was around a ninety-minute drive, this morning, however, it could be at least double that time.

He fought through the London traffic, the sick feeling in the pit of his stomach in full force as he jabbed the brake and clutch. He opened the window, gasping for air, closed it, then cracked it slightly open again, playing with the controls like a baby in a crib.

Sweat formed on his brow and he furiously wiped his forehead with the back of his hands, his arms like wiper blades in a storm. Meagan's voice played in his ears, over and over as he drove: *"You need to finish what you started."*

*Fuck you, Meagan. This is on you too. Thanks for the help. Next time I won't bother.*

He saw gloved-man's corpse lying in the trunk, the image flashing in his head like a bolt of lightning.

Oliver reached the M25 at 9.23am according to the clock on his dashboard. The traffic was unusually light, just the tip of the rush hour remaining. The only people left were either running late or going to mid-morning meetings with their lattes in tow.

He glanced at the traffic on the other side. Vehicles were practically reduced to a standstill. He watched a couple of the drivers, pushing their hands through their hair, leaning backwards in frustration, a guy with a phone balancing on his shoulder and pressed to his ear, his voice raised as he rolled his vehicle forward, forcing another driver out of his lane as they tried to get into the string of traffic.

He wondered if anyone suspected what he was about to do.

Forty minutes later, Oliver drove along the M3 following the signs for Tilford.

It was just gone 10am. The roads were quiet, his surroundings comforting.

A mile past the Tilford sign, Oliver swung a left, driving along an old dirt track. The lake was to his right. A couple of cottages appeared on the left side of the road. Oliver noticed a clothesline crammed with jeans and T-shirts. A kid's slide was in the front garden and there was a fountain on the go, pumping water around a large rock.

The second house had a jeep in the drive and all its windows were curtained.

Further down, an elderly man walking a dog stood aside on the grass verge, beckoning him to pass, waving with his right arm. Oliver wasn't in the mood for niceties.

The road narrowed with sharp bends and potholes causing him to swerve. He slowed, finding an entrance to his right leading along to the water. Oliver quickly glanced in the rearview mirror and pulled over at the opening of the path. He killed the engine, opened the driver's door and stood outside.

The tranquil silence was welcoming. The sky was a dull grey and thick, deep clouds were forming above, ready to burst at any minute.

Oliver stood for a moment, immersed in his surroundings. He took a deep breath, moving to the boot of the car, working out a route. He eyed the path leading to the water and was pleased to see it was slightly downhill. Manoeuvring the trunk shouldn't be too much of a problem, as the terrain was stony, and the grass was longer by the water, which would hide Oliver slightly.

He knew the water was shallow where he stood; he'd worked that much out. While looking for a place to dump the trunk, he read that Tilford Lake boasted a small café, occasional activities and a boat hire. He'd need something robust enough to hold the trunk. He didn't need anything flash. A small boat on an hourly charge would be perfect.

He made his way to the small wooden cabin by the lake, keeping watch, sizing up the area. From what he could tell, the place was perfect to trunk-dump.

As Oliver approached, he saw a plastic window at the front; the lights were off and the front door chained. The cabin was shabby, in need of wood-staining.

He cupped his hands to the window, peering inside. There were a couple of canoes neatly stacked on a shelf towards the back, a small reception with a till, papers, a cup filled with pens and a roll of Sellotape.

*Shit, don't do this to me, please.*

Oliver went around to the side of the hut. This door was also locked with a security chain fastened across the entrance.

Then he saw a sign: *Opening hours 10am–2pm.*

*Wow, what a grafter. This person's a real high flyer.*

He noticed a phone number for general enquiries underneath.

Oliver called the number, and a guy answered on the third ring, sounding like he'd been up all night. His voice was rough, deep, and by the sound of his telephone manner, he wasn't used to calls. 'Tilford Lake.'

'Hi, I was hoping to take a boat out for an hour or so. Would it be possible?'

The guy paused – Oliver thought he'd hung up – then he spoke, unenthusiastic and sounding like he couldn't be bothered. 'It's the middle of winter, mate. The boats were chained up weeks ago.'

*Wow, entrepreneur of the year in action right here. What a guy.* 'I understand, I just need to take a boat for an hour, that's it. A bit of relaxation, clear the head, you know. I'll pay you treble.'

The guy sighed, blowing out a hard breath into the mouth-piece, sounding like a poorly-tuned radio. 'Fine. Go for it, knock yourself out.'

He gave Oliver a code to unlock a padlock, then took his card details.

Ten minutes later, Oliver had rowed back to where his car was parked.

He got out, returned to the parked vehicle, then opened the

boot, placing his foot on the bumper for leverage, pulling to one side the blanket he had used to cover the trunk.

Oliver quickly checked over his shoulder, looking into the distance, then heaved the trunk out of the boot, dragged it to the edge, removed his socks and shoes and stood in the icy water.

It was beyond cold; his feet were instantly numb as he balanced, feeling his legs sink into the silt. He quickly grabbed the trunk, manoeuvring it onto the boat, then pulled himself over and in. The boat rocked back and forth as he steadied himself. For a moment he thought he'd drop over the edge and into the murky water.

He sat for a second, gaining control, composing himself, then picking up the oars, he rowed into the middle of the lake. Every so often he paused to jab the oars into the water, and when he couldn't touch the bottom, he stopped. He looked around and then tipped the trunk over the side, watching it drop to the bottom of the lake and out of sight.

Twenty minutes later, Oliver had chained up the boat, dumped the oars and was back at the car.

He stood for a moment, looking out across the calm lake, selfishly gulping fresh air, clearing his mind, filling his lungs, stretching.

He stepped back, aware someone was approaching. Oliver ducked, seeing the old boy from earlier standing at the entrance. His Jack Russell dog was taking a pee, sniffing, then looking towards where Oliver stood. *Go, please. Just move on, for Christ's sake.*

The dog moved further down the path, heading to where Oliver was crouched, barking furiously and pulling at his lead.

'What's up, boy? You found something?'

Oliver stood, making out he'd just seen the elderly guy. 'Hi,

I've just got a flat tyre. I pulled in here so as not to cause an accident.' Oliver waited, hoping the guy would move on and leave him to it.

'I'll give you a hand. Come on, Roofus, there's a good boy.'

'No, really, it's fine. I've almost finished.'

'Don't be daft, it's no trouble.'

Oliver watched as the dog pulled harder, anxious to get to the water; he could smell something. The elderly guy seemed pleased for something to occupy his time. Any second now, the guy would phone for help, reporting suspicious activity.

'I'm Roy, good to meet you, squire.' The elderly guy extended his arm, struggling to restrain his four-legged companion.

Oliver shook his hand, giving his name and then turning away. He didn't need this. He hadn't worked out how to deal with being seen.

The old guy let the dog go, watching him race to the edge of the lake, lapping the water like it was an ice cream on a hot day. The guy wore a smart waistcoat, white shirt and light blue cords. He removed his flat cap, wiping the top of his head. 'Hard work having one of them,' he said, pointing at the dog. 'They keep you fit, mind.'

Oliver was crouched on one knee, making out he'd replaced the tyre. 'Right, that's it. Good to go. Well, it was nice meeting you.' He made for the driver's seat.

'Course, we get fly-tippers here a lot. Forever dumping their shit on our land.'

'Yeah, nasty business,' Oliver stated, unsure whether the old guy was suspicious. 'Anyway, I've got to make tracks. Good to meet you, oh, and Roofus too.'

As Oliver got into the driver's seat, he closed the door and started the car.

The elderly guy walked to the side to clear a path. 'You wouldn't be dumping stuff now, would you, young fellow?'

Oliver thought, *if only you knew.* He pulled out onto the

narrow country lane, turning right. In his rear-view mirror he watched the elderly man standing by the gate and waving him off.

Oliver thought about what could have happened if the guy had turned up earlier and seen him dragging the large trunk down to the edge. He shuddered.

The road was quiet ahead; the sharp bends forced him to stay in second gear. He pictured the body of gloved-man lying in Tilford Lake, wondering if he'd ever be recovered.

His mind wandered to Claire and her visit late yesterday evening. He wanted to call her but didn't want to look desperate. She was the only person he could speak with about the situation. Maybe she could help, give him advice. God they'd been so in love, shared great times, and he had to talk to someone. How much he told her was up to him.

He battled with his thoughts and his conscience, justifying his way of thinking. *Why shouldn't I call? Ask her to come over... After all, she made the first move.*

He reached a fork in the road with signs pointing left and right, but was unsure which road would lead him to London.

He reached for his mobile and tapped in Claire's number. He heard the ringtone. Then, 'Hi, it's Claire. Leave a message, and I'll call you back.' Beeeeeeeeeeeep.

'Hi, Claire. It's Oliver. I need to see you. I-I don't know where to begin. Last night was great. Seeing you, I mean – the best. I know I'm waffling on, but just call. It would be great to hear your voice.'

He hung up, stared at the screen for a second before placing the phone back on the passenger seat.

Oliver rubbed his face, pulling down hard with the palm of his hand, the frustration taking over his body. He glanced at his reflection. He looked tired, worn out. He'd had enough and needed sleep.

He drove for another mile or so, and saw a billboard to the left: *Harcombe Lodge. Bed and Breakfast. One mile ahead.*

Oliver decided to pull over, take a break, have some time out, make a couple of calls and sort his head.

As he approached, Oliver saw a sign for the car park pointing towards the back of an old public house, with lodges and barns to the side and rear of the building. He parked next to a transit van, shut off the engine and got out.

The wind had ramped up. A strong breeze howled through the open fields making it difficult to move.

As Oliver walked to the reception, a woman came out from one of the barns. She was dressed as if she'd been riding a horse, with long boots, tight leggings and a round black hat strapped tightly under her chin. 'Getting a little blowy, I'd say. We'd better get inside,' she suggested.

Oliver smiled, offering no communication. His head was too full to think straight. He opened the large wooden door and was greeted by a middle-aged woman who was flicking through the guest book behind the counter. She looked up. 'Afternoon. How can I help?'

Oliver stepped forward, watching the lady closing the book, pushing her glasses to the top of her thick blonde hair.

'I'd like something to eat. Is the bar open?' He nodded towards the eatery to the left.

'We're always open. It seems my husband and I never leave this place. Take a seat, and I'll get Siobhan to take an order. I'm Margaret; make yourself comfortable.'

Oliver thanked her and went to the first table in the left corner.

His head throbbed from the stress, and he wished he could plonk himself on a barstool and sink a bottle of whisky.

Once he'd given his order to the friendly young Irish girl, she returned a few minutes later with a pot of coffee. The smell of bacon wafted from the kitchen, and a radio played an old Bruce Springsteen classic, *Dancing In The Dark*. How very apt.

His phone beeped, alerting him to a message. Oliver glanced at the screen. It was Meagan. She had nothing on him now and no way to prove where the body was.

He stood, took a sip of his coffee then moved outside to the doorway where he read the message in private.

Oliver. It's me. You need to help me; I'm desperate. You need to finish what you started.

He suddenly felt sick, tired of her games, worn out. He had to call her, however much it went against his better judgement, however it made him feel. He needed to speak with her and sort it once and for all.

He dialled the number and Meagan answered almost instantly. 'Hello.' There was a slight optimism in her voice.

'Meagan. It's Oliver.'

'Hey, Oliver. Thanks for calling. How are you?' She sounded tired, as if she'd just woken.

'What the fuck are you playing at?' he hissed.

There was a brief pause. Oliver heard her sigh, then she spoke softly. 'I don't know what you mean, Oliver.'

'Don't play fucking games. The picture you sent of the trunk, trying to blackmail me. You know exactly what I'm talking about. It's as much your fault as it is mine, you hear? If I go down, you'll come with me; I'll make sure of it, Meagan.'

'Oliver, I opened up to you, I confided and put my trust in you. I thought you wanted to be with me, make a life together. I don't know any other way to make you finish this.' Meagan waited for a second; she was sniffing, sounding like a little child. 'I had to send the picture, I couldn't think of any other way to make you listen. I had to get your attention. I'm risking being caught, and I'm aware I'm as much a part of it as you are. So you see, you need to finish what you started. We can have a life together.'

'You're nuts, that's it, isn't it? You're off your fucking trolley. Let me make this clear, Meagan, because I don't think you're getting it. We will never be together. I've had it with you. The body is gone. It's off my hands. Do you hear me? Gone, Meagan!'

Oliver suddenly realised what he'd said, instantly regretting letting Meagan know he'd moved the body. He waited, hoping the forceful tone of his assertions had finally sunk in, made her listen and understand.

'Why don't you come over tonight? Rob should be out. We can talk.'

Oliver paused, working out what to say. 'Meagan. I can't say it any more clearly. We're over.'

'Oliver. I'm scared. I have no one to turn to, no one. I thought Rob had changed. In the last week he started treating me differently, looking at me, really noticing me, interested. He brought me out, treated me like a lady, but it didn't last long. He's going to kill me, Oliver. The guy has been back, looking for his partner, making threats at the door. He attacked Rob. He knocked again last night while Rob was out.' She screamed, 'I need help!'

Oliver waited, soaking up the words Meagan had said. 'Don't answer the door. When he comes, pretend you're not home.'

'He's coming back, Oliver. He thumped on the door last night, he stayed for ages. He's coming back, and I don't know what to do.'

'Meagan, pull yourself together. Listen, how do you know he'll be back? It's possible he's knocking at everyone's door, did you think about that?'

'No. He saw us; he knows something isn't right. He's going to kill me, Oliver.'

As Oliver listened, thinking what to do, he heard Meagan's buzzer. He pulled the phone from his ear. He listened to Meagan lifting the handset, her shaky voice.

'Hello. No. I don't know anyone by that name. Well, I'm sorry, leave it downstairs. No, I'm not pushing the buzzer. You'll have to take the parcel away, I'm afraid.'

Meagan replaced the receiver, and the buzzer rang again, longer this time. Meagan tried to speak over the loud vibration.

Suddenly it stopped.

'Oliver, I'm so scared. I think it was him. He's onto us. What if he knows?'

'Meagan, calm down. You don't know that for sure.'

'Oliver. Can you come over?'

Oliver screamed, 'I told you for fuck's sake! No. I'm not doing this anymore, you hear? I'm done. Don't call me again.'

'Then you leave me no choice.' Her voice was raised, louder than he'd heard her talk before.

The phone went dead.

Oliver looked at the screen, struggling to make out what Meagan had meant. *You leave me no choice.* What the heck was that about? *You leave me no choice.* It wasn't as much a threat as total desperation.

He stood outside the lodge for several minutes, dissecting the conversation. As Oliver went to close the phone, a JPEG arrived.

He pressed the square with his right thumb, and a second later, the image appeared.

Oliver eyed the picture, widening it with his thumbs to see more clearly.

There was a note pinned to a door. He could make out the words: Oliver Simmonds at the top. Underneath, an address on the Kings Road. His address. There was a picture – a still from the video of Oliver placing gloved-man into the water.

Meagan had pinned the A4 page to the front door of apartment seven.

Oliver gasped, more of a desperate groan as he listened to himself cry out. The echo of his voice was penetrating through the fields close by.

His heart raced, nausea causing a feeling like his head was swelling, like a pumped-up balloon about to explode, with his brains spilling over the path where he stood. He stepped backwards, gripping a handrail, gasping for breath.

He went quickly towards the lodge, making his way into the breakfast area, and took his coat. His food had been placed on the table; the works, a full English breakfast.

The waitress looked across as she moved away from the table. 'Can I get you anything else?'

'The bill, I need the bill.'

She straightened her name badge, looking awkward. 'Is it not to your liking? I can bring–?'

Oliver cut into her speech mid-sentence. 'You don't understand. I need to leave.'

'Are you okay, sir? Can I help in any way?'

'Just get the bill.' Oliver raised his voice. 'Please. I have to go.'

'Certainly, sir. Come this way.'

Oliver followed behind as the waitress led him to the foyer. Margaret was talking on the phone, unaware they were standing next to her.

'That's all booked then. Two nights for a family lodge. Fine, looking forward to seeing you all.'

Oliver motioned to the waitress, tapping the watch on his wrist, mouthing for the bill, forcing a sense of urgency. He listened to Margaret, still deep in conversation. 'Oh, there's loads to do, wait, let me get a brochure, bear with me.'

'For fuck's sake. Here, this will cover it.' Oliver dropped a twenty-pound note on the counter and raced out through the front door.

A minute later, he pushed his car into reverse, jabbed the accelerator and swung onto the country lane. He drove at a fast, steady pace. Although desperate to get home, he couldn't draw attention to himself, so it was too dangerous to speed. He eyed his reflection in the rear-view mirror. Beads of sweat had formed on his forehead and he wiped at them with his fist.

He ferociously shouted at the screen, calling Meagan. It went straight to voicemail. He tried Claire, again leaving a message, trying to keep calm. 'Claire. Hi, it's me, Oliver. Just wondered if you got my message earlier? Call me back.'

His head raced with the events of the past week. How could Meagan ask this of him now, knowing what they'd done?

*Why is she doing this now?* Oliver pictured the A4 sheet hanging on the door of apartment seven. He tried desperately not to imagine what would happen if it was found, with his details on display like a card placed in the window of a shop.

He tried both numbers a couple more times as he reached the A3. At last, he could put his foot down and sort out this mess.

Oliver pulled into his apartment on the Kings Road at just gone 1.30pm. He struggled to recall the journey, remembering only vaguely waiting in the forecourt of the lodge after speaking with Meagan, the heavy traffic as he joined the M25 and the last couple of minutes in central London.

He needed sleep, wanting nothing more than rest, a hot bath and to sink as many cans of beer that his body would tolerate.

He jabbed the fob on his key ring, locking the car and moving up to his apartment.

As Oliver entered his front door on the fourth floor, his phone rang. He quickly ripped it from the back pocket of his jeans, glimpsing Claire's name. She was returning the call from earlier.

He needed to speak with her. How much he'd tell her was debatable, but Oliver had to talk to someone. 'Hi, Claire. You okay?'

'I'm good. Just returning your call. I didn't expect to hear from you so soon. What's up? You sounded worried earlier. Is everything okay?'

Oliver took a deep breath, then paused for a few seconds, contemplating his response. 'No. Look, can you come over this evening? I need a chat. It's urgent.'

He listened for a gap in the conversation, a telling sign, an indication it was too much trouble for her. He didn't notice anything.

'Yeah, sure. Say around six. I have a couple of hours left. Paperwork, don't you love it? Then I'll call over. I'll bring wine. We can make a night of it.'

'Sounds good, Claire. Thanks. See you then.'

He pressed the end button. Then he waited, hesitating, knowing what he had to do.

Oliver had taken twenty minutes to walk to Albuquerque House, keeping his head down, avoiding eye contact, steering in and out of pedestrians and evading families staring at maps.

He stood outside, looking up at the old brick building, struggling to see straight. His eyes were watering from stress and his face was reddened and numbed by the cold breeze.

As Oliver approached the communal door, he looked at the buzzers to his left. He contemplated jabbing the button for apartment six, then racing up the stairs and carrying Meagan out in his arms and away from her troubled life. *She's not a bad person, just desperate to escape.*

Oliver waited. He stamped his feet with the cold, struggling to warm himself. He tried to see inside, pushing his face to the glass doors, cupping his hands, his cold breath condensing on the glass.

Finally, a figure moved inside. He watched as the person appeared on the stairs and walked along the corridor.

Oliver pushed himself to the side so he was concealed behind bushes and listened to the front doors opening. Oliver glanced at the man as he passed. He was sure he had seen him before. Was he the guy who had threatened him and Meagan? He could only see the back of the guy's head as he walked down the path and out onto the street. He wore a black jacket, grubby blue jeans and his hair was short, greying and cut tightly. He had something in his hand which he folded and placed inside his jacket pocket, then he turned right, heading in the direction Oliver had come from.

Next to come to the door was the old lady from the fourth floor, slowly making her way down the hall with her trolley bouncing behind as she struggled to pull it along the carpet. She fought to push the main doors, and Oliver stepped forward to help.

'Oh, thank you, dear. My bones aren't as strong anymore; it's old age you see, gets us all in the end.'

'It's no trouble. Here, let me get the trolley.'

'Oh, you are kind, dear. Bless you. My husband Ken was a gentleman, held the door for me, pulled out a chair, not many of you left, I'm afraid.'

'He sounds like the perfect man.'

'Oh, don't get me wrong; he was an arsehole at times. But you must always try and see the good in people, dear. My Ken had a great heart; he always spoke to people, that was his charm, you see, he made time for everyone.'

As she edged down the steps, Oliver placed the trolley beside her. She leant into him. 'Not like that ignoramus who's just come down here.'

Oliver looked behind. 'What do you mean?'

'Well, let me tell you. I know everyone here, all of them, I've seen people come and go. 1967 I moved in, they'll have to carry me out in a box.'

'What ignoramus?'

'Oh, let me tell you, dear. I was coming down the stairs, blasted lifts, on the second floor it was. A big guy, ripping something off the door of number seven. He barged past me, all manner of profanities, nearly knocked me flying. I tell you, if I was fifty years younger...'

Oliver turned and raced off down the street.

## 30

Meagan had known that once she sent the image of the A4 page she had pinned to the door of apartment seven to Oliver, he'd have to act. He'd have to take her seriously.

The buzzer sounded again. She lifted the handset and heard a neighbour talking, asking who was there. Meagan heard the clunk as the front door to Albuquerque House opened. She quickly replaced the handset. Moments later, she heard footsteps coming up to the second floor. Heavy boots, walking in her direction, pausing, turning back along the communal hall.

Suddenly there were voices; she listened as trolley-lady from upstairs fired questions, her curiosity taking charge. She was the longest-staying resident here and didn't like intruders. After a few seconds, it went quiet. Meagan wanted to open her door to find out what had happened. Instead, she placed the chain across the front door and moved back from the hallway.

As she sat at the breakfast bar in the kitchen, sipping on her lukewarm coffee, she heard Rob stirring from the room above.

Her heart sank. Her body was numb with the pain he'd put her through.

A few seconds later, he appeared in the doorway, still dressed in his shirt and pants. His hair was unkempt, and his eyes had the usual menacing glare she'd never get used to seeing. 'Afternoon. Wow, what a late one last night. What's for lunch?'

Meagan sipped her coffee, looking across to her husband. 'I can make you eggs; there's not much as I haven't had a chance to shop. Here, take my seat, and I'll rustle up something.'

Rob was snorting and croaking like a farmyard animal. 'What's your plan for today?' He asked the question more sarcastically than inquisitively.

Meagan thought. *Oh, you know? I've taken a lover, and we're plotting your death. I wanted to hit you over the head with a club, bash you until your head exploded over the kitchen floor, but he has other ideas. Just wait, you bastard, time is running out fast.*

'I'm going to attempt to sort out the paperwork from the club; there are unpaid bills, the VAT's due soon, the usual. I'll get it all up to date,' Meagan said.

'Great. Can you get me a glass of water? There's a box of headache tablets in the drawer, pass them over. I'm heading to a meeting in a little while so I'll need a clean shirt ironed and a fresh pair of trousers.'

Meagan flushed as she realised she'd put on a wash last night and forgot to remove the items from the machine.

As she placed the coffee beside Rob, he looked up. 'Meagan, Meagan, how many times? You don't learn, do you? You'll mark the table. Honestly, it's like dealing with a fucking imbecile.'

She froze halfway between the table and the fridge, waiting for the next order.

'Come back here and place the cup on a saucer.'

Meagan reached into the cupboard above her head, her hand shaking. She took the saucer, lifted Rob's cup and placed it down, spilling a small drop onto the floor.

'Now look, go and get some kitchen wipes and mop it up. You have the mind of a small child. I've never met anyone so fucking thick. Honestly, what is your problem?'

'I'm sorry,' she replied.

'Sorry, sorry, that's all I ever hear. It's so tiresome, Meagan, so very fucking boring all the time.'

Meagan returned a second later with a handful of kitchen roll, kneeling at Rob's side, wiping the floor. He placed out his foot, which had a coffee splash, and Meagan wiped it.

'Good girl. Now that's better, isn't it?'

As Meagan stood, drops of hot coffee splashed onto Rob's legs, causing him to wince.

'Well, that's just plain fucking stupidity.' Rob stood, watching his wife and her mortified expression.

'I'm sorry, Rob. Here, let me get some cold water. I'm sorry.'

As Meagan turned to the sink, Rob grabbed her hair, pulling it back, ripping downwards like he was trying to remove her head from her body. He reached for the steaming hot coffee, throwing the contents into her face.

Meagan lay on the floor, writhing in pain, holding her face, the heat raging across her skin.

Rob stood calmly. 'I'm going to take a shower. Be sure to have my shirt and trousers ready when I come down.'

Oliver raced along the King's Road, trying to get a glimpse of the guy who had exited the front door of Albuquerque House.

The road was still busy with cameras clicking, teenagers arranging selfies, holding phones on the end of poles and smiling like they'd never visited a city before.

Oliver ran next to the pavement, avoiding crowds of people who were oblivious to his desperation. As he ran, he scouted the side streets, desperately trying to catch up with the guy, unsure what he'd say, how he'd play it out. He had to find him, tackle him, try his best to convince this lunatic that he had nothing to do with his partner's death. The problem was, the guy had Oliver's address and a picture of him.

He reached his apartment block. He stopped across the street and waited in a doorway.

The sky opened and heavy rain pelted down onto the streets. People were running for shelter and car headlamps lit the darkened road.

Oliver backed up, keeping low, watching for anyone acting suspiciously or loitering. Oliver lifted his hand to divert the water from his face. He eyed the car park across the road. The doors at the front of the building remained motionless.

The rain eased to a drizzle and Oliver stood in the doorway for a few minutes, certain that the guy who had come out of Albuquerque House had gone somewhere else. *Perhaps it wasn't him. But if it was him, I'm in trouble. Give it more time; I need to make sure it's safe to get inside, then I'll lock the door, stay put and let all this blow over.*

Oliver gave it another ten minutes, then slowly crossed the street, heading to his apartment. He reached the communal doors, glancing behind, darting his gaze along the street, looking into the distance, trying to study people, checking and rechecking.

The vibration of his phone in his back pocket made him jump. *Jeez, calm down. Get it together and take the call.* He eyed the screen.

'Hello. Oliver, it's me.'

Instantly recognising the voice, he tried to keep calm, steering his emotions elsewhere. 'Claire, hey. You okay?'

'Yes, look, I've finished early. What do you say I come over in an hour or so?'

Oliver looked at the phone, feeling calm for the briefest of moments. 'Sounds like a plan. Looking forward to seeing you. Oh, Claire, call me when you're outside.'

She paused for a second. 'What, you don't think I'm capable of climbing the stairs by myself? Will do. See you in an hour.' She hung up.

Oliver's mind raced with the consequences of Claire coming to his apartment. He craved normality. He needed her now more than ever. He fished the key from his jeans pocket, pulled the heavy door towards him and entered the building.

Oliver stood for a few seconds at the bottom of the stairs, listening for movement. The building was quiet. Most residents were at work, leading busy lives. He'd been here for over a year, but no one had ever knocked on his door. There had been no welcome from the neighbours when he and Claire moved in, no baked pies or bottles of champagne or flowers to say how close the small community were and how they appreciated another career-minded normal young couple taking residency.

Oliver thought, *If only they knew.*

Inside his apartment, Oliver went to the window and lifted the blind so he could look out over London. How he wanted to be away from here, in a hut on a warm sandy beach, a barge on the Norfolk Broads, a cold drink as he watched the sunset, anywhere but his apartment.

He closed the blind, letting it drop roughly to the floor, then stepped back, scouting the room. Something felt out of place. He eyed the shelf to the right-hand side, his junk collection, the breakfast bar, the kettle resting by the fridge, the Banksy pictures on display over his head.

He peered at his phone, flicking through his recent messages, still shocked by what Meagan had sent. She had pinned to the door of apartment seven the A4 image of Oliver tossing the trunk containing gloved-man into the reservoir. *What was she thinking? How desperate must she be to do something like this?*

He wanted to go over to apartment six and have it out with her, take her phone and dump it as he had the trunk. He could get rid of the evidence and cut the noose from around his neck.

Oliver placed the phone in the back pocket of his jeans and

turned off the kitchen light. He needed a quick nap before Claire arrived. His body was exhausted, and he needed to rest.

The door to his bedroom was open, with a slight gap so he could see inside. He pushed the door and removed his T-shirt, placing it neatly over the end of the bed. *I'm sure I shut the bedroom door when I left this morning.*

Oliver took off his jeans, pulled the sheet back and lay down, enjoying the sensation of clean bedding, the soft pillow. A breeze from outside seeped through the small gap in the window above.

He lay still, his eyes staring, struggling to settle his racing mind. He listened intently. There were sounds he'd never noticed before: water circulating through the pipes; the humming of the fridge; a clock ticking from the kitchen, the second hand pounding like a hammer on a wooden stake. Oliver pictured himself lying on the floor, and gloved-man escaping from the lake, hunting him down.

Tick, tick, tick.

Oliver woke a little after 4pm. Opening his eyes, he peered around the bedroom, across to the door. It was slightly open, allowing him to see into the hallway. He listened for anything unusual. Something had woken him; a noise from outside the bedroom. Suddenly the buzzer sounded, a deep drone bellowing through the apartment.

'Shit, Claire.'

He leapt out of bed, moving to the hallway, picking up the intercom phone, balancing it on his left shoulder, while peering into the kitchen.

'Hello.'

'Oliver, shit, I've been out here ages. Did you forget about me or what?'

'Sorry, Claire, I'll be right down.'

'Hurry up, it's freezing.'

Oliver pulled a pair of jeans from the drawer nearby, threw on a clean T-shirt and headed downstairs to the communal front door.

Through the glass he could see Claire stamping her feet, wrapping her arms around herself to keep warm. Her smile grew as he approached until she was beaming, obviously glad to see him.

'Claire, I'm sorry, I must have drifted off. It's been a little hectic the last few days. Come in, hun, you must be freezing.'

She leant forward, kissing him on the cheek. Oliver found himself wanting more.

Oliver followed Claire down the hall, watching her, thinking how great she looked in skinny jeans and high heels; little effort, maximum attraction. He briefly thought how much he'd missed her, glad they were back in contact. They had so much to discuss, and Oliver was trying to work out how much he needed to tell her.

Claire stopped, turning suddenly. 'Shit, Oliver. My phone, I've left it in the car. I'll only be a second, okay.'

'Seriously? All right, I'll wait here. Hurry up, hun.'

Claire opened the front door and went around the building towards the car park.

Oliver waited. Finally, something was happening in his life to make him smile again. God knows he needed it now. He wanted to talk with Claire. There were things left unsaid, after all, she just upped and left him one morning, kissing his forehead, leaving behind the life they had. They were good together. She was beautiful, intelligent, often humorous. She had never explained what had happened, why she left.

Oliver stood in the communal hall, lost in his own thoughts. He'd talk with her, find out her story, listen to her explanation, and do his best not to be judgemental. Everyone deserves a second chance. He'd decided to play it out and enjoy the evening, so an immediate, full-on interrogation wasn't the way to deal with this.

All of a sudden, it struck Oliver how long he'd been standing in the hall. *Where is she, for crying out loud?*

He went outside.

The car park was empty, Claire's Ford Mondeo was alone in the far corner. The car doors were shut, the lights off. Oliver went around the side of the building, working his way closer to her vehicle. He swung his body round, looking behind in case she'd walked back a different way or decided to use the side entrance. But you needed a key to open it from the outside.

Oliver walked towards the fire escape at the back of the building. He felt panic as he quickened the pace, charging to the building's front entrance, back towards the car park. He peered inside the car. The engine was still warm, the vehicle empty. *What the fuck is going on?* He had a bad feeling. Claire had gone to the car to fetch her mobile, but in the space of a couple of minutes, she'd vanished.

Oliver went to the street, jumping the three steps down to the main road, frantically searching, wondering if she'd gone to a shop to get more alcohol. *Surely she'd tell me, but then she didn't understand the danger I'm in. Shit, where the hell is she?*

His mobile phone was upstairs. He should call her and see what had happened. He glanced along the street, watching the faces of pedestrians frustrated at having to change direction around him. He stood on the pavement deciding his next move. He thought about watching Claire's car. If she'd had second thoughts, fine, it wouldn't hurt him as much this time around. He'd deal with it.

*Surely she wouldn't leave and abandon her car, would she?*

He wondered if he was being paranoid. Had all the shit that had gone down recently made him overprotective?

Oliver had to get upstairs and call her. He made for the

communal doors at the front of the building and dashed along the hall and up the stairs.

Once inside his apartment, Oliver fetched his phone and tapped Claire's number then listened for a dialling tone. It went straight to voicemail. Oliver hung up and redialled. The same thing – her voice, asking the caller to leave a message, with the promise of a call back.

'Shit. Where is she?' Oliver stumbled dizzily into the kitchen. He felt like he'd just returned from a heavy drinking session. He took a glass from the cupboard overhead, turned on the tap and gulped some water, poured more and threw it back.

He turned slowly, sure he could hear someone.

The guy from apartment seven, gloved-man's partner in crime, knew where he lived, he knew what he'd done and was now coming for him. Oliver was sure of it.

He stood in the kitchen alone, the fridge humming like an irritating wasp at a picnic, and the clock was pounding, causing an ache in his eardrums. He looked around the kitchen. Something was out of place, something not right. He had felt it earlier.

Along the breakfast bar he saw a pile of bills, electricity and gas demands. Lying on top were two items of jewellery; a necklace Oliver had bought Claire when they first started dating, and a bracelet he'd seen dangling from Meagan's wrist.

## 31

PRESENT DAY

As Claire went to retrieve her phone from her car she had been excited about the evening ahead. She regretted walking out on Oliver a few months ago.

He was a good person and he looked after her. *God, shouldn't that be the priority in a relationship?* The problem was that Oliver was demanding, hard work. They'd go out for a drink, and he'd ask that they sit in the corner, with Claire facing the wall so she could only look at him. He was jealous, insecure, with low self-esteem, and paranoia. She had to keep reassuring him – praising him, telling him over and over how great he was.

The night before she left, they'd been at a party; a friend of Claire's. Oliver had too much to drink and was jealous when she'd spent time talking to a male colleague. She had seen Oliver grow angrier by the minute until he walked over and made a fuss, demanding they leave.

Her friend had made a stupid comment, a joke.

'Oh, it's like that is it?' Oliver had inquired.

'No, it's not like that,' Claire had replied. 'Oliver, we're not going anywhere. Come and join us.'

He had stormed out. Claire had joined him at home a half hour later.

She walked out the following morning.

But the weeks apart had made Claire realise she could deal with this, so she'd made up her mind. She was very much in love with Oliver and could work through anything for the sake of their relationship.

As she locked her car, checking her phone for messages, she saw a tall guy by the side doors of the car park. He was wearing a boiler suit with the words *LIFT ENGINEER* on the back. He smiled at her. 'Got a key to get inside? It's urgent. The lift alarm's sounding: someone stuck between the first and second floor.'

Claire tried the door. 'Wait there. My partner is in the hall at the front. I'll get him to open it. Give me a second.'

'Thanks, I appreciate it.'

As Claire turned, heading towards the front doors of the building, something soft came over her face and she felt herself being dragged bodily across the car park.

She struggled, kicking out, screaming under the face cover. Her heart was racing and she felt like she'd vomit at any second. Claire's chest was about to explode. She tried desperately to rip the cloth from her head, struggling to breathe. She shook uncontrollably, her body spasming and she feared she'd faint. 'Please let me go. I beg you,' Claire screamed, managing to overcome the numb feeling in her lips.

'Shut your fucking mouth, or I swear I'll snap your neck right here.'

'Please don't do this. I beg you, don't do this.'

As the guy pulled her body along the rough path, he punched her in the side of the head.

He dragged her further, then stopped, loosened his grip for a moment, but she was too shocked by the punch to react. The hood over her head slipped and she caught sight of the back of a truck.

The guy in the boiler suit tied rope around her, circling her body several times, making sure she was secure. He reached for another shorter piece of rope, wrapping it around her face and pulling tight. She heard a door open, and he threw her trembling body into the cargo area.

She felt the truck shift and start to move.

She thrashed and struggled, trying to get free.

The driver shouted at her, 'Don't make it more difficult for yourself. Your air is limited, so I'd keep as still as possible if you don't want to suffocate.'

She lay still then, moaning.

The man said, 'Your boyfriend is a very fucking stupid man. He doesn't know who he's dealing with. Did he tell you? I bet he didn't mention what he's done, huh? This is what happens when you fuck with people like us. How's the breathing going back there?' He paused.

Claire tried to move herself into a less uncomfortable position.

'Your boyfriend fucked with the wrong people. Now, it's payback.'

Claire lay in the back, bound so tightly with rope that her body throbbed. It felt like her airways were blocked and the bottom half of her body was hanging on by a thread. She was staring into the darkness. The hood was smothering her and her breathing was becoming more rapid and desperate. She kicked out, thumping the side of the truck with her heels. Her mouth was open, but nothing was coming out. She could hear the driver shouting about something Oliver had done.

*Why did I go back for the fucking phone?* She wriggled like a fish on the end of a line, wondering if it was the end of the line for her too.

Suddenly, she heard something in the back next to her. She stopped, listening to the sounds of the truck moving across London.

*There it is again, something beside me, next to me.* Claire heard a moan, followed by a whimper, close to where she lay.

Someone else was tied up next to her.

~

A short while earlier, Rob had showered, and was standing by the full-length mirror with a towel around his waist. He eyed his shape, impressed at how good he looked for his age.

He thought how he deserved so much better than Meagan. *She brings me down. She ruins my image. She holds me back.* He thought about the parties he could have back here, the late nights, the drugs, the sex. She ruined everything. He could never let her mix with the same people he liked to hang out with. They'd laugh at how pathetic she was, mock her innocence, her casual take on life, her laid-back approach. Rob liked to live life in the fast lane, playing dangerously, taking risks, and he loved his job. The nightclubs, the late-night gambling, the orgies, the trips to Europe where he was free to be who he wanted to be.

Rob had a plan: a definitive vision of the future. It wouldn't be long now. He'd open the club in Spain and make it a success. The only thing holding him back was his pathetic wife. She would no longer be part of his dream.

Rob was going to get rid of Meagan, her and her pitiful little life. If he didn't act now there'd be a divorce settlement, she'd get hold of the money he'd made from the club. The business he'd built himself. He recalled a conversation they'd had when they first met. Meagan had told him if he ever got tired of her, she'd fleece him for everything he had. He'd have to pay her off. Well, now Meagan had no choice. She wouldn't get a penny of his money. He couldn't wait to see her face as he placed the rope around her neck, crushing her windpipe, watching her beg, her final plea for him to spare her life.

Now as he dropped the towel, he wanted Meagan. He needed

some relief, then he'd finish her. She hated it, despised being intimate with him, although she'd never say it to his face. She wouldn't fucking dare.

Rob grabbed the thick rope from the drawer beside his bed, feeling the excitement flood his body. This was it. Showtime.

He called down the stairs, 'Meagan, you'd better have my shirt and jeans ready. I have an hour before I need to leave. Did you hear me, Meagan?'

He walked into the kitchen, finding it empty. As Rob turned towards the front door, he noticed it was slightly ajar, gently swinging on its hinge.

Meagan was gone.

～

Claire estimated the pickup truck had been driving for almost an hour.

The music was still playing loudly from the front. The guy had been quiet, occasionally talking on the phone to a voice on the loudspeaker. The figure lying next to her hadn't moved for some time.

Claire wondered if the person had died or was unconscious.

She struggled to stem her distress, breathing deeply with slow, calm breaths. Claire could hear her yoga instructor's voice. 'Keep your back straight, darling, let the air flow, my love. Think of yourself as a vessel, clear your mind, a blank canvas. Now stretch. That's it, girl, reach that body forward, tall and proud. Tall and proud. Now fly.'

*All I've learned in the past means shit now. It's pointless. The fucker's going to kill me, and there's little I can do to stop him.*

The truck slowed and gravel crunched under the tyres. Claire's body was thrown around like a suitcase in the hold of a plane going through heavy turbulence.

Suddenly the truck stopped. The music went off. There was

the sound of the driver's door opening and footsteps moving towards her.

The figure lying next to her suddenly moved. Something pushed against Claire's body.

Claire needed to get out; she was struggling to keep calm. She shook her head, desperately trying to remove the hood, needing to escape. She was claustrophobic, terrified of enclosed spaces and being confined or held down. She heard the boot open.

Then she heard the guy's voice close by. 'Don't make this difficult, or I promise I'll slit your throats right here.'

Claire listened to his words, needing to co-operate with whatever he said. Regardless of his demands, she needed to follow the instructions.

He dragged her body towards him, dropping her on the ground with a heavy thud. She landed awkwardly on her head, her aching frame collapsing.

She heard the person who had been lying next to her falling on the ground and crying out, begging to be released. It was another woman, her voice hysterical.

The boot was shut hard, then Claire was lifted and placed over the guy's shoulder. She kicked out.

The guy walked calmly across the gravel like he was strolling along a sandy beach watching the sunset. Claire tried to imagine warm water lapping the coastline. The sensation eased her racing mind, if only for a few seconds.

As Claire bounced on his shoulder, she sensed some steps, her body lowering, heading towards a basement deep below. She pushed ferociously, thrusting her legs in desperation. She heard a door open and the air changed. They were in a dank, cave-like room. She was sure she was going to die there.

## 3 2

Oliver had tried Claire's phone numerous times, each call going to voicemail until eventually he'd memorised the message and found himself mouthing the whole sentence, then hanging up and redialling.

He was frantic. It had to be gloved-man's partner. It had to be.

He called Meagan, getting an answer message.

'Fuck.' Oliver shouted louder than he'd expected. He pounded his fist on the breakfast bar, then stood still, staring at the jewellery.

*The guy has been in here, inside my apartment.*

Oliver wanted to go to the police, let them know what had happened, have them deal with it, find this arsehole and bring him down. But how could he? Firstly, the guy had the photo showing Oliver dumping a body at the reservoir. It was only a matter of time before the police put two and two together. *They'd bang me up for the rest of my sad little life,* he thought.

Secondly, Meagan has a video recording. If this lunatic has got to Meagan, he'd more than likely get into her phone and see the film. There was the possibility she would talk. If Claire had been taken, Meagan was also on his radar. Gloved-man's partner already had suspicions; calling to her door, making threats while Oliver hid in the lift. He had all the evidence he needed and it was only a matter of time before he came for Oliver.

*He's been in my apartment. He'll come for me.*

Oliver thought about Claire and Meagan. He couldn't break down now. He had to be strong. Claire had been such a big part of his life, they'd shared so many laughs together, so many wonderful moments, it couldn't end like this. Oliver wouldn't allow it. His mind moved to Meagan, the life she'd lived, the torment and abuse she'd suffered. How could he put them both in such a predicament? He was going to help them. He was going to rescue Claire and Meagan at any cost.

Oliver raced through the hall. He pushed the chain across the front door, twisting the key, engaging the double lock and checking it.

Now he could only wait and see how it played out. Whatever happened, he was in deep shit; and he had no idea how to escape.

Suddenly he found himself angry. Angry at how Meagan had acted, her foolishness and naivety. One thing was for sure, if trouble landed at Oliver's door he'd blame Meagan and pin it on her. Oliver would bring her down with him.

Claire sat strapped to a flimsy chair. She pushed her body forward. She thought the wooden legs might snap any second, dropping her to the hard floor.

She gasped for breath, each time swallowing part of the hood. With her tongue, she forced the cloth away from her mouth, taking hard breaths in and out, trying to work it away from her face by locking her jaw open and swinging her head frantically.

She listened to the strange noises coming from her throat. She was unsure why she was being held captive.

A rancid waft came through the hood as she gulped for air.

The basement stank of piss, mildew and something else. Claire tried to recall what it was. The smell of a butcher's shop. A childhood memory of her parents treating them to steak on a Saturday night. She hated the stench. She stood in the middle of the shop, watching the animals on display like a freak show, the ringmaster standing at the front door, beckoning people to come in and take a look. *'Roll up, roll up. Do we have a surprise for you today, ladies and gentlemen? A pig's ear, a sheep's head! Don't fear little one, they're most certainly dead.'*

Claire's head was full of senseless imagery and she was unable to control her thoughts. Her mind was racing and confused through sheer exhaustion. Her head was suddenly heavy, like a foreign object that had been planted on her shoulders. She was going to faint. Any second now she'd pass out. Fear caused her to kick her legs forward, desperately trying to free herself.

The door opened with a slow creaking close to where she sat. There was a shuffling just in front of her. Claire listened, hearing something being dragged, then the muffled screams.

Something was placed on the seat next to her. She heard footsteps moving closer. Someone was standing in front of her face, leaning in towards her.

Hands suddenly grasped her neck.

*This is it – the end, where my world finishes. A dank, piss-smelling basement.*

The guy's hands moved around the back of her head, and suddenly the hood was whipped from her face. She felt relief from the heat which had suffocated her the last hour, welcoming the coolness of the darkened room.

Claire's eyes darted around. There was the abductor in her peripheral vision on the left, but she was too frightened to turn and look directly towards him. She flicked a look across to the woman tied beside her on her right, a hood still over her head.

Suddenly, the abductor came into view, stepping to the front of the basement room. A tall figure; he had broad shoulders and was wearing a menacing-looking mask. It was stitched up at the sides, like flesh had been sewn together and placed over his face, the mouth a large hole.

His left arm rested by his side, holding a gun.

Claire listened to the pleas for help coming from the woman next to her, and the terrifying sobs emanating from her own throat.

He suddenly started speaking – a deep, husky voice, authoritative, confident. 'You can play this one of two ways. Either you both die here, now, or you go for the other more sensible option. I want answers.' The guy leant forward, pushing his head into Claire's face. 'Your boyfriend didn't tell you, did he? What he's done, I mean.

'See, my partner Tony was a complex character. Good at his job, he worked hard with only the best intentions. Yeah, he could be brutal, but sometimes you have to be in this game, if you know what I'm saying. Anyway, your fella, Oliver, is it? I'm thinking he knows more than he's letting on. I think he knows where Tony is, but he's too frightened to come out and face the consequences. He broke into his apartment, that's what I'm guessing. There was an argument, some shit or other went down and to cut a long story short, your fella killed him, dumped him in a trunk and got rid of the body.'

He pointed to the woman who was sat next to Claire, then reached forward and ripped the hood from her face. She started wailing like a baby.

The abductor looked at her closely. 'See, I remember you. Meagan, isn't it? I might look fucking stupid, but I never forget a face.'

The other woman was throwing her body one way, then the other, twisting, trying as best she could to free herself. Claire edged away as she tried to push backwards off the chair.

He smirked then continued. 'Now it's payback time, an eye for an eye. You both understand this, right? The thing is, I very much doubt he worked alone. It was too complicated, and besides, there's something being kept from me, something I'm not being told. He most certainly had help, an accomplice to guide his actions. Look at the size of the trunk in this picture. I think he had help, don't you?' He leant forward, his forehead pressed against the other woman's, holding an A4 page in front of her face. 'Yeah, I remember you all right. How's your husband, by the way?'

The abductor continued, 'Someone planned it, organised the show, but she didn't think about the fucking consequences. The way I see it, maybe you saw Tony doing his thing. He's a debt collector. It's his job; he roughs people up a little.'

He stood back, taking a deep breath. A dim bulb next to the door provided some welcome light. Claire stared at the crumbling wall behind him, the blackened damp marks, specks of paint lying on the watermarked ground. She was trying to figure out where they were. They'd driven for an hour, but she was unsure in which direction. She could feel the walls closing in on them.

The guy directed a question at Claire. 'Where's your phone?'

'In-in my back pocket.'

The abductor untied her, struggling to loosen the knot in the rope, pulling her body forward. He fished the mobile from her jeans and placed it in her hands. 'Call him!'

Claire lifted the phone, focusing on the screen, squinting her eyes to try and adjust her vision. She dialled Oliver's number, and he answered instantly.

'Claire. Thank God. Where the hell are you? I've been worried si–'

The phone was whipped from her hand. 'Listen, dickhead. She's with me.'

Oliver paused, trying to think what to say. He needed to keep calm and in control. 'Who is this?'

'Oh, I think you know full well who it is. So here's what's

going to happen, Oliver. I have two women tied up in the basement. You should see them; it's pathetic. They are begging for their fucking lives, an embarrassment. Anyway, let's get to the point. You have twenty-four hours to wire money to an account I'm going to give you. If in that time the money doesn't arrive, then you make a choice.'

He instructed Oliver to get a pen, reading out the account details, informing him again of the repercussions if he failed. He also stated the sum of money he wanted: £50,000.

The abductor hung up. He took a picture of the two women on the phone. 'Smile, girls! I'm sending that to your boyfriend.' He then placed the phone into the front pocket of his boiler suit, tied the rope around Claire's hands, wrapping her body tightly to the chair.

'You're going to wait here.'

He turned to the other woman – Meagan, he'd called her – and rammed the gun into her mouth.

Meagan frantically tried to shift away from the weapon, the chair bouncing on the concrete floor. She was gagging and Claire feared she would vomit and choke to death. Her mouth was open, saliva spilling from her lips.

The man leaned forward into her face, pulling the gun from her mouth. 'You'd better start talking.'

The woman gulped air, trying to release her body from the rope. 'I'm sorry. I'm so fucking sorry. Your partner was in the wrong place at the wrong time. We didn't mean it; it wasn't supposed to happen this way. It should have been my husband.' She was hysterical, completely breaking down. She screamed out, crying uncontrollably. 'Oliver made a mistake. It should have been my fucking husband.'

Claire sat still, listening to Meagan's confession, waiting for the gun to go off, worried she'd be next in line, regardless of whether Oliver paid the money. She wanted Meagan to keep quiet, close her mouth and never speak again.

The man placed the hoods back over their heads. 'Well then, thank you for clearing that up. Now someone's going to fucking pay.'

~

Oliver stared at his phone. The picture of the two women had just come through, showing them held in a basement. He had goose pimples, his skin started to itch.

Claire and Meagan were tied up in a grotty room somewhere. He had to co-operate and pay this psychopath, but he feared it would not be the end. *People like this never stop.*

He'd come after Oliver, and maybe he'd pay, but the women would be killed for the fun of it. He knew these people were ruthless. *Gloved-man pulled a woman into his apartment and drowned her in the bath, for Christ's sake.*

It might only be the start of his problems, but Oliver wasn't going to delay. Two women's lives were in danger, that was the reality. He had to deal with one thing at a time.

He looked at the piece of paper on which he'd taken notes during the call. The account number was a haze of digits lined up. He wondered how much these bastards had made from lending money to desperate people who needed cash for an electrical bill, heating, a phone that had been cut off, or to put food to the table.

*Yes, certainly we can help. We'll have the money sent to you immediately. Oh, I can imagine. It must be freezing. Well hey, light a candle for now, and you'll be warm in no time. Oh, just one thing before I go, our terms. There's just a little interest on the payment. Call it our hidden service charge if you like. Oh, and another thing, If you don't pay, we'll kill you. How about that? Have a great day now, won't you!*

Oliver had a crazy thought. He wondered what would happen if he called back and asked the abductor if he could borrow the ransom.

Oliver paced the kitchen floor, rubbing his face, his heart racing like a greyhound just released from the traps. He'd pay, what choice did he have? The money was a worry, but the greater concern was the hold this guy now had over him. He knew what Oliver had done. He'd taken Claire and Meagan, he'd seen the picture, knew where he lived. It was impossible for Oliver to go to the police. He contemplated going back to the lake in Tilford, cutting up the body and dumping it down the toilet. Even so, it could still be found.

He would pay the fifty grand, then what? What's to say he won't come after him again, demand more money, or even worse.

He sat by the breakfast bar, trying to keep calm. He opened his laptop and accessed his bank account. He had the money: he could just about scrape it together, but it would cripple him to send it over. Maybe if this was the end of the matter, it wouldn't be so bad, but Oliver knew this was wishful thinking.

He stared at the money in his account, fearful for Claire and Meagan tied up, bound and gagged in a room and begging for their lives.

*Tick, tick, Oliver. It's in your hands now.*

Claire and Meagan sat in the basement, their hands tied, rope marks on their wrists. They heard scuffling noises coming from the corner of the room. The sound seemed to be getting closer. Claire moved her feet, scratching the stony ground, fiddling with her fingers, trying to summon the strength to untie the rope. It was tight so it would take her hours to work it loose.

Their captor had left a few minutes ago, slamming the door and pulling a bolt across to secure them both inside.

Claire wanted so badly to remove her gag and speak to the woman next to her so she could get the story straight and understand what Meagan and Oliver had done. It was clearly a plan that had gone horribly wrong.

Meagan hadn't stopped squealing since she'd been placed next to Claire; a cacophony of noise, panic, hysteria, penetrating her gag.

They both waited, listening for a sign that the guy was outside, observing their surroundings. Claire sensed the room they were in was surrounded by fields, a large open space. There had been little traffic on the drive here; the roads were rough, and she recalled bouncing around like a rag doll in the back of the truck. When she'd been taken out of the boot, the air seemed different, wholesome if you like. There's a sense you get in the countryside that the atmosphere is lighter, the breeze fresher.

Claire quickly focused, listening to heavy boots coming down the steps, moving towards the door. She could hear Meagan gasp, like she'd woken from a nightmare.

The door opened. The figure walked slowly across the basement floor to stand behind the girls, casting a menacing shadow as he stood still, silent.

Both women tried to talk, groaning noises coming from deep in their throats. The room had filled with uncontrolled panic. Claire was pushing her mind to cope, to muster the strength. She struggled to tear away from the bonds that held her. *You can do this. Stay calm and breathe. You will get through this.* She was coughing, forcing sharp breaths from her nose. Her head was dizzy, her mouth aching from the hood.

The guy leant in. Claire could feel his breath on her earlobe. 'You better hope this goes smoothly. I promise, if it doesn't, I'll destroy you both here. No one will hear your screams.'

Again, he left the basement, leaving the words going over in their minds.

*No one will hear your screams.*

Oliver pressed the transfer button, watching the money dissolve from his account. His savings, disappearing down the plughole. He may as well have taken a match to the notes, sat by a campfire and watched it all go up in smoke.

He stared at the laptop screen: his mind flooded with a barrage of hatred towards this guy. His account had been almost emptied; the procedure so easy. A couple of buttons and boom, everything was gone; his life savings, the dream of a better life, disappearing out of the window.

Anger was seeping through his veins, working its way towards his neck. A pulse was developing, his heart pumping rage through his body. He wanted to find this guy, rip his head off, humiliate him, and beat him to within an inch of his smug fucking life.

He thought about Claire, mixed up in this shit, at the wrong place at the shittiest of times.

He thought about Meagan making threats, asking Oliver to finish the task, pinning the fucking picture to the door and bringing all this shit to their lives, messaging him again and again asking for him to finish what he started.

He blamed Meagan. She was gutless, spineless; everything Oliver could think to describe a total walkover, nothing but a punchbag for her vicious partner. If she'd left when Oliver had asked her to, none of this would have happened.

He wanted to rescue Claire now that the money had been paid and leave Meagan to rot in the room, tied to a chair, the rats eating her sad, pathetic little body. Maybe he'd persuade the captor to finish her off and take her out of the equation. Slip him a bundle of cash and ask politely. *I could offer to dump her body.*

Oliver called Claire, again getting her answering machine, then he tried Meagan's number: the same thing. *Fuck this.*

He debated whether to go for a run to try and stem the anger. Maybe he could take a walk, hit a bar and down as many shots of Jack Daniels as his body could hold until he passed out in a slumber, temporarily paralysed from the thoughts which were festering inside.

He needed to temporarily disengage, concentrate on something else, occupy his mind.

Again, he picked up the phone, dialling both numbers: the same outcome. He reached above his head, about to slam the phone on the kitchen floor when a single beep sounded, alerting Oliver to a message and pulling him back from his thoughts.

He slowly opened his phone, his left hand trembling.

Be here at 9pm sharp. I don't need to explain what will happen if you're late.

Underneath was an address in Read Hill, around an hour from where Oliver lived.

He quickly opened the laptop and googled the place where he'd been ordered to go – a farm which seemed like the back end of nowhere with fields and open space for miles.

He didn't like it, but Oliver had little choice.

He glanced at his watch, 6.58pm, then he reread the message: *I don't need to explain what will happen if you're late.*

Oliver watched the clock ticking, the second hand dragging, the minutes elapsing like hours. He'd need to leave shortly. Another hour and then Oliver would make the drive over to the address that the guy had given. He couldn't call anyone. The one person he could trust was tied up in the basement room. Oliver would have loved nothing more than to turn up, break the door in, lift Claire out from her seat, biting through the rope with his teeth. He would meet the captor at the door on the way out and pummel him, break his body in half and see him beg for mercy.

Oliver killed time by taking a shower, then he dressed in a pair of tracksuit bottoms and a thick jumper. He was nervous, his body weak from the stress, his mind poisoned against the person who had taken Claire and Meagan, and all his money.

He checked over the apartment, then headed to his car, opening the text on his phone with the address the guy had sent.

~

The digital display on his dashboard showed the time: 8.32pm. He had just under half an hour. He was unable to recall the journey as his head was too full, like a blanket had been placed over his mind, smothering his thoughts.

He was on an A-road, surrounded by fields. There were lights in the distance glaring towards him, temporarily blinding him. It was dark and the roads were empty. Every so often he'd take a sharp bend too fast and slow up, jabbing the brake with his foot.

The address was less than two miles away. The nearer he got to the place where the girls were held, the harder his heart thumped through his jumper.

His satnav instructed him to turn up a side road leading to woodland. *Shit, Oliver, what are you doing? Maybe it's a trap; the guy has my money now, perhaps he has no intention of letting Claire and Meagan live. He could be waiting, hiding, wanting to make an example of me.*

It was half a mile to where Oliver had been instructed to go. The road was stony with deep potholes filled with water, and miles of trees either side of the path. His view was obstructed by a mist that was thick in the air. The area was in total darkness and uninhabited, but this was the place, he was sure.

Oliver heard a voice. 'You have reached your destination.' He rolled the car towards the side of a ditch, killing the lights and getting out, stepping onto the rough ground.

Oliver took the heavy-duty torch that he'd brought from home out of the glove compartment. He shut the driver's door and waited, slowly scanning the area and listening hard.

He walked forward, more of a creeping action, keeping as quiet as possible, trying to duck to stay obscure. Ahead, he saw a glow from a small window, a barn or stables, he thought. Oliver couldn't see any movement.

He walked across the ground, heading towards the barn, checking behind every few seconds. He heard a twig snapping beside him and had the feeling that someone was watching him, waiting for his arrival.

'Hello?' He realised the stupidity of his action after he said the word. If someone was waiting, they most certainly knew he was here.

As Oliver reached the barn, he opened the door and went in. He swung his torch left and right, trying to scan the area. The place was empty.

He stepped backwards. His heart was racing and he was struggling to stem the coldness penetrating his body, fighting thick cobwebs which had clung to his head.

Back outside, Oliver crept along the edge of the barn, finding steps leading down to a basement. He went slowly, trying his best to keep calm: deep breaths, in and out.

The door was solid with a metal bar across the outside. The area was wet under his feet, damp and contaminated with faeces.

Oliver listened, placing his ear to the cold wood, trying to gauge the situation. He needed to open the door, face what he had to face, and get to Claire and Meagan.

He lifted the heavy bolt, pulling it backwards, the squealing noise penetrating, grinding like an old machine.

As he opened the door, he lifted the torch, guiding the light towards the back of the room. He saw a single figure sat alone strapped to a chair, a hood placed tightly over their head.

He walked forward, moving slowly towards the figure, conscious of the urgency. The empty chair troubled him. Oliver scanned the room, looking for the other woman, knowing the abductor could be lying in wait, ready to pounce at any second.

He thought, *Could this really be it? Will it end here?* It sounded too easy. Surely the abductor wouldn't just let them leave. Oliver had to take the chance. This guy had a picture of what he and Meagan had done. But he still hoped this was the end.

Suddenly, the figure in front of him looked up, their head turning sideways, listening, hearing someone in the room. 'Hello. Who's there? Help me, please.'

Oliver reached forward, undoing the rope, pulling off the hood.

Claire was sitting alone, pitiful, fighting her tears. She looked up, gasping for breath, her face completely flushed. Oliver listened to her break down in uncontrollable sobs.

He quickly released her from the chair, then searched for Meagan, thinking maybe she'd been moved to another room. He contemplated whether to leave her here or not. He knew he couldn't; she'd acted stupidly, made mistakes, but Meagan didn't deserve to be left behind.

Oliver crouched beside Claire. 'Where's Meagan?'

She held him, falling forward, holding onto him. 'I think he's killed her. He came back a short while ago, saying I could stay as I'd done nothing wrong. He said I was caught up in the wrong place, all that shit. He said that you'd paid the ransom and were coming for me. I felt him in front of us, crouched down. I heard the excitement in his voice. He picked her up. I heard her kicking, the chair fell, she pleaded for her life, begging him to forgive the two of you. She kept screaming that it was supposed to be her husband. I heard the door open; he was struggling to drag her body out. Then I heard crashing noises, like a pole or some other heavy object. He hit her, Oliver, over and over. He dragged her body out of the basement, and I heard the metal bar being placed across the door. That's the last sound I heard. I think he's killed her.'

Oliver placed his arms around Claire, helping her stand. He was numb, utterly sick in his stomach. He knew this wasn't over. He knew he'd be next. 'I have to help. I have to find Meagan.'

## 33

Oliver drove with Claire in the passenger seat. Her cold aching body was wrapped in a blanket and the heat was turned up full.

Oliver's mind went to Meagan. He wondered if he'd see her again. The guy had the money but what would stop him coming for Oliver, demanding more? What would stop him breaking into his apartment in the middle of the night, torturing him, murdering him and placing his body in a trunk?

Oliver drove along the M25, pleased it was quiet. He looked across at Claire, placing his hand in hers. 'I'm so fucking sorry. I didn't mean for you to get caught up in this shit.'

He watched her as she turned towards the window and closed her eyes. She didn't have the energy.

Forty minutes later, Oliver pulled up outside Albuquerque House. Claire was asleep. He needed to see if Meagan had got home. Somehow, he knew she hadn't.

As he stood outside on the street, he dialled her number, but it went straight to voicemail. Oliver didn't want to leave a message.

He had to see her and try and help, but where would he start? He contemplated going to the reservoir. Images flashed in his mind of her body in a trunk, lying at the bottom of the water.

He slowly walked towards the main door, cupping his hands against the glass, looking at the buzzer for apartment six and picturing Rob, alone, frantic, a baseball bat in hand, enraged and smashing everything in sight.

Maybe he was out looking for her. Oliver didn't care; he hoped he was suffering.

He stepped back from the doors, thinking this was a ridiculous idea. It was too late, there was nothing he could do tonight.

As he stood by the front door, a voice startled him. 'Hello, Rob.'

Oliver spun round, looking at the person in front of him; the small, frail figure, the headscarf wrapped tightly around her head, a trolley beside her.

He smiled at Mrs Sheehan, the elderly lady from the fourth floor, wondering if she ever slept.

'Hi, how are you?' Oliver asked politely.

'Oh Rob, how are you, more like it?'

Oliver played along. 'I'm good thanks. Is everything all right?'

She squinted at him. 'Out already? You must have a good lawyer.' She placed her hand on his arm, smiling. 'It's a lot of nonsense, I know. I'm a good judge of character, always have been, dear. I said it, I told that officer, while he held you on the ground earlier, "He's a good man, a gentleman, so let him loose!" He was quite rude, you know, the officer I mean, him telling me to mind my own business. I've lived here longer than his father's been alive more than likely. These youths, think they own the world. I told him while he leaned on you, you'd never mess around with that stuff, you know, drugs. He was shouting all manner of profanities at you, saying they'd found things at your club. Illegal substances, but it's just not true, you're not like that. Anyway, I'm glad you're out. And how's the lovely lady?'

Oliver stood, his mouth open, trying to grasp what she had

told him. Rob had been arrested. *Well, good riddance,* he thought. 'Yeah, she's fine. Thanks for asking.'

'Take care, dear, I'll see you soon no doubt, if I haven't croaked it walking up them bloody stairs. I shall speak with the service company, those lifts have been out for so long now, I'm sick of it. They don't care, that's the trouble with the world nowadays. People don't look after one another.'

She climbed the steps, fishing a key from her handbag and placing it into the lock. He held the door open, watching her walk towards the communal hall.

'Thank you dear, you are a gentleman, I must say. Oh, before I forget.' She turned round, facing Oliver as he stood at the front door. 'Did you get your parcel?'

'Parcel? Which parcel was that?'

She placed her hand on her forehead, her mouth open, deep in thought. 'Let me see now. It was last week, I think. A charming young man he was, dressed in uniform, smart looking. I passed him on the stairs, the second floor, it was early morning, he was standing outside your apartment. I told him I'd take it, well, you never know do you? When they'll come back, I mean, and it's a bloody nuisance going to pick it up, so I took it from him. I came down early afternoon, maybe one or two I think it was. I can't remember to be honest. I was confused though; I remember that much. Your door, the top of the stairs on the left, had a number seven on it. Well, I know you live at number six as I've passed your place hundreds of times over the years, and I know everyone here. I went along and lo and behold: number six was on the other door further down the hall. Anyway, I left it outside your door. The numbers were back to normal when I passed by the next morning. I know I'm not crazy, well, not yet anyway. Probably kids, you know how they like to play tricks. Anyway, take care Rob, I'll see you soon, young man.'

Oliver watched as she made her way along the communal

hall. The wheels of her shopping trolley were the last thing he saw disappearing up the stairs.

He stood alone on the path outside Albuquerque House. It was like he'd been stabbed, and he couldn't let his breath out. What the old lady had just said to him... It couldn't be true.

But then, insanely, it made sense.

The numbers had switched: the numbers had changed, with apartment six becoming apartment seven temporarily. She said the numbers were back to normal the following morning. Could Meagan have done it? Swapped them around, tricked him, making him kill the wrong guy?

*For fuck's sake.* The more he thought about it, the more realistic it seemed. Meagan had begged him to kill her husband; she'd said the second floor, the first apartment on the right past the lift, then she changed her story, insisting she'd told Oliver the apartment was on the left. She'd definitely told him apartment six was on the right side. Oliver was one hundred per cent convinced.

She could easily have swapped the numbers and made him break into the wrong apartment. Oliver thought hard, wondering why she'd done it. What was the purpose of making him kill the wrong man? Unless... He tried to figure it out, his head rushing, his brain on fire, trying to piece it all together. Unless she worked with someone and had planned it all in advance. His mind drifted to the guy who kidnapped both Meagan and Claire. The guy who asked Oliver to transfer fifty thousand pounds. The same guy who'd turned up looking for his partner and making threats. It would explain everything.

Oliver stepped back, holding the side wall, realising the truth of what had happened. It was the only thing that now made perfect sense.

Meagan and the kidnapper had both fucked him over, used him and then spat him out. They'd planned it together all along. She had tricked Oliver into breaking into the wrong apartment, making him kill the wrong person. She had framed him, blackmailed him and then run off with the money. He knew it now, it made sense; she did it, knowing Oliver's hands were tied. He was unable to go to the police, unable to go after her. She had something over Oliver that would see him locked up for the rest of his life.

*Meagan was a fucking genius. She reeled me in, shafted me and threw me to the lions.* Oliver dropped to his knees, and holding his head in his hands, he screamed on the steps outside Albuquerque House.

## 34

PRESENT DAY

Phil drove with Meagan sat in the passenger seat of the pickup truck. She had the music blaring, her feet on the dashboard, her head buried into her hands and she was laughing uncontrollably.

The events of the last few weeks were running through her mind, and she was barely able to contain her excitement, the reality of what they'd achieved.

Phil screamed out, 'Fifty fucking grand, Meagan. Fifty grand! Can you believe that arsehole?'

She yelled, hysteria taking over, her body tingling, unable to contain her emotions. She looked across at him and stroked his face, watching the motivation in his eyes, the wild expression.

'It was so easy; I can't believe the arsehole fell for it. Happy days, Phil. Happy frigging days.' She picked up the mask which was sitting between the front seats. 'I love this. Very effective. Bloody scary though.'

Phil looked across. 'You did fucking amazing. A right little actress in the making.'

They'd conned Oliver with a plan they'd hatched when they met in a psychiatric hospital.

After Meagan had killed her mother, she'd gone off the rails, unable to cope with the guilt.

Her father went to prison, taking the blame for the death of his wife, keeping the secret to his dying day a couple of years back. Meagan had nothing to do with him. She had decided that being placed in a cell for a crime he didn't commit was punishment enough. Meagan guessed he'd suffer in much the same way as her mother had.

Aunt Anne had stepped up to the mark, taking her niece in, looking after her, acting as her legal guardian and adoring her. And Anne had watched Meagan's destruction as she rebelled against society.

During her early teenage years, Meagan was constantly in trouble; petty crimes at first on a small scale, getting into drugs, dealing, mixing with the wrong crowd. When she'd committed one too many offences and was arrested for grievous bodily harm, they locked her up. 'You'll serve time,' her solicitor had explained.

Meagan pleaded with the court, playing the victim card.

She had a psychiatric evaluation. The diagnosis was paranoid personality disorder, often delusional. It was attributed to the trauma she had watched her mother suffer.

Meagan had been so damaged by her father's cruelty to her mother that she subconsciously distrusted men. Men in general. But Phil was a tool, a way to help her get what she wanted. She was using him as a revenge mechanism. So far, it worked for her.

Phil had been locked up for fraud; he was a conman of the highest order. He'd faked a bipolar condition and gained entry to a hospital where he'd be loosely monitored. Anything was better than prison.

Meagan and Phil had struck up a relationship, eating meals together, talking whenever possible. The attraction was instant, but not sexual.

Phil had a plan, but he'd need help. He explained the idea to

Meagan, and it was something they'd put to work as soon as they left the hospital.

He'd planned the con for years, and all he needed was help; someone who could play the victim, entice the opposite sex, get what she wanted. Meagan was perfect.

Meagan was released a couple of years before Phil. She'd taken regular medication, put her head down and it seemed like she'd finally got her life in order.

Once outside, she was down on her luck with nowhere to turn and no money. Her aunt had died years ago, willing the farmhouse to a charity. It was her final response to the shit that Meagan had put her through.

Meagan met Rob and fell for him hard. He was the perfect gentleman at first, treating her like a lady, showering her with gifts, providing a home; all the comfort she needed until he started slapping her about. The abuse was verbal at first, she could deal with that, just about, but it became severe, until he was knocking her about and beating her daily. She feared for her life, needed a way out. Meagan was trapped with nowhere to turn and nowhere to hide.

She received a text message from Phil. He'd been released, let out earlier than expected for good behaviour. He wanted to meet her and put the plan in action immediately. Meagan was worried, as she couldn't even take a piss without asking her husband.

Rob had a trip planned, telling Meagan he'd be away for a couple of nights. That was perfect; she used the opportunity to meet Phil and get the ball rolling.

A couple of weeks later, it was time. She'd been attacked by her husband, kicked and punched like a rag doll, so it wouldn't be difficult to find someone who would offer a helping hand.

Meagan had her eye on someone; he seemed perfect. She'd kept hidden, observing him, watching. She knew where he lived, what he liked, what he ate. While standing behind him at a cash point, he jabbed in his PIN. He requested a receipt that showed his balance, then he got distracted, removing his cash but leaving the printed receipt hanging from the machine.

Meagan watched him disappear into the crowd, knowing how much he had in his bank account. It was so easy observing people and monitoring their behaviour; you can get into anyone's life. You'd be amazed at the stuff people throw into their bins: folded up pieces of paper, telephone bills, electric bills, bank details, money they owe, places they visit.

That morning at the train station, a tall, good-looking guy introduced himself. Meagan just had to play the game and act like the perfect victim.

The stage was set. Meagan was slowly starting to show interest in Oliver, leading him on then playing hard to get; exchanging numbers, telling him she worked as a nanny, her excuse for meeting more often on their commute to work, calling him and making out she was worried that her neighbour had killed someone.

Meagan had invented a character so believable that she was almost convinced herself.

She met with Oliver while Rob was out of the country, convincing him to kill her husband with the promise they'd be together. This was the part Meagan was most concerned about. She knew how difficult it would be to convince someone to commit murder, so she and Phil planned it carefully. Meagan had to act desperate as if her life depended on it. Rob helped in a perverse kind of way; the cuts she suffered at the hands of her husband were very much real, proving that he was a wicked human being.

Before Oliver arrived to poison Rob, she had swapped the door number on her apartment, number six, with apartment seven, which was empty. And so apartment six became apartment seven.

It was perfect. Phil broke in and waited in the bedroom upstairs, face down on the bed, while Meagan left what Oliver believed to be an autoinjector containing poison in the basement.

It was all played out in the vacated apartment next door to where Meagan lived, but as she waited in the café, she turned her phone on, and received a message from Rob while he was still in Spain. She'd never planned on bringing Oliver into her apartment, but realising her husband would be staying in Spain for an extra night, she quickly set it up for Phil to make a phone call, posing as Rob and telling her he wouldn't be returning today. Oliver knew no different. It was the icing on the cake to convince Oliver he'd broken into the wrong apartment and killed the wrong man.

While they lifted the body into the trunk, Meagan made out she was going to look for a chain to secure it, while instructing Oliver to go home and get the car.

While he was gone, Phil stepped out of the trunk, and the plan was in full swing. They loaded the trunk with bricks wrapped in cloth.

Meagan and Oliver brought the trunk to the reservoir, and while Oliver rolled it into the water, Meagan stood behind him, recording everything. Evidence for blackmail.

All Meagan needed to do was torment Oliver, asking him over and over to kill her husband and finish what he started.

Phil watched Oliver closely, keeping tabs in case he really did try to kill Rob.

Once Meagan sent the video to Oliver's phone, they knew he'd panic, and this would drive him into their hands.

Meagan and Phil worked convincingly together: he'd ring the buzzer when she spoke on the phone with Oliver, or provide a voice out in the communal hall, thumping on the front door, stomping around outside while Meagan pretended she was worried about gloved-man's partner.

The only problem they hit was when Meagan went over to Oliver's apartment. She brought some rope and placed it around her neck. She'd planned to make a racket in the communal hall, then stand on the side rail, pretending she was about to jump. As Oliver came out, she got more into the character. As she stood on the handrail, ready for his pity, her leg slipped and she fell, almost breaking her neck.

Rob was easy to deal with. Meagan had contacts, people who dealt in everything from a dodgy passport to heroin. She had bags of cocaine delivered to the club, paying for everything on Rob's credit card. She made a copy of Rob's key, giving the delivery driver the code to disarm the security system.

Once the shipment had been planted in a storeroom out the back, Meagan made a call to the police. It would be enough to see Rob arrested and the club closed down for good.

The final piece of the puzzle was working out how to force Oliver into a corner. They'd planned on staging a kidnap, with Meagan tied up, bound and gagged. But Meagan had seen Oliver the previous night with Claire, and they worried he may not come to Meagan's aid. So they decided to take Claire.

It was the tipping point, and Oliver made the transfer.

As soon as the money appeared in their account, they ran.

Phil made out he'd beaten Meagan to a pulp at the basement door, with a large pole that he whacked against the mud bank.

Meagan hadn't planned on making love with Oliver, but the passion and excitement was too much. She saw the wheels turning and the pound signs were so close. At that moment when they had sex, it was real, and it meant something. Meagan was attracted to him, that much she'd admit: no one said she wasn't human.

Phil parked his beaten-up truck in the car park of Stansted Airport, dumping it with the keys in the ignition. A few hours later, they were drinking cocktails in Paris.

Gabriel Thomas stood on the platform, wiping the rain from his coat. It was a drizzly Thursday morning in Paris and the Metro rush hour was in full swing.

The train pulled into the station, the driver eyeing him, looking bored.

Gabriel turned, stepping back from the platform, waiting for the train to stop, the wind from the tunnel tossing his hair forward. He was dressed impeccably, wearing a long brown coat, smart black trousers and a white shirt. He gripped a briefcase tightly in his right hand.

As the passengers pushed off the train, he noticed a woman standing next to him. She had her head down, slumped forward, looking like she was carrying the weight of the world on her shoulders. Gabriel stepped closer to the train, moving his arm and banging it against the woman next to him. She looked up and Gabriel noticed the cuts on her face, her split lip.

'I'm so sorry. Are you okay?' he asked, watching as she forced a smile, noticing her eyes and the sadness behind them. She was beautiful, elegant, and completely breathtaking. He observed her as she boarded the train through the crowd, disappearing into the barrage of people. Gabriel followed, moving forward, pushing through the commuters. He gripped the handrail overhead as the train pulled off. As he steadied himself, he saw her and was certain she directed a smile towards him. Gabriel wanted so badly to talk to her. He smiled back, thinking he'd literally kill for a woman like that.

# ACKNOWLEDGEMENTS

I'd like to thank the wonderful admin and members of The Fiction Cafe Book Club, The Reading Corner Book Lounge and Page Turners Book Nook. You have all helped me on my journey and I'm forever grateful to all of you. Love you guys.

Finally, thank you to Betsy and the amazing team at Bloodhound Books for believing in me and giving me the opportunity to show my work to so many people. I'll be forever grateful to the Bloodhound team and I can't thank you all enough.

I love to speak with my readers and will always get back to you. Please get in touch if you have any questions or would like to find out about future thrillers I'm working on.

Facebook: Stuart James Author

Twitter: @StuartJames73

Instagram: Stuartjamesauthor

Bookbub: @Stuartjames

Website: stuartjamesthrillers.com

Printed in Great Britain
by Amazon

35374283R00173